THE EDEN STORIES

THE Mercury Protocols

TERRY TOLER

The Mercury Protocols

Published by: BeHoldings, LLC

Unless otherwise noted, all Scripture quotations are taken from the Holy Bible, New Living Translation, copyright © 1996, 2004, 2015 by Tyndale House Foundation. Used by permission of Tyndale House Publishers, Inc., Carol Stream, Illinois 60188. All rights reserved.

Book Cover: BeHoldings Publishing

Book Editor: Jeanne Leach
For information, address terry@terrytoler.com.

Our books can be purchased in bulk for promotional, educational and business use. Please contact your bookseller or the BeHoldings Publishing Sales department at:sales@terrytoler.com

For booking information email: booking@terrytoler.com.
First U.S. Edition: September 2021
Printed in the United States of America
ISBN 978-1-954710-04-7

OTHER BOOKS BY TERRY TOLER

Fiction

The Longest Day
The Reformation of Mars
The Great Wall of Ven-Us
Saturn: The Eden Experiment
The Late, Great Planet Jupiter
Save The Girls
The Ingenue
Saving Sara
Save The Queen
No Girl Left Behind
The Launch
The Blue Rose
Body Count

Non-Fiction

How to Make More Than a Million Dollars
The Heart Attacked
Seven Years of Promise
Mission Possible
Marriage Made in Heaven
21 Days to Physical Healing
21 Days to Spiritual Fitness
21 Days to Divine Health
21 Days to a Great Marriage
21 Days to Financial Freedom
21 Days to Sharing Your Faith
21 Days to Mission Possible
7 Days to Emotional Freedom

Uncommon Finances
Uncommon Health
Uncommon Marriage
The Jesus Diet
Suddenly Free
Feeling Free

For more information on these books and other resources
visit TerryToler.com.

Based in part on true events.

PROLOGUE

In the beginning, God said, "It's not good for Us to be alone." He was speaking to the Word, who was with God, and the Word was God. Also, with God and the Word was the Spirit of God who hovered over the waters.

"What shall we do about it?" the Word asked.

"Let Us make man in Our own image, in Our likeness," he replied.

So, God created mankind in his own image. Male and female. He placed them on Asiminia, the planet closest to the sun. The name, Asiminia, means silver because of the abundance of the element on the planet.

Pleased with his creation, God placed mankind in a Garden and called it Eden and gave them dominion over it and all the living creatures.

Man was called Adam; the woman was called Eve.

In the center of the garden, God planted a tree of life and a tree of the knowledge of good and evil. He instructed Adam and Eve not to eat the fruit from the tree and warned them that if they did, they would die.

The evil one tricked Adam and Eve, and they ate of the fruit bringing sin and death to Asiminia. They were cast out of the garden and cursed.

The evil one renamed the planet after a false god.

It became known as Mercury.

1

16000 years later
First Quadrangle, Mercury

"What are we going to do about the Disorderlies?" Herodius asked the group of five men in the room with him.

"Why do we have to do anything?" Incubus asked.

"Because they're a threat," Zagan answered angrily, his voice boomed through the room. "They ignore our orders and preach against the Mercurian law. They claim, and I quote, 'The hypocrites look beautiful on the outside, but on the inside they are unclean.' Imagine them calling us hypocrites. They are the heretics!"

"I agree," Herodius said, with no intention of calming the hostile feelings in the room. He had called the meeting, was in charge of it, and was perfectly happy to let the group air their collective hatred for the Disorderlies.

In fact, Herodius added, "The Disorderlies *are* a threat. They have made a mockery of Mercury Protocol 660."

The room seemed unanimous in agreement. While technically, the men in the room were equals, Herodius the Supreme Leader, and his opinion usually carried the day. That didn't mean the debate didn't sometimes get spirited, and everyone was free to disagree without repercussions.

"The goal of the protocol is to eliminate life unworthy of living," Incubus continued to make his case. "It seems to me that the Disorderlies are doing us a valuable service. They're making my job easier."

Incubus was in charge of carrying out Protocol 660. His official title was Prime Minister of Health and Medicine, and the protocol fell under his jurisdiction as did a lot of issues pertaining to who lived and who died.

"How's it doing us a service when they are adding to their numbers daily?" Zagan asked, in a way that raised the tension in the room another notch. "At some point, there may be more of them than there are of us," he added.

"They have no money or power," Botis chimed in for the first time. "We can squash them like ants anytime we want."

Botis was the richest man on Mercury. He owned all the silver mines. Hundreds of them. If there were such a thing as seniority, he would have it. His ancestor was one of the original members of SCOTE—The Secret Council of the Eliminati.

Botis attained his position for obvious reasons. His riches were used to fund all of the activities of the Eliminati and helped them maintain control over all the institutions. The men in the room would have no power if not for him. As it were, their power was nearly unfettered. The Council answered to no one but themselves.

"They say they get their power from God," Zagan retorted. "That's how they're able to render the protocol irrelevant."

Zagan was in charge of the state religious institutions which was why he was so concerned about the Disorderlies—the name given to the followers of Christ who constantly spoke against the state religion which Zagan ran from behind the scenes.

"As I said... I don't see how they're hurting the protocol," Incubus said. "The less sick people in the world, the better."

Herodius was confused. Mercury Protocol 660 had been Incubus's idea. The Disorderlies were rendering the program of mercy killings unnecessary. That didn't seem to bother Incubus. Herodius figured Incubus should be the most upset.

"Shall we have them arrested?" Lechies asked, causing a mixed reaction in the group. His solution to every problem was to arrest offenders and question them later. Some voiced agreement while others laughed at him.

"That'd be impossible," someone said.

"That's a good idea. Do it," another retorted.

Lechies was in charge of the political and judicial branches of government. He controlled them like a puppet master controlled a puppet. His strings were Botis's money which allowed him to buy every judge, policeman, soldier, and politician. Actually, he didn't need to buy them all. Just a majority. Enough to maintain control.

For those who couldn't be bought, Lechies had his own way of controlling them. By manipulating the elections with Botis's help. Botis owned the company that made the election machines. The result of every election held for the past six thousand years had been predetermined. This had made all of their jobs much easier.

Herodius let the arguments continue for a few more minutes while he mused. After he'd had enough, he finally decided to bring the argument to a conclusion.

"There are too many Disorderlies to arrest them all," Herodius said strongly. "We don't have enough prisons to house them. And the people love the Disorderlies. Especially now that they've disrupted the protocol. We'd have an insurrection on our hands if we started arresting them."

"We could add them to the protocol list and terminate them," Saleos said.

Saleos was in charge of the educational institutions. The intellectual scholar of the bunch, he generally had good ideas.

"Interesting," Herodius said, as he rubbed the stubble on his chin.

"But they aren't infirmed or disabled," Incubus argued. "The protocol doesn't cover them."

"One could argue that a belief in a false god is a mental illness," Zagan said with a chuckle.

Mercury Protocol 660 called for the death of every person who was "unworthy of living." That included the mentally challenged. The disabled. The elderly. The blind and deaf. Incubus had great latitude in determining who made the list. The unfortunate souls were given a lethal dose of mercury in the form of an AXX-E. Something Incubus had developed that was used to control the people against their will. More than half the population was medicated with his concoctions, thinking they needed them for various ailments. In reality, most were caused by the secret ingredients in the AXX-E.

Getting the people hooked on medicines and relying on AXX-E was one of Incubus's biggest accomplishments. Most people on Mercury had taken as many as a dozen in their lifetimes. Many of the Disorderlies refused to take them.

"This could get out of control if we don't do something," Zagan said roughly.

"I was concerned this might become a problem," Herodius said. "Might I remind everyone that I voted against the protocol."

The vote had been five to one in favor. Herodius had cast the lone vote against the measure. Not that he opposed it. He was worried about his power. With the title of SLOTE, Supreme Leader of the Eliminati, he was the most powerful man on the planet and didn't intend to give that up easily. The protocol seemed like a risk. The people might rebel.

His concerns had come to fruition. The existence of the Council was at stake. That's why he had called the emergency meeting. Incubus didn't grasp the full danger they had created by their own foolishness. The Disorderlies were gaining power. The protocol wasn't having the desired results.

Not that anyone knew about the vote or even who was behind the protocol. The Council was a shadow organization. No one on Mercury, other than the six in the room, knew the full extent of the Council's power. No one even knew that SCOTE existed. The Council met in secret and everything they did was behind the scenes. The protocols were rolled out through the institutions. The people were oblivious.

It had been that way for more than ten-thousand years. With each generation, the Council strengthened their hold over the planet. While Herodius had no fame, he had power. If given a choice, he'd choose power any day of the week. He wouldn't rest until the Eliminati had absolute power. Hence the name. They had to eliminate every threat.

The Disorderlies were a threat. As the prophet Jesus had been when he was alive. A danger that had been dealt with by his predecessors. Namely Herodius I, his great grandfather several times removed. Herodius I was the one who had Jesus arrested and killed. History recorded that Jesus was raised from the dead, although his ancestor didn't believe it. The Christ followers did, though, and the movement spread rapidly.

Over time, the Council regained control over the Disorderlies, but it took several centuries. The so-called Christians had been mostly impotent for thousands of years. Now they were making a revival. Mercury Protocol 660 had something to do with that as Herodius had feared. They were using some of Jesus's same methods. The self-proclaimed Son of God ingratiated himself to the people by performing miracles. Healing the sick. Opening blind eyes. Performing other such magic tricks.

The Disorderly preachers today were doing the same thing. When they learned that the sick were being eliminated through the protocol, they called for everyone to bring the sick and infirmed to the church. They laid hands on them, and they recovered. Miraculously. Herodius wasn't sure how they were healed, but many of the results had been documented.

By all accounts, nearly a third of the list identified for mercy killings, had been miraculously healed of their infirmities. At that point, killing them was unjustified. The number of mentally ill, disabled, and infirmed, was dwindling daily. By unprecedented numbers. Which was a good thing from Incubus's point of view. Not to Herodius. The power the Disorderlies had amassed was concerning.

Botis argued another point bringing Herodius back to the debate at hand which was now raging. "The purpose of the protocol is to eliminate the dredge of society and lessen the drain on our resources. We need to kill everyone on the list to accomplish that goal."

"How many people have we terminated to date?" Saleos asked. Being a professor, and in charge of the educational institutions he liked to deal in facts and figures.

"Seven thousand," Incubus answered.

A gasp went through the room. That was a lot of people. The entire population of Mercury was only seven hundred thousand. They didn't have space for many more than that. Because of the close proximity to the sun, the surface of Mercury maintained a year-round temperature of roughly eight-hundred degrees. Life could not survive on the surface.

When the planet formed millions of years ago, the only place inhabitable was under the ocean. A protective layer held the water in place above the dry land and kept the bubble a balmy seventy degrees most of the time. The sun's rays were so strong, they still provided the area with light. However, without the protective layer, the only area on the planet that would sustain life would flood, and they'd all die.

For years, the Eliminati spread the propaganda that the Strata-zone layer, as it was called, was thinning. It wasn't, but this was their way of keeping the population under control by creating fear among them. People always responded to doomsday predictions. This had been one of the more effective ruses.

The debate in the room continued and interrupted Herodius's thoughts.

"Part of the purpose of the protocol was to thin out the population," Botis argued. "We already have problems providing enough food and water and general supplies to the masses. Must I remind everyone that, eventually, we need to eliminate two thirds of the population."

"Seven thousand has made a good dent in the numbers," Incubus said.

Everyone seemed to agree.

"But the Disorderlies saving the others defeats the purpose," Botis said.

Incubus interrupted. "The Disorderlies pose no threat. So, they heal a few people with magic tricks. It's just a fad. They'll fade away like others before them."

Herodius knew better. The only way the Eliminati could exist was by keeping the power away from the people. Even giving power to a God who didn't exist was a threat to his power.

In this case, six men controlled an entire planet. Only because the people ceded their power. A delicate, fine line existed between power and absolute power. Herodius wanted absolute power and wouldn't stop until he got it. The only way for that to happen was for the people to not realize they were losing their rights. Eventually, they'd only have the rights that he gave them.

The change in thinking must be voluntary and gradual. The Eliminati had to take away their rights incrementally. Without them even realizing it. Like a frog in a pot of boiling water. Keep turning up the heat gradually, and the ignorant frog will die before he realizes what's happening.

That was Herodius's monumental task. A job that kept him up at night. How much could he turn up the heat on the stove without the frog jumping out? The frog being the people of Mercury. More specifically, the Disorderlies.

They had protested Protocol 660 vehemently. Preachers took to the pulpits once a week to speak against it. As he had feared, Herodius knew almost immediately that the Council had made a mistake. The protocol 660 had turned up the heat too much. People were upset that the law was inhumane. Barbaric.

Not that the Eliminati weren't prepared for the backlash. They countered their arguments. The greater good was the mantra. Relieve their suffering. That argument didn't resonate. After all, the victims were loved ones of somebody.

Eventually, they were forced to do the killing behind the scenes. They kept the actual lethal injections out of the spotlight. Disposed of the bodies discreetly. Thwarted any legal challenges through subversive means. Squashed any political investigations. Arrested violent dissenters.

Eventually they regained control over the dissent by controlling the spread of information. The actions taken in the protocol went unreported. The news outlets refused to cover it at their insistence. The Square Groups were policed. The Square was a fairly new phenomenon. Social groups. People entered squares. Within the figurative four walls of cyberspace, they could communicate freely. Voice opinions. Interact socially and politically. The groups had spread like wildfire.

The Eliminati had to get control over the Squares, and they did. Posts were deleted and labeled as disinformation. Any dissent was blocked. People were removed from the Squares for repeated violations.

This infuriated the masses even more. Talk of a secret council spread like a virus. An emergency meeting of the Council had been called, and the Eliminati took steps to squash the threats. Eventually, their efforts paid off, and they were able to gain control of ninety-five percent of the disseminated information. A small portion of the squares was still out of their control.

What they couldn't control was what the preachers said in their churches. Converts could spread information by word of mouth in a way they couldn't control. That's why the Disorderlies had to be stopped.

Herodius decided to put an end to the vigorous debate raging in the room and get to his plan.

He stood to his feet.

The room got immediately silent.

"Here's what we're going to do," he said. "I'm creating another protocol. Number 661."

Several people leaned forward in their chairs. Saleos began taking notes. His job was to record the decisions made in the meetings.

"We'll tell the people that we've discovered a hole in the Stratazone layer of the atmosphere," Herodius said. "We'll say that our atmosphere is warming at a record pace. Until further notice, everyone is confined to their homes for sixty days until we can fix it. If we even can. All nonessential persons are to remain indoors. Only essential businesses will be allowed to operate. Churches are closed until further notice. One person from each household can travel to get food once a week. All violators of the protocol will be arrested."

"Brilliant," Zagan said.

Others voiced their approval.

"That will shut the churches down," Herodius said. "At least temporarily. That'll also give Incubus time to terminate the remaining people on his list."

Incubus nodded in agreement.

"How long do you think the people will be fooled?" Saleos said skeptically.

"As long as we want them to be fooled," Botis said with a smug grin.

"We'll tell them that the lockdown will only be for sixty days," Herodius said. "But we can continue it indefinitely. However long it takes to get control of the Disorderlies."

"And when the people realize it's all a sham?" Saleos said in a questioning tone.

"We'll write another protocol, if necessary," Herodius answered confidently. "And another. Then another, if need be."

"And if the protocols don't work?" Saleos asked.

"Then we'll kill every last one of them."

2

Revelation Church
Fifth Quadrangle, Mercury

Gohn had long since gotten used to the smell of human suffering. He'd probably never get used to the sight of it.

He stood at the front of his church and looked out over the standing-room-only crowd. The sign in the back of the small sanctuary caused him some concern. *Maximum capacity: 143.* By order of the Fire Protector, backed by Mercurian law.

More than three hundred people crammed into the small space today. Another two thousand lined up outside. If the authorities chose to make a visit, he wasn't sure what the consequences would be. Maybe imprisonment. Certainly, they'd be shut down. He couldn't let that happen. Although he wasn't sure how he could stop it.

Standing room only was somewhat of a misnomer. Those who could, stood in the back. Most were in no condition to stand. It broke his heart every time he took the time to look over the crowd. Every manner of sickness and diseases were present. All waited patiently for one touch of his hand on their forehead.

So far, it had worked every time. For nearly two months, twelve hours a day, seven days a week, Gohn stood in that exact spot. One by one the sick and infirmed made their way to the front. He did the same thing each time because he was afraid if he deviated from the way in which he did it the first time, the power to heal might somehow leave him.

Marta, his long-time assistant, stood next to him with a cask full of anointing oil. She handed him the already opened vial. He put a couple of drops on his finger, dabbed the oil on the person's forehead, raised his free hand to the heavens, and thanked God for having mercy on this poor soul.

Without fail, whatever sickness or disease the person walked in with, they left free of it. Perfectly and beautifully healed. He'd seen blind eyes opened. The deaf could hear. The mute could speak. The lame walked.

The crowd cheered after each one. To the extent they could. Every gamut of emotion ran through the church like a flood. The celebrations were almost as draining as the long hours of standing.

He couldn't ever remember being this tired. It was worth it though. He'd never been happier or more fulfilled in ministry. After the people received their healings, the elders of the church prayed the prayer of salvation with each one. There'd never been a single person refuse. The logic behind Jesus's ministry had come into focus for him. It made perfect sense to heal a person from their sickness first. Then get them saved.

The person was then encouraged to go to the doctor and get a clean bill of health so they could get their names off the Mercury Protocol 660 list. The mercy killing list, as the authorities called it. Many with verifiable internal injuries and diseases came back to the church with their clean bill of health from a physician. Gohn often stopped the healing line to give an opportunity for testimonies.

He felt this would encourage the others. Give them hope so they wouldn't lose patience and leave. Those were some of the best times for him. Hearing the testimonies and the joy in their voices. He made sure it was a time when they could all praise God for his wonderful blessings. He remembered the Bible verse when Jesus healed the blind men, and only one came back to thank him. Gohn saw to it that they didn't make that same mistake.

The testimonies only spurred the faith in the crowd and were the reason for the long lines. Word had spread that Gohn was a faith healer. He tried to dispel that myth and hated the term. He had nothing to do with it. The Holy Spirit healed these people. No way he could do it on his own strength. He didn't even believe he could do it. Gohn was surprised every single time it happened. Maybe eventually it wouldn't, but Gohn was determined to keep it up for as long as God provided the favor.

One of those walking miracles had the microphone in her hand at that very moment and shared how God healed her from a disease that had emaciated her body. She'd spent all her livelihood on physicians and could not be healed by any. That's why her name was on the Protocol 660 list. She'd dodged a bullet. Or literally an AXX-E. A deadly toxin filled with mercury that the law insisted she take because she had become a drain on society.

The Mercury Protocol 660 infuriated Gohn. It went against everything he believed about God and the sanctity of life. That's why he put in the tireless effort. He'd keep going until he had no strength left. When he could no longer lift his hand in the air, someone would have to lift it for him.

The testimonies also gave him time to rest. Gohn leaned back on the platform and sat down and let out a huge exhalation of air. Truthfully, he could never do it in his own strength. He felt the power of the Holy Spirit giving him the energy and stamina to keep it up.

Marta had voiced her concern for his health on more than one occasion.

"As long as there is one person in need, I must continue," he said to her.

At her insistence and with the advice of the elders of his church, Gohn agreed to take a thirty-minute break three times a day and end the healing services by nine o'clock each night. They always ran longer than nine. How could he tell the people in the crowd that they had to suffer one more night?

He didn't quit until they made him. The next morning, he got up and started the same routine again. The people in the church didn't leave. They were afraid to lose their places in line. The members of his congregation tried their best to keep the sick fed and hydrated. A difficult job considering the numbers.

The conditions were also not sanitary. Hence the smell. Nothing he could do about it other than keep pressing forward.

The people kept coming.

He remembered the first one.

Two months before.

Gohn was in the pulpit preaching to a crowd of thirty-five people who were mostly bored. The sermon was fiery, but the congregation wasn't matching his intensity. The Last Days was the topic. They'd heard it before. Jesus was coming again. We needed to be ready. He used a passage in the Bible where Jesus spoke about the Last Days and warned the people that there would be perilous times ahead.

Many would oppose the truth, Jesus had said. It seemed like they might be living in those last days, he argued in his sermon, although no one acted like they believed him.

Gohn used the sermon to lash out at the government and religious institutions who imposed inhumane and barbaric protocols on the people. Something that could get him arrested. That got a little more response from the crowd. He got the occasional amen, but he could see that his congregation had grown cold. Another thing Jesus warned would happen in the last days.

"Because lawlessness will be increased, the love of many would grow cold," Jesus had said.

The sermon was about to end. Gohn raised his voice to a crescendo and said those words, "You have grown cold."

"We have grown cold," he corrected himself to lessen the vitriol. He couldn't help it. He was angry. At his congregation. Faithful followers but Gohn had been frustrated that he'd been at the church for more than seven years and attendance had dwindled every year.

Angry at himself. He felt like a failure.

A loud noise in the foyer interrupted his planned ending.

What was it?

A gunman?

He remembered feeling dread. Wondering if an armed man had entered the building. Several churches had been attacked by gunmen. One pastor was even killed. Gohn suspected the government or church state might be behind the killings.

One of his congregants, Will, was a conspiracy theorist. He spouted all kinds of wild ideas. Talk of an Eliminati. A secret council. Godless men behind the scenes who ruled the world from an ivory tower somewhere. Gohn dismissed the talk as wacky ideas. Craziness.

Now he wasn't so sure.

To his relief, the noise didn't come from a gunman. Four men carried another man on a stretcher. Everyone turned in their seats and stared at them as they walked down the aisle and brought the man to the front of the church and sat him on the floor right below where Gohn delivered his message.

He was too stunned to speak. Then annoyed at the intrusion. Who were they?

One of the men had a piece of paper in his hand. He handed it to Gohn. Tears streamed down the man's face. The man on the pallet strained to raise his head but was too weak and fell back to the prone position. He reeked of medicine and bodily fluids. Gohn put his hand over his mouth to keep from gagging.

"What's this?" Gohn asked the man.

"Read it," he said.

The paper was addressed to Luo Long. On official Department of Health and Medicine letterhead. With a seal. Gohn assumed the man on the pallet was Luo.

Pursuant to Mercury Protocol 660, you are compelled to present yourself to the Office of the Medical Examiner no later than noon on the tenth day of the month.

That was today.

What was Mercury Protocol 660? Gohn hadn't heard of it. He kept reading.

In the pursuit of a more perfect union, you have been chosen to receive a new AXX-E for people with mental illness, infirmities, and incurable diseases.

What was the problem? That sounded like a good thing. He kept reading.

Failure to do so will result in immediate imprisonment for you and every member of your family.

It couldn't be a good thing if people were forced to be there. What was the catch?

"I don't understand," Gohn asked the man.

"When people show up, they're never heard from again. They disappear."

A murmur went through the crowd who could hear every word.

"What happens to them?" Will asked. He had come to the front of the church and read the protocol.

Then answered his own question. "I have a guess," he said. "The AXX-E kills them. This is the work of the Eliminati."

The murmurs intensified.

Gohn tried to calm his congregation. "Let's don't jump to any conclusions," he said. "Not until we have all the facts."

The clock in the back of the room read ten to noon. Gohn liked to have everyone out of church by noon.

"What do you want me to do about it?" Gohn asked, as he handed the paper back to the man.

"Help me," the man cried out from his pallet. "Have mercy on me."

A pain went through Gohn's heart like a dagger. "What's wrong with him?" Gohn asked the men who had carried him in.

"His body is ravaged by Sarcona that eats away at his internal organs," one of them said.

"Is it contagious?" Gohn asked, immediately concerned for his own health and the safety of his congregation.

"No, it's not contagious," the man said bitterly. "But he'll die soon."

"Like I said, what do you want me to do about it?"

"You're a preacher. Pray for him. Heal him."

Gohn didn't believe in healing. His theology was that miracles ceased with the Apostles. Not that God couldn't heal, he just no longer chose to. Gohn started to speak the words and present his arguments, but his mouth was suddenly frozen shut. Like a vise held it in place.

He cleared his throat and moved his head from side to side to release the tightness in his jaw. He tried to speak again. His lips moved but nothing came out. Like he was suddenly a mute.

What's going on? Was he being hit by an illness? Was the man's sickness contagious after all?

A sudden warmth came over him. Gohn felt hot. His body tingled. Before he realized it, he was kneeling next to the man, although he didn't remember doing it.

"Marta, go get me the healing oil," Gohn said, as his speech returned.

In his office was a cask full of healing oil. It used to sit next to the pulpit. One of the first things he did when he started as pastor was move it back to his office. He had put it in one of the drawers. Marta would know which one. She was as detailed as any person he'd ever met. He couldn't function without her.

She got up from her seat and left the sanctuary. Her sister, Aria, stood and walked over and knelt next to Gohn. She placed her hand on the sick man's head and began to stroke his matted hair.

He let out a moan.

Aria looked up and smiled at Gohn. He tried to return it, but his face felt like it was frozen. Probably in fear. He had no idea what was happening.

Was he going to lay hands on the man? He'd never done that before. What if it didn't work? It wouldn't work. God didn't heal today. How could he explain it to the man in a way that he'd understand? Gohn didn't even fully understand it.

It seemed like Marta was gone for a good ten minutes, but the clock had not yet struck noon, so it had been less than two. When she returned, she handed Gohn the cask. He opened it.

A pungent and vial smell immediately filled the air and caused those around him to wince.

The hotness returned.

This time in his hands.

They were on fire.

What's going on?

They didn't hurt which added to the confusion.

Without thinking, Gohn took his finger and placed it on the top of the vial. He shook it up and down keeping a finger on the hole, so no oil escaped. He had no idea why he was compelled to shake it. He poured more oil into the palm of his hand. Then placed his palm on the man's forehead.

Power surged through him like an electric current.

The man's head jolted like he'd been struck by a bolt of lightning.

Aria let out a slight scream. Marta reacted and grabbed Gohn from behind.

Gohn kept his hand on the man's head. Then he raised his other hand in the air and said, "Thank you God for healing this man. For making him whole. In the name of Jesus. Our Lord and Savior."

Gohn felt the power leave his body and go into the man.

The man sat up.

The crowd gasped.

The man's eyes were fully alert. He grabbed Gohn's hand. Hard. Gohn tried to pull away but couldn't. The man suddenly had tremendous strength in his grip.

He threw his arms around Gohn.

Aria let out a louder scream. Marta took the man's arm off of Gohn and helped him to his feet.

The congregation erupted in applause. Gohn slumped back to the floor. All his energy was gone. Aria helped him stand. Gohn started to fall backwards. If Aria wasn't holding him up, he would've fallen down again. His knees were that wobbly.

The man hugged his friends. They jumped up and down and screamed at the top of their lungs, words of praise for God.

Gohn was stunned. The skeptic in him suddenly reared its ugly head.

This was a trick.

The man wasn't even sick.

You're a fraud.

Then Gohn heard a still small voice. He recognized it as Jesus's voice, but he wasn't sure how he knew.

"He who believes in me will do the works I've been doing. And they will do greater works than these."

A Bible verse. Gohn knew it well.

Gohn looked around to see if anyone else heard the voice. No one seemed to as everyone focused on the man who was now running around the sanctuary. He went from person to person to thank them.

Then Gohn heard the voice again.

"In the last days, I will pour out my Spirit on all flesh. Gohn, you shall prophesy. You shall see visions. You will dream dreams."

Gohn heard the words as if someone was right there, speaking them to him. He didn't know what they meant.

Two months later, he did know. It was happening right in front of his eyes.

* * *

The woman with the microphone finished giving her testimony. Gohn stood slowly to his feet and returned to the line of sick people that stretched to the back of the room. Thankful for the respite, but ready to go back to work.

He felt hot again.

The fire was on his hands all the time now. He'd grown used to it. The power flowed in and out of him like the waves in a body of water. He'd also seen visions and dreamed dreams. Someday he'd share those. Up until now, he hadn't mentioned them to anyone. Whether he was caught up into heaven or not, he wasn't sure. But the dreams were vivid. Violent. They revealed what would happen in the last days. He was sure of it. Which was why he hadn't shared them. Most people would think he was a crazy man.

At some point, he might pen them as a letter to the other churches. Revelation Church wasn't the only one going through a revival. Hundreds of churches across Mercury were full of the sick and infirmed. Just like his. Everyone who was sick was healed by the laying on of hands and the anointing of oil.

There were counterfeits. Jesus warned of them. He said that "false Messiahs and false prophets would appear and perform great signs and wonders." Gohn could tell the difference. Those people were full of themselves. Taking credit for the power to heal. Preaching a false gospel.

He didn't worry about those people. God would judge them. He had enough to concern himself with.

Gohn looked over at Marta and their eyes met. He smiled and she returned it. He felt rejuvenated. The short rest had renewed his strength like the eagles. They got back to the line of people.

The next man was blind from birth. Gohn touched his eyes. In an instant he could see.

The next in line was a young child. Crippled. In a wheelchair. Her hands were mangled. Her head contorted to the side. The young girl forced a smile from her lips causing drool to run down her face. Aria was there in a second and wiped it off with the sleeves of her shirt.

Gohn hurried. He didn't want the poor child to suffer for one more second.

Within a minute, she was out of her chair. Running. Another aspect of the miracles that couldn't be explained. Even though the girl had been confined to a chair all of her life, her muscles somehow responded as if she had been walking and running all her life. The healing was complete. She was restored to how her body would've been had she aged properly.

The once contorted face now beamed with a smile as broad as any Gohn had ever seen. Aria ran with the girl, and they laughed, played, and danced around like little schoolgirls.

Marta's face was emotionless. Not because she didn't care. She was on to the next person in line. Focused on her job. The two sisters couldn't be any different.

Aria was happiest when she read the Bible or worshipped God. Marta was constantly working. Flitting around. Always on the move. Going from one task to the other. It'd been pointed out to him by more than one person that both girls had crushes on him.

He quickly put that thought out of his mind and got back to the task at hand. While he would like to take the time to rejoice with the ones who were healed, he couldn't take his focus off of those who still suffered. In fact, he wanted to pick up the pace. Find a way to move the line along faster. Marta would have some ideas.

A man lumbered toward him. With a cane. Every step registered on his face as the grimaces gave away the intense pain he obviously felt.

Marta had the vial in her hand prepared to give it to Gohn.

A loud noise.

In the back of the room. Outside the double doors in the foyer.

It startled him. The sound was eerily reminiscent of the day two months ago when the service was interrupted by the man on the pallet.

He heard shouting.

The two double doors opened.

To his horror, two armed men entered the sanctuary with their guns drawn.

3

Gohn was slow to react to the two armed soldiers who had just entered the church. His attention had been on the man with the cane who he was about to lay hands on to receive his healing.

Will, on the other hand, reacted quickly. He'd been in the corner praying the prayer of salvation with someone. Now he was on the move trying to cut the men off before they could get to the front of the church. The line of sick and infirmed blocked the way and made it difficult for the soldiers to make it all the way to the front and kept Will from reaching the soldiers right away as well.

"Move!" one of the soldiers shouted angrily to the people in line.

Most of them seemed frozen in fear. Having dealt with soldiers before, Gohn knew the best approach was to remain calm and non-confrontive. Most in line weren't in any condition to challenge the men anyway.

A woman and small child didn't move fast enough, and one of the soldiers roughly pushed them to the side, knocking the child to the floor. That set Will off. He was impulsive and often acted out of emotions. Seeing the helpless woman pushed aside and the child thrown to the ground caused him to react with a fury.

"You have no right to be here!" Will yelled at the men. "This is a house of worship!" His shouting caused a crescendo of screams to echo through the building. The sick were beginning to panic. Gohn saw some heading for the exit.

"Back off," the soldier said, as Will got in the armed man's face. Their eyes were no further than six inches apart.

Aria was fearless as well and had helped the woman and young girl stand and get out of the way of the inevitable confrontation.

Gohn left the altar and walked quickly to the aisle to try and diffuse the situation if possible. "What is the meaning of this?" he said to the soldier, strongly but with a tone of respect.

After he said it, he heard the Holy Spirit say to him, "Don't worry about what to say or how to say it. I'll give you the words to speak."

A peace came over Gohn.

He put his hand on Will's shoulder and was able to move him away so that he was now between the two men.

Gohn stood face to face with the man. In the soldier's right hand was a piece of paper.

"Why are you here interrupting our church service?" Gohn asked.

"The room must be cleared immediately," the man said in a deep and gruff voice. "All churches have been ordered closed until further notice."

"On whose authority?" Will said, as he pushed his way past Gohn and was once again within striking distance of the soldier. Gohn tried to hold him back with his hand.

"On this authority," the soldier said, as he waved the piece of paper in Will's face.

"May I see that?" Gohn asked.

The soldier handed it to him.

Gohn began reading to himself.

Mercury Protocol 661

In order to ensure the public health and safety, all residents of Mercury are ordered to stay indoors at home and in their places of residences except as needed to maintain the continuity of operations of the national government, hereinafter called essential workers and businesses.

The Department of Health and the Department of Commerce have identified six essential business structures. They are listed in Addendum A. Essential businesses may continue their work because of their importance to the ongoing operations of the government. All other nonessential businesses are ordered closed.

Churches are considered nonessential and are to be closed immediately.

Pursuant to Mercurian Law and to be enforced by the armed guard of the Mercurian Proctor. All violators will be subject to fine, imprisonment, and even death if they resist.

The order will continue for a period of sixty days or until further notice.

The letter had the official seal of the government of Mercury and was signed by the Chief Proctor of Mercury.

After Gohn finished reading the protocol, Will snatched it out of his hand and read it quickly.

"This is ridiculous," Will said, throwing it to the ground. "There are no businesses on this planet more essential than churches."

The soldier raised his weapon a little higher, so it was pointed directly at Will.

"I have my orders," the man said.

"The order says that residents are to remain indoors," Gohn retorted. "As you can see, everyone is indoors. We're also providing a valuable service to the government. These people were sick and are leaving here completely healed. We'll send them home after we've ministered to them."

"My orders are that the building is to be cleared."

"Over my dead body," Will said.

"You're under arrest," the soldier said, taking a step toward Will.

"I'm not afraid of you," he retorted.

Before Gohn could react, the soldier raised his weapon and struck Will in the side of the head with the end of his gun.

Will staggered but somehow managed to stay on his feet.

A gash opened above his eye. That didn't seem to deter him. Will lunged at the soldier and knocked him to the ground. The second soldier was on Will in a flash and yanked him off his partner and threw him hard against the side of the pew. Will let out a huge exhalation of air as the breath was clearly knocked out of him. In a flash, the soldier had Will on his stomach with his knee against his back. Gohn could hear Will struggling to breathe.

The other soldier regained his feet. He took a pair of wrist braces and tied Will's hands together behind his back and then pulled him to his feet. Roughly. Angrily. Gohn could see the hatred and evil in his eyes as they burned like hot pieces of black coal.

Blood flowed down Will's cheek from the blow to his head.

"You're going to die for this," the soldier said to him.

Touch the braces, Gohn heard the Holy Spirit say.

Gohn stood behind Will. He reached his hand out which was hot as fire. When he touched the braces, they fell off Will's hands.

"Hey!" the soldier said.

Once free, Will lunged toward the soldier a second time. This time, the man was ready. He pointed his weapon and fired. The gunshot reverberated throughout the church with a loud cracking sound. Will was less than two feet away from the armed man. The bullet hit him in the chest. He slumped to the ground.

Aria was beside him in a second. Gohn initially stepped back at the sound of the gunshot. Once he regained his composure, he started toward Will. Marta grabbed his arm to stop him.

Gohn pulled away from her.

Aria knelt beside Will and felt for a pulse. "He's dead," she said, as her voice cracked, and her eyes welled up in tears.

"You murdered him," she cried out to the soldier.

More people were panicking and had fled the building.

Gohn still felt an unexplainable peace and wanted them to stay.

Lay your hands on Will, Gohn heard the Holy Spirit say in a still small voice.

He's dead, Gohn thought.

He's not dead. He's just asleep.

What can I do for him?

Jesus raised the dead. Remember what he said. Greater works than these shall you do.

Gohn got on one knee beside Will and laid his hands on him. The soldier pushed Gohn roughly away from Will's lifeless body. Blood had saturated the carpet and was on Gohn's hands as well.

Aria sobbed almost uncontrollably.

Marta shouted at Gohn trying to get his attention, but to no avail. His focus was on Will. He was oblivious to everything else.

Tell Will to wake up, the Holy Spirit said to Gohn.

What should I say?

The power of life and death is in the tongue.

The soldier was between them so Gohn couldn't lay his hands on him. Wasn't even worth the risk to try. By the look on the soldier's face, he was ready to fire the weapon at Gohn if he took one step closer.

The Holy Spirit said to speak the words. So, Gohn raised his hand in the air and said aloud, "Thank you God for healing Will, in the name of Jesus, our Lord and Savior."

Gohn could feel the power of the Holy Spirit pulse through his body, starting at his heart, racing down his extremities to his hands. Out of his hands and into the air.

"Will. Wake up!" Gohn said at the top of his lungs, not knowing what else to say. He thought that the louder he said it, the more power there'd be behind it, so he screamed it out. Then he remembered the power in the Holy Spirit's still small voice.

He said it again. This time softer. In his own still small voice. "Will. Wake up."

Marta looked at Gohn with her mouth agape and her eyebrows raised in confusion.

"Our brother, Will, is not dead," Gohn said to her. "He only sleeps."

Will's body twitched.

Then they heard him moan.

Aria screamed in delight when Will raised his head.

"Help him to his feet," Gohn said.

Will stood. A radiant glow shone from his face. Almost like he was transfigured.

Both soldiers raised their weapons to fire at him again. Their guns jammed. They also must've gotten extremely hot because they dropped them like they were holding a hot frying pan. The men took one more look at Will, and then at their guns that lay useless on the floor and let out their own screams. They took off running down the aisle. Toward the door which was still crowded with people trying to escape.

The soldiers pushed them to the side until they cleared a path out.

"Don't leave," Gohn said to the people once the soldiers were out of the building. "You're safe now. Come back to your seats."

One by one they returned.

Gohn and his core team huddled together. Will. Marta. Aria. Several of his elders and other members of the church who were there to help with the sick.

"They'll be back," Will said.

Something Gohn already knew.

For now, he just stared at his friend in amazement. If he hadn't seen it with his own eyes, he'd never have known that moments before, Will lay on the ground dead from a gunshot wound. The only evidence of the event was the bullet hole in his shirt and the blood that stained it. The carpet where Will had fallen was stained with blood as well. Will acted like nothing had even happened.

"Yes, they will be back," Gohn said. "With reinforcements."

"What do we do?" Marta asked.

"I'm not afraid of them," Will said. "We'll lock the church and not let them in."

"What about the people who are still outside?" Aria said, with deep concern in her voice.

Lord tell me what to do.

Gohn knew immediately what to do.

"Help everyone into their seats," he said. "We're going to see God do a great miracle today."

No one questioned him. Instead, they spread out across the room and helped the ones in need get back in their seats. They encouraged everyone to stay calm. When the seats were filled, they let more in from the outside, so the church was filled to capacity. The line outside was beginning to form again.

They continued until no one else would fit in the building.

It broke Gohn's heart that some had left out of fear. He prayed that they would have the strength to come back.

Gohn stood at the front to address the crowd. He raised his hands to quiet them. By the looks on their faces, most were still in shock. Terrified. Obviously concerned as well that the soldiers would return.

"The Proctor has ordered all churches closed," Gohn said. "A protocol has been released and states that all persons are confined to their homes for sixty days."

In unison, a protest rose from the crowd as they began to shout and speak against the protocol.

"The soldiers will return," Gohn said, after he quieted them. "So, we must hurry. There's still a long line outside. And there's no time for us to lay hands on each of you to receive your healing."

Again, in unison, the room cried out. Gohn could feel their pain. Their hopelessness. He immediately regretted the words. He'd spoken them out of his own flesh. Not under the leadership of the Holy Spirit.

He wouldn't make that mistake again.

Gohn paused to give himself time to hear from the still small voice.

After he did, he lifted both hands high in the air. "In the name of Jesus, our Lord and Savior, be healed!" he shouted with authority.

The sound of a rushing wind filled the room. Swept through it from one end to the other. Gohn could feel the coolness of the breeze.

Immediately, everyone in the room was healed. Of every affliction, disease, and infirmity.

From the front, he could see the change in the people. Unspeakable joy radiated from their faces as the agony, fear, and hopelessness left them.

"Do you believe in Jesus?" Gohn shouted out to the crowd. The sound in the room had risen to a frenetic level to the point that Gohn could barely hear himself speak.

He said it again. This time even louder.

The din slowly subsided.

"Do you believe that God raised Jesus from the dead?" Gohn asked.

"Yes," they shouted.

Leading them in the prayer of salvation became Gohn's priority now. What good did it do for them to be healed physically if they weren't healed spiritually?

"Then confess with your mouth that Jesus is Lord," Gohn said. "Say these words after me. I confess with my mouth."

"I confess with my mouth."

They repeated his words.

"Jesus is Lord," Gohn said.

Again, the people spoke in unison.

"And I believe in my heart." Each time Gohn spoke, he waited for the people to respond.

"That God raised him from the dead."

"So that I might be saved."

"And spend an eternity in heaven with Christ my Lord."

Gohn paused to let that sink in.

Suddenly, all across the room, those formerly sick began to praise God. The loudest noise Gohn had ever heard engulfed the room. The people clapped and shouted, and some raised their hands to heaven, others looked up to the heavens with their eyes.

Gohn's heart overflowed with jubilation as he saw the power of God heal and save so many people at once.

When the praise finally began to die down, Gohn said, "Everyone go home. The Proctor has ordered that every person remain indoors for the next sixty days. He's also ordered all churches to close. We're going to close today, but we'll be open this Sunday as usual. Bring with you anyone who is sick or in need of salvation."

The crowd cheered.

"Please make your way to the exit. There are more people outside who need to be healed."

As the crowd left, the group huddled again.

"That was amazing," Aria said, with a huge smile on her face. "God healed everyone at the same time."

"I wish we'd known that sooner," Marta said. Almost predictably. "That would've saved us a lot of time and effort." She didn't say it bitterly or sarcastically. She was only pointing out the obvious.

The thought had already occurred to Gohn. Healing everyone at once took a lot less effort. "Well, at least now we know," he said. "It's my fault. My lack of faith. Sometimes I limit God."

"You have more faith than anyone I've ever met," Marta said. She took his hand and squeezed it. An unusual show of affection.

"The way you stood up to those soldiers was incredible," Will said.

The side door to the church opened. Will's wife, Alcie, walked in. As soon as she saw her husband, she ran to him. She'd been home taking care of their young kids.

They embraced, and Alcie kissed him profusely.

"Someone said you were dead," she said, as tears welled up in her eyes.

"I was," Will said. "But Pastor raised me from the dead."

"God raised you," Gohn corrected.

"They said someone shot you," Alcie said.

He responded, "Like I said, God healed me."

"I don't believe it," she said. "I'm confused."

Alcie had always been a skeptic. A faithful member, but one who kept on the fringes. Gohn had had many long conversations with her about her faith. She often questioned it. Wasn't sure what she believed.

"It's true. Look at my shirt," Will said, pulling it away from his body. "Here's the bullet hole. Touch it. See for yourself."

Alcie's eyes were as wide as humanly possible. She touched his shirt. Then put her finger through the hole. The shirt was still stained with blood.

"Is that your blood?" Alcie asked.

"It is."

Alcie looked at Gohn who nodded. Alcie collapsed into Will's arms and began to cry.

"Don't cry, honey. I'm okay. Everything's okay."

"Your husband was amazing," Aria said. "He stood up to the soldiers."

Alcie squinted her eyes and furrowed her brow in what appeared to be a look of confusion.

"Two soldiers came to the church to shut us down. I tried to stop them," Will explained. "One of the soldiers shot me. I don't really know what happened next. They said I died."

"That's when God healed him," Gohn said.

"He was dead," Aria said. "I checked for a pulse myself."

"You fool!" Alcie said, patting Will on his chest. "Promise me you won't do anything that stupid again."

"I can't promise that," he said with a chuckle. "I imagine the soldiers will be back at some point."

"Which is why we'd better get to work," Marta said. "Looks like the next group is in place."

For several hours, they brought in group after group. Around three hundred at a time.

Each time, God faithfully healed everyone present. After a while, Gohn didn't feel as rushed and allowed more time for praising God and even a few testimonies.

Around nine o'clock, the last group left. The soldiers hadn't returned. Gohn wasn't sure why they hadn't.

"Is there anyone else out there?" Gohn asked, as exhaustion finally set in. None of them had eaten since that morning or had taken any breaks.

"That's everybody," Marta said.

"I'm so proud of all of you," Gohn said.

"Should you have promised the people that the church will be open this Sunday?" Marta asked. "You could be arrested."

"We can talk about that later," Gohn said, dismissively. "Let's just focus on today. And thank God for the miracles we've seen. He protected us. I'm sure he'll protect us Sunday if someone comes to arrest me."

"I'm surprised the soldiers never returned," Will said.

As if on cue, they heard a noise in the foyer. A door opened and then slammed shut.

In walked one of the soldiers. The one who had shot Will.

Don't be afraid, the Holy Spirit said to Gohn.

The soldier walked quickly down the aisle.

"Stay here," Gohn said to Will.

Gohn met him halfway. The others didn't listen and were standing right behind Gohn.

The soldier wasn't carrying a weapon.

"All the people have left," Gohn said. "We're all going to our homes now as well. I'm afraid your trip here was unnecessary."

Tears had formed in the man's eyes. One tear escaped and ran down his cheek.

"What is it?" Gohn asked, as he suddenly felt compassion for the man.

His voice cracked as he answered, "Do you... think... God could save... someone like me?"

"Of course, he can," Gohn said. "What's your name?"

"Cloyd."

Gohn turned to Will. "Could you lead Cloyd in the prayer of salvation?"

Will's jaw was tense. His shoulders raised. His fists clenched. He was ready to fight the man again. Suddenly, his demeanor changed. All of that tension immediately left his face when Gohn spoke the words.

"Come with me," Will said gently to Cloyd.

They went and sat down on the first pew on the right side of the church.

Gohn let out a huge sigh of relief. Then he took Aria and Marta in his arms and hugged them tightly.

"That may be the greatest miracle we've seen today," Gohn said, as he let a huge grin of satisfaction form on his face.

"God is so good," Aria said.

"Yes, he is," Gohn answered. "But the Holy Spirit just told me that things are about to get a lot worse. Our faith is going to be tested in ways we never thought possible."

"I don't see how things could get any worse," Marta said.

If what Gohn had seen in his dreams and visions were about to come to pass, things were going to get way worse.

Nearly unbearable.

4

M arta was in love with Pastor Gohn and didn't know what to do about it.

She was in the spare bedroom of his apartment cleaning it up. When Mercury Protocol 661 was issued and everyone was restricted to their homes, the decision was made for Marta to move into the second bedroom of the church parsonage. That way she could still do her job as Gohn's assistant.

Of course, a single woman living in a single man's apartment would be considered highly inappropriate. So, Aria, Marta's sister, moved in as well. A source of consternation for Marta. They hadn't shared a room since they were kids. Marta hated it then and the last two days had reminded her why.

She looked around the room. Her side was perfectly straightened and organized. The bed was made. Her clothes were hung neatly in the closet. A Bible lay on the bedside table. Aria's side was a mess. Her bed was mussed. Clothes were strewn on the floor and piled up on the bed. Dirty dishes sat on her bedside table.

Disgusting.

Marta had mentioned to Aria several times that she needed to keep her side clean. Each time she was met with the same response, "I'll get around to it."

She never did.

Marta wanted to bring it up again. For Aria to keep her room messy at their house was one thing but quite another to leave it in disarray at Gohn's apartment. Technically, the church's apartment. What if a member of the church came by? What if Gohn came in and saw it? It reflected badly on her.

Rather than keep harping on it, Marta decided to clean it up herself. Easier than nagging her sister into doing it which didn't work anyway.

Marta picked one of Aria's shirts off the floor and threw it across the room toward the dirty clothes basket. Then shuddered her shoulders to release some of the tension and anger.

She loved her sister, but sometimes...

Marta began making Aria's bed as her thoughts returned to her predicament.

The feelings.

For Gohn.

They were excruciating sometimes.

No matter how hard she tried to suppress them, they wouldn't go away. They started shortly after she began working for him. A slight attraction had grown into an infatuation which had blossomed into a full-blown, head-over-heels love.

She could do nothing about it even if she wanted to. She couldn't tell Gohn. It'd ruin everything. She worked for him. He was a pastor. While they were both single and nearly the same age, the situation was complicated. If she told anyone, Gohn would find out. He'd have to tell the elders of the church. She'd be forced to quit her job.

Embarrassing.

It'd be hard to ever show her face in that church again.

But what if he felt the same way? Was she missing her one and probably only opportunity for happiness?

Not possible anyway. It took two. Gohn had never shown the slightest bit of interest in her. He'd always been the consummate professional. That would make it worse. If the feelings weren't reciprocated, she'd feel like a fool.

Marta quickly tamped down the thoughts. Things were better this way. Gohn was obsessed with his ministry anyway. The End Times. The Eliminati. His visions and dreams. Something she admired about him. His love for the Lord and his passion for ministry were two of the qualities she was most attracted to.

Really, a moot point. Marta wasn't the kind of girl men noticed or had romantic feelings for. Boys didn't when she was younger and in school, and men didn't now, even though she was older.

She let out a sigh of resignation and flung Aria's pillow to the floor. Then picked up an article of her clothing from the bed and sent it flying through the air. A lame attempt at letting out her frustrations which were now directed toward her sister.

Why did her feelings for Gohn make her mad at her sister?

She knew why. Those old feelings of inadequacy and jealousy of Aria had plagued her most of her life. She thought she'd dealt with those. Now that they were living together, they were coming to the surface.

Why did she feel inadequate? She hated feeling that way. Aria was the one who should feel inferior to her. Marta was the dependable one. Hard working. Made straight, level top grades in school. Never got into trouble. The one her parents were always proud of.

But Aria always got all the attention. She was the pretty one. Her hair was long and flowing. Her features, perfect.

In contrast, Marta was homely. Slightly overweight. Her teeth were a little crooked which caused her to hide her smile. Marta's hair and dress were always understated. She was the one overlooked in school. The only reason anyone even noticed her was because she was smart. Boys were more likely to ask her to help them with their homework than out on a date.

Since she'd come of age, Marta had only been on a handful of dates and those were a disaster. The boys were immature and lacked ambition. The men were grabby with only one thing on their minds. Even the Christian men seemed to have zero interest in the things of God. She needed someone who was her spiritual equal.

Someone like Gohn.

That isn't going to happen.

She had to let it go.

Marta felt a pang pierce her heart. She threw Aria's bedspread to the ground. Roughly.

The thoughts flooded her soul like a storm cloud had been unleashed.

She'd be a good wife to Gohn. A helpmate. A virtuous woman like the Bible described. Gohn deserved someone like her. Not someone like Aria.

Where did that thought come from?

Was Gohn interested in Aria?

Did her sister have feelings for him?

Aria was a flirt. Even toward Gohn. But that was how she was. She didn't mean to flirt; it just came naturally to her. Men found Aria attractive. Fun. Sexy.

The thought made Marta bristle inside. She'd die if she found out Aria liked Gohn. Surely, he'd never be attracted to someone like her.

Or would he?

Now, she wasn't so sure.

A knock on the door interrupted her thoughts.

"Come in," Marta said.

Gohn opened the door. Of course, it had to be him. No one else was there. Aria had gone to the store. According to the protocols, one member of the household was allowed to leave the house one time during the week to gather food and supplies. They decided that Aria should go this time and get everything they needed.

"Are you available?" Gohn asked, in a serious tone. "I have something I need to talk to you about."

"I'm just straightening the room. Give me ten minutes," she said.

While the room was still a mess, at least he saw her working on it.

"I'll meet you in my office," he said, and then flashed her a smile that sent her heart racing.

He closed the door, but the image of him still lingered in her mind. Along with a strange feeling. What did he want? It sounded important. He seemed deeply concerned about something. Of course, these were difficult times. He was concerned. About the church. The protocols. The tyranny of the Mercurial Proctor.

Having seen Gohn, Marta was now fully distracted from the task at hand. Gohn was ruggedly handsome. A shorter man, but strong. His arms were muscular. Not in a bulky way but toned and defined. His grip was hard and firm. People at church sometimes complained about his handshakes. They were too firm. Several also complained about his hair. Gohn had a medium-length beard. His curly locks were dark brown and covered his ears and went below his shoulders. Longer than what some thought was appropriate.

His eyebrows were bushy and accented his steely brown eyes which were like embers of coals when he was angry. Gohn had a temper. A fiery personality. Generally, only when he was dealing with an injustice, but sometimes he could erupt if the situation called for it. Part of it was that his face always looked like he was angry. His nose was crooked and jagged with a slight hump, and his nostrils flared when he spoke. That added to his ruggedness.

She'd also seen his softer side many times. When ministering to the sick. Helping a family dealing with grief. Gohn had the heart of a lion but could be as gentle as a lamb when he wanted to be.

Gohn was a unique person. He didn't have the charisma one would normally expect from a pastor. He was socially awkward. But he loved people. He worked hard and was obsessed with the truth. Part of why they got along so well. Marta was a stickler for the truth too. Everything was black and white to her. Gohn saw things that way as well.

She admired everything about him. Which made her desire him even more.

Marta finished making Aria's bed as the anger toward her sister returned with a fury.

What would Gohn see in her?

Marta was hard working. Aria, flighty. Marta paid careful attention to detail. Meticulously planned out her day and her future. Aria flew by the seat of her pants. Lived in the moment. Hardly gave a thought to anything other than what she had to do today. Marta was never late. Aria was never on time. Marta was a perfectionist. Aria never met a detail she paid attention to.

Infuriating.

Surely that wasn't what Gohn wanted in a wife.

Why was she worried about that?

Because...

Marta felt tears well up inside of her again.

She and Gohn had actually talked about it once. The subject of marriage came up. Marta said she was destined to be single all her life. To die an old maid. Gohn reminded her that the Bible said it was better for a woman to remain single than to marry so she could focus on serving the Lord and not her husband. Marta regretted mentioning that because Gohn would never look at her in that way because of it. But as Marta grew older, she suddenly had an overwhelming desire to be married. To have babies. To be married to Gohn.

That wasn't going to happen.

She looked at the clock on the wall. Ten minutes had passed. Gohn was waiting for her in his office. The room wasn't finished but would have to wait. She looked in the mirror to see if she was presentable. She ran her hands through her hair. Then brushed away the remnant of the tears from her eyes and off her cheeks. Took a deep breath to compose herself.

Gohn's office was in another part of the building. Once there, she stopped by her desk which was just outside his office door to get a pad and paper so she could take notes.

As she started to enter his office, her heart began to race. Her palms were sweating. The normally strong knees suddenly felt weak. Marta got that way around Gohn. Even after all these months of working with him.

When she walked into the office, he surprisingly said, "Close the door please."

An ominous feeling came over her. Gohn never told her to close the door. He felt like it was inappropriate for them to be in a room alone together.

"Please have a seat," he said, soberly. For a moment, Marta wondered if someone had died.

She sat down in the chair slowly. Gohn sat at his desk and leaned forward with his hands clasped in front of him with his chin against them.

"I need to talk to you about Aria," he said.

Marta's heart did a complete somersault in her chest.

"What about Aria?" Marta asked, dreading the answer.

"We talked... yesterday... She came... to my office." Gohn stuttered as he tried to force out the words. Marta had never seen him like this. Gohn was a wordsmith. An eloquent preacher. In difficult situations, he always seemed to know exactly what to say.

You're scaring me, she wanted to say but resisted the urge.

Instead, she said, "What's wrong? What did Aria say to you?"

"She told me that she's," he hesitated again. Then blurted out, "She told me that she's in love with me."

Had Marta not been gripping the side of the chair with a vise grip, she would've fallen out of it.

5

"Aria told you she loves you?" Marta said incredulously. Hardly able to believe the words she heard come out of Pastor's Gohn's mouth.

Gohn nodded his head yes and then leaned back in his chair.

"That's what she said," Gohn replied hesitantly, almost like he was embarrassed. "Two days ago. Right here in my office. Right where you're sitting."

"Was she serious?" Marta asked. "Maybe she was kidding. You know how Aria is."

"That's what I thought at first. Then she started crying. Even apologized. It seemed like she immediately regretted it because she said shouldn't have told me."

That sounded like Aria. The Drama Queen. She'd always been the emotional one. As kids growing up, Aria would cry at the slightest provocation. If they watched a sad movie, Aria would cry. When their cat died, Aria cried for weeks.

Another way the two girls were total opposites. Marta couldn't remember the last time she'd cried. It wasn't her nature to get emotional.

That wasn't completely true.

Tears had welled up in her eyes a few minutes before. Back in her bedroom, when she thought of the possibility that Aria might be in love with Gohn. Now, her worst fear had come to pass. Had she sensed it? Subconsciously? Perhaps in the far recesses of her mind, she already knew that Aria had feelings for Gohn. That's why she felt such angst about her own feelings. If it came down to a competition between her and Aria, she could never win. Boys always preferred Aria to her.

Although, Gohn wasn't a boy. He was a man. Surely, he wouldn't fall for someone like Aria. Young and immature. Flighty and flirty.

She had to ask. But... did she really want to know?

"What did you say?" Marta blurted out before she could stop herself.

"I didn't know what to say."

Wrong answer.

You should've told her that you aren't in love with her. That you never would be.

"I was flattered," Gohn said pensively. "But I was confused. Aria is a member of my congregation. How would it look to them?"

Was he considering it? He certainly hadn't come right out and said he wasn't interested in pursuing a relationship with Aria.

Marta wanted to slink out of the room. Instead, an idea popped into her head.

She hated what she was about to do.

"I wouldn't take it seriously," Marta said. "You know how Aria is. She falls in love as often as I change my clothes."

Guilt raged inside of her as her heart sped up from the fabrication. She'd always prided herself on telling the truth. But she couldn't stop herself. Marta waved her hand in the air in an exaggerated fashion. "I'm sure it's just a silly schoolgirl crush." She wanted to remind Gohn of the age difference.

"I didn't know that about her," Gohn said. "I've never known her to have a boyfriend."

Aria had never had a serious boyfriend. Or been in love as far as Marta knew. Boys fell in love with her all the time, but she never reciprocated. Hadn't to this point at least. Aria telling Gohn she loved him was out of character. Her sister must've struggled with the decision for days. Marta was surprised Aria hadn't mentioned it to her. Maybe Aria could sense Marta had feelings for him as well.

"Are you in love with her?" Marta asked hesitantly. She winced as she said it.

"I'd never really thought about it until she said something."

You've had time to think about it now, Marta wanted to shout at the top of her lungs. Typical man. Keeping his options open. It's a simple question. Was he in love with her? His face didn't give away an answer, and Marta searched it carefully.

She started to rattle off a list of arguments against dating Aria. Having grown up with her, she was aware of her every fault. Or she could stick with the obvious.

Aria's a member of his congregation.

He was so busy with the church.

The protocols.

These were difficult times that would be complicated by a romantic relationship. Then she realized she'd be making the case against a relationship with her as well. A convincing case that he shouldn't date Aria was an equally convincing argument that he shouldn't date her. Not that he was even considering her. He didn't even know she was an option. Still.

So, she bit her tongue to keep from saying anything.

Telling Gohn about her own feelings was out of the question now. That's the last thing he needed. Two sisters competing for his affections. Talk about complicated.

She began to seethe. How could Aria do that to her? She ruined everything. Dashed any hopes Marta ever had of having a relationship with Gohn. Also complicated things at the church. People were going to find out about it.

Then she wondered. Who else has Aria told?

What if Gohn returned the love? Marta didn't think she could stand to be around that. If that happened, she couldn't keep working for Gohn. Seeing him and Aria together would be too much to bear.

If he told Aria he wasn't interested, that would complicate things as well. Aria would be hurt. Especially if she and Gohn ever started a relationship. Aria would feel betrayed.

What a mess!

Could they still live in his apartment? Should they move out? Who would help Gohn at the church?

What was Aria thinking?

Telling Gohn was a stupid thing to do. That's why Marta hadn't done it. It made things too complicated.

"Why are you telling me this?" she asked, somewhat coldly, suddenly realizing she opened her mouth before really thinking it through.

"I wondered if she had talked to you about it. I thought maybe you knew. You might be able to tell me what to do."

"She hasn't talked to me, but I'm thinking it's just a crush. Aria is too young to be in love." More guilt. Technically, twenty-four was not too young. Marta kept making every argument she could think of.

"She doesn't even know what it means," Marta said. "She's been sheltered all her life. I would just ignore it if I were you. It'll pass."

Gohn had a far-off look as he stared at the ceiling.

"Maybe so," he said.

"Are you ready to talk about Sunday?" Marta asked, as she adjusted her position in the chair, crossed her legs, and got the pencil and pad in the ready position. She didn't want to talk about Aria anymore.

"Yes. We should talk about that. What are we going to do if three thousand people show up on Sunday?"

"Is that even possible? The checkpoints are set up all around the quadrangle. How will they get here?"

"They should defy them," Gohn said strongly.

Marta was glad things were back to normal. Gohn had returned to being his fiery self. Get him talking about ministry and everything else was put on the backburner. If the subject did come up again, she'd be better prepared. A plan was already formulating in her mind to confront Aria about it.

She tried to keep her focus on the conversation at hand. "They'll be arrested if they defy the protocol."

"They can't arrest everyone," Gohn retorted. "If the people of God rise up and defy the authorities, they'll have no choice but to back down. The only way they win is if God's people do nothing."

Gohn's tone sounded angry and defiant.

"The soldiers will be armed," Marta said. "They might even have orders to kill all the Christians who defy the order."

"God will protect us. Like he did against the soldiers who came to the church last week."

"The Protocol says that all churches are to remain closed for the sixty days. Sounds like you intend to defy that order."

Gohn slammed his fist on his desk.

Marta jumped and uncrossed her legs.

"The Bible says that we are not to forsake meeting together. We're not closing our doors just because the government tells us to. We answer to a higher power. God didn't say to meet every week unless the authorities tell you not to."

"Some people argue that the Bible says we are supposed to submit to government authorities. I'm not saying that we should," she quickly added. "I'm just trying to anticipate the arguments."

"The authorities told the disciples not to preach in the square. They did it anyway. The authorities told the early church that they couldn't meet in their churches. They ignored them. If they hadn't, the church would've died out before it even got started."

"And many of them were arrested and some were executed for defying the authorities." Marta wasn't being argumentative. Just practical. They needed to think through all the ramifications of defying the protocol.

"A martyr's death," Gohn said. "There's a special reward in heaven for those who defy the tyranny of the government and are martyred for the sake of the gospel. I'm not afraid to die."

"Neither am I. But... like you said, what do we do if all those people show up?" she asked.

"That's a good problem to have," Gohn said.

"A problem, nonetheless. It's not like we can set up several service times at this late date. Sunday is two days from now."

"I know," Gohn said, staring off at the ceiling again.

At least he wasn't thinking about Aria at the moment. Hopefully. She wouldn't give him a chance.

"We also have all of our leaders to consider," Marta said. "How are they going to get here? We can't do this alone."

"I know. I've thought about that but haven't come up with a solution."

An idea came to Marta. "What if they used Sunday as their day to leave the house?"

"What do you mean?" Gohn asked, now fully engaged. He was sitting on the edge of his seat, with his hands on the desk in front of him.

"The protocol says that nonessential workers are only allowed out of the house one day a week. To go to the store and get supplies."

"Right. Aria is at the store as we speak. Getting everything we need."

Marta bristled inside. Why did Gohn have to bring up Aria's name? She already knew what Aria was doing. Gohn knew she knew as well.

She decided to ignore it. This was the new reality. Something she was going to have to get used to. "My understanding is that the first time you go out, the soldiers give you a protocol 661 card. I haven't seen one, but from what I hear, it has eight holes. One for each week. The soldiers punched a hole in each person's card each week when you try to go through the checkpoints. That's how they know if you go out more than one time in a seven-day period of time."

"Tyranny!" Gohn said in a raised voice.

Marta thought he was going to strike the desk again.

He didn't this time. "It's their way of controlling us. There's no hole in the stratazone layer. Even if there were, what difference does it make if we are inside or outside. If it breaks, we're all dead anyway. I don't believe God will allow that to happen."

"I don't disagree. What I'm saying is that those are the rules of the protocol. Why don't we have our leaders use Sunday as their one day to go to the store? They can have their cards punched at the checkpoints, but then come straight here."

"After the services are over," Gohn said, excitedly as his face lit up. His eyes brightened and his bushy eyebrows were raised. "They can go to the store on their way home."

"Exactly. Their families won't be able to come with them, but at least the leaders can come to the church and help."

"Marta, that's brilliant!"

For the first time that day, Marta let a momentary feeling of joy overwhelm her. Even if she knew it'd be short-lived.

"That still doesn't solve the problem of the soldiers," Marta said. "If they come to the church, which I'm sure they'll do, then they'll find that we're open."

"Cloyd is working on that," Gohn answered.

Marta didn't respond, so Gohn continued. Cloyd was the soldier saved at the last service. The one who shot Will.

"Cloyd is trying to get put in charge of monitoring the churches in our Quadrangle. If he's successful, he'll report back that they're all closed."

"That's risky. For him especially. Eventually, someone will find out. He'll be the one arrested."

"He's willing to take that risk. We'll just have to trust God to protect us. We're living in the last days. I'm certain of it. Jesus said the suffering would be such as has never been seen before on Mercury. The only reason the days will be cut short is for the sake of believers. Nothing we can do about the persecution. We just have to endure it."

The pain Marta felt inside was not the type of suffering Jesus was referring to. Now that the conversation with Gohn was winding down, the thoughts of Aria and Gohn came flooding back like a heavy gale. Aria would be home soon. How could she look her in the eye? More importantly, how could she keep from confronting her?

Gohn's tone suddenly softened. "Thank you, Marta. I don't know what I'd do without you. Are things working out okay with your living arrangements? Do you and Aria have everything you need?"

No! Aria is a terrible housekeeper. She leaves everything in the room a mess all the time. Do you want that in a wife?

It was all Marta could do to fight back the words.

"Everything's fine," Marta said instead. "The bedroom is cramped but workable. Given what you told me earlier, it's a good thing I'm here. I'll try to make sure that Aria is never alone with you. You know how people talk."

"That's probably a good idea."

Probably?

What was with all the mixed messages? She still didn't know how Gohn felt about Aria. He hadn't given her the slightest hint about his intentions. The worst part of that was he had definitely not ruled them out.

A door slammed.

So loud it resounded all the way into Gohn's office. Even with his door closed.

It startled Marta, and she could see that it startled Gohn as well. He bolted out of his chair and hurried out of the room with Marta following him.

A figure darted down the hallway and into the living quarters. It looked like Aria.

They followed her down the hall into the living area and kitchen which made up one big room.

Aria was sitting bags on the counter. She turned toward them, blood dripping from her forehead.

Before Marta could react, Gohn was at her side. He had his arm around her.

"What happened?" he asked. "You're hurt."

Aria had clearly been crying as well, and she roughly brushed tears off her cheeks.

"It was just awful. One of the soldier's hit me," Aria blurted out.

"Hit you!" Gohn said angrily.

"Yes. It was horrible. I didn't do anything to deserve it."

"Why did he hit you?"

Aria was sobbing now. "I got the groceries and was on my way home. He asked for my ID card. I tried to get it out of my bag. You know the new card. The Protocol 661 card that they gave me earlier when I went through the checkpoint. I couldn't get it out fast enough. So, the soldier pushed me aside and took my bag. I fell to the ground and hit my head on the walkway."

"Doesn't sound like he actually hit you," Marta said.

Aria glared at her sister.

Gohn squeezed Aria's shoulders more tightly in an obvious attempt to console her. Her head collapsed onto his chest.

Oh, good grief!

Marta thought it was a little much. Considering what they'd been talking about in Gohn's office. About the persecution to come.

See what I mean, she wanted to say to Gohn. *Aria's a Drama Queen. Is that what you want in a wife?*

6

Sunday morning
3:00 a.m.
The Fourth Watch of the Night

I was awakened by a loud voice. Calling my name.
"Gohn."

In an audible voice.

Accompanied by a thunderous sound. The wind rushed around me, but I was not shaken nor caught up in it. Lightning flashed around me, but I was not afraid. At least, not at first.

Was I dreaming?

I couldn't be. I was fully awake.

Whether in the body or out of the body, I wasn't sure. God knew. All I knew was that I was caught up in the spirit. Somehow, I was in the third heaven. Don't ask me how I knew. In that state, you have a greater awareness of the things around you. Everything was in vivid color. My senses were more alive than at any other time in my life.

Even though I was in the third heaven, I was also in the bedroom of my apartment. I looked out the window and could see that the night was still dark.

Strange.

The blinds were closed, but I could see outside.

The lights in my room were off, but the room was illuminated by a great light. A beautiful, bright, glorious light.

The voice spoke again. He called my name again. "Gohn," he said. "Write down what you see. Speak the words I give you to the seven churches of the quadrangles." The seven churches made up all the peoples of Mercury.

I turned to see where the voice was coming from. A man in a white robe walked toward me. His eyes were radiant and glowed like embers of coal. His hair and head were white. Without spot or blemish. Pure as the piece of white paper from the notepad that sat on my desk. When I started having dreams and visions, I put the pad there so I could write down everything I remembered from my visions.

A stack of several hundred white papers with my handwriting on them lay on the corner of the desk. Held down by my Bible.

"I am the living one," the voice said.

I fell to my knees by the side of my bed. Knowing immediately that I was in the presence of my Lord.

My entire body shook. I could no longer look upon his face. I cowered before him. He was still at a distance, and yet I felt like I could reach out and touch him.

I didn't dare.

"Do not be afraid," the kind and gentle voice said.

I suddenly found strength and stood to my feet. Like a force lifted me.

"Write the things you are about to see and hear," he said again.

My desk was in the corner of the room against the wall. Without knowing what was causing my body to move, I started to walk toward it. My knees were wobbly at first, and I staggered. But then I caught my balance and steadied myself when I grabbed the corner of the side of the desk, and I managed to sit down in the chair.

I took the writing instrument in my hand.

The storm around me intensified as the man in the white robe was almost upon me. Storm was the only way I knew how to describe it. Loud claps of thunder echoed through my room. Then bright lightning bolts.

I thought thunder came after the lightning.

Nothing I saw made sense.

Did Marta and Aria hear it?

How could they not? They were in a room on the other side of the apartment, but the sounds were so loud, it seemed like they would be heard for miles.

Why had the girls not come to see what the commotion was about? Part of me wanted to run and wake them, but I was restrained. By what, I hadn't a clue.

The man hovered right over me now. His arms were outstretched. Controlling my movements but not touching me.

The Lord God said, "Gohn. My faithful servant. To you I give the mysteries of the last days on Mercury."

His voice was like the sound of a loud trumpet.

"The things I give you are for the saints," he continued. "I will explain to you the things that are, the things that are to be, and that which shall take place after these things."

I felt unworthy.

If not for the seat holding me up, I would've fallen to my knees again.

Images suddenly appeared on the wall above my desk. Like a movie playing on a screen. I reached out to touch them, but nothing was there in the physical realm. Yet I could see it as plain as if I were actually in the picture. I saw with spiritual eyes.

A room came into view.

In the room were six men. They sat around a conference table. I didn't recognize them.

The room was lavish. The men were obviously of considerable means. Dressed in expensive clothes. The time piece on one man's arm cost more than twenty years of my salary at the church.

My eyes could see more than their physical bodies. I could see into their souls. I could read their thoughts. Their motives were laid bare like the core of a sliced apple. What I saw made me shudder.

Pure evil.

The evil presence was inside of them but also lingered over the room. I felt the evil one even though I couldn't see him. The vileness in the room was so strong, I wanted to run.

But something held me back. The words "Do not be afraid," kept overwhelming the urge to flee.

One of the men in the room spoke. The man who sat at the head of the table. He appeared to be the leader. Or the Holy Spirit revealed that to me. I could understand what he said. Could still see inside of him. His thoughts and motives.

My mouth gaped open. I was looking at the Eliminati.

They were real!

Will was right. The conspiracy was being unveiled right before my eyes. A secret cabal. The men who ran the world. Like puppet masters. With an evil plan orchestrated by Satan. Every thought and action taken upon his command.

I furiously wrote what I heard and saw. Barely able to keep up with it.

"The Disorderlies are a threat," the leader said.

"We can squash them like ants any time we want," another man added.

The Holy Spirit continued to give me discernment. The Disorderlies were the Christians. We were the threat.

"There are too many Disorderlies to arrest them all," the leader said.

When I heard those words, I suddenly knew what the Lord wanted me to do. I wrote it down and highlighted it on the paper.

"How many people have we terminated to date?" a man asked, with an evil grin on his face. His eyes were filled with hate. They burned with rage at the mention of the Disorderlies. His nostrils flared, and he bared his teeth like a snake about to strike its prey.

Strange.

On the outside he looked perfectly normal. I could see into his heart.

"Seven thousand," a man answered. Once again, on the outside, the man spoke the words in a calm and emotionless manner. On the inside, he was laughing. Hideously. I could see the snarling, sneering, gnashing of teeth as his jaw clenched tighter than a vise. A vein pulsed on the side of his neck from the rage inside of him. The laughter was his way of releasing the tension inside that was about to explode and would if not contained by his physical body.

I gasped out loud.

My heart broke as my eyes filled with tears. I knew what he meant. Seven thousand innocent souls were killed by the Eliminati. I suddenly knew why they chose that name. To eliminate every threat. Particularly the Christians.

"Part of the purpose of the protocol was to thin out the population," one of the men said, confirming what I already knew.

A righteous anger filled my heart. They were manufacturing protocols to eliminate Christians. Control the churches. Keep the people under their control.

The leader stood to his feet. The room grew quiet. His demeanor changed on the inside. His bulging eyes were filled with rage. His nostrils dilated and pulsed in and out as his breathing increased to a rapid pace. His face turned slightly red. The tight lips from the clenched jaw suddenly curled.

On the outside, he looked perfectly normal to the others in the room. I could see the effect the evil one had on his emotions which churned inside of him like a pot of boiling water.

"I'm creating another protocol. Mercury Protocol 661."

And there it was! This meeting was from the past. The day Mercury Protocol 661 was enacted. God had allowed me to see what happened in real time and where it had come from.

The Eliminati was behind it.

The leader continued with words that sent chills down my spine, "We'll tell the people we've discovered a hole in the stratazone layer of the atmosphere. Our atmosphere is warming at an alarming pace."

Lies!

A verse in the Bible came to mind. I wrote it down on a separate piece of paper.

"No one will be allowed to leave their homes for sixty days. That will shut the churches down," the leader said.

My mouth flew open for a second time. It all suddenly made sense. The lockdown was to shut down the churches. We'd seen thousands healed from Mercury Protocol 660. They needed a new decree. Protocol 661. Something to make it impossible for us to minister to people in need.

The movie playing above my desk suddenly disappeared. As fast as it had come.

The man in the white robe appeared in the blink of an eye. This time he didn't speak. An angel of the Lord spoke for him.

"Gohn. As a fellow partaker in the tribulation and the perseverance which is in Jesus."

I wrote the words down furiously.

"Because of the Word of God and the testimony of Jesus."

Before I could write those words, a picture of Revelation Church suddenly appeared on the screen above my desk.

The sanctuary was empty.

I began to cry.

I knew why it was empty.

No one was coming to the services that day. The people were too afraid.

A small group sat in the corner on the first two rows of the church.

My leaders. I could see them. Will. Marta and Aria. Roux. Jass-ron. Lars. Hawke. It warmed my heart.

Pret was also there. Why? She wasn't a leader. Pret was Will's daughter. I assumed she came to church that day to help with the kids.

The Lord spoke to me. "In the last days, I will pour out my spirit on all people. Your sons and daughters will prophesy."

The Holy Spirit reminded me of a verse in the Bible. *God was no respecter of persons. Women could prophesy along with men.* Pret was there because God wanted me to invite her. I needed to make her a leader. God was going to give her dreams and visions. She will prophesy.

The Eliminati suddenly reappeared on the screen, replacing the meeting with my leaders.

The evil leader still stood at the head and addressed the group. "We'll tell the world that the lockdown will only be for sixty days," he repeated. "But we can continue it indefinitely. However long it takes to get control of the Disorderlies."

"What do we do when the people realize it's all a sham? That there is no threat to the climate?" someone in the room said.

"We'll write another protocol, if necessary," the leader answered confidently. "And another. Then another if need be."

The Holy Spirit told me the leader's name. Herodius.

"And if the protocols don't work?" Herodius was asked.

He answered. "Then we'll kill every last one of them."

The image suddenly disappeared.

* * *

For what seemed like hours, I wrote down the things I'd seen and heard. When I finished writing, I looked at the clock. One minute to six. The fourth watch was over at six. I knew from Scripture that a number of strategic events took place during the fourth watch.

The solemnity of the moment was not lost on me. From three in the morning until six, God had met me in a remarkable way. Many of the prophets had divine encounters with God during the fourth watch.

None more significant than the one I'd just had.

Right before the clock struck six, an amazing thing happened.

A rainbow appeared in my room. The colors overwhelmed it. At exactly six, the rainbow disappeared.

A sign.

I had the revelation for the church of the first quadrangle.

* * *

6:30 a.m.

Gohn was alone.

With only his thoughts and his papers. He rifled through them, although they were etched in his mind.

Still wearing his bed clothes, Gohn quickly changed. The sun had risen, and light crept in the window through the shades.

After he dressed, Gohn walked through the living room to the other side of the apartment and knocked gently on Marta and Aria's door.

Marta answered it. She hid partially behind the door.

"Is something wrong?" she asked.

"I need your help," Gohn said.

7

N o one showed up for church.
Just as Gohn had expected.

He had a vision earlier that morning of an empty sanctuary. The fact that no one showed up was confirmation that the vision was from God.

A few leaders did make it. Also, as Gohn had expected. The same ones he'd seen in his vision. More confirmation.

Marta and Aria were there. Nothing more had been said to either of them since the conversation with Marta a couple days before. It seemed to be a topic they were all avoiding.

Will was there and showed no effects of having been shot in the chest only a few days before. Gohn couldn't wait to tell him about his vision. The Eliminati was real. He'd seen it with his own eyes. They were behind the Protocols. Will would be beside himself when he heard the news.

Four of the elders, Lars, Jassron, Roux, and Hawke, were there.
And Pret.

Will's daughter. She came to church with Will to help with the kids. As it turned out, no kids came that morning. The fact that she was there was divine providence though. Before the meeting, Gohn asked her to join them.

A fog of disappointment hung over the group. A sharp contrast to the excitement from a few days before when more than three-thousand people were healed and saved. Gohn struggled to keep the group's optimism up. He felt the depression as well but had the benefit of the vision. He knew things they didn't know.

His mission was clear. For whatever reason, God had chosen him for such a time as this. To fight the Eliminati. To reveal to the world his visions and dreams. To help usher in the last days. It wouldn't be easy. The church had to stand up to the ungodly cabal that operated in secret. People would be skeptical. He'd be labeled a lunatic. A conspiracy theorist. A madman.

However, Gohn knew the reality of the situation. If the church succumbed to the pressure of the protocols, then the Eliminati would have won. Mercury Protocol 661 was a lie. A ruse to try and close the churches. There was no hole in the stratazone. The people needed to know the truth. He was going to give it to them.

"Don't be sad that no one showed up today," Gohn said to the group "Soon this place will be packed with people."

"I love your optimism," Will said. "And I agree with you. But people are afraid of the soldiers. Pret and I barely got past the checkpoint. The soldiers said that only one of us needed to go to the store at a time. I convinced him that we had a large family, and it would take two to carry everything."

"I'm glad you mentioned Pret," Gohn said. "I've invited her to join us for a reason. Will, your family has faithfully served this church for decades."

The group applauded in agreement.

Gohn continued. "Last night I had a dream. The Lord said that in the last days he will pour out his spirit on all people. He said, 'Your sons and daughters will prophesy.' I'm convinced, we are living in the last days."

"Amen!" Will said enthusiastically and the others echoed him. The mood seemed to be getting better.

"As such, I believe it's time we added Pret to our board of elders."

Dead silence. No one voiced opposition, they just didn't say anything.

"I agree," Aria finally said.

"Me too," Marta added.

Gohn thought he saw Marta give Aria a glare but ignored it.

"Why Pret? She's just a child," Will said.

"Pret has found favor with the Lord," Gohn said. "God showed me that in a dream."

Total stunned silence. Pret seemed genuinely touched by the gesture.

"It's funny you should say that," Pret said. "Last night I too had a dream."

Pret was normally soft-spoken. This was the first time Gohn had heard her speak with such authority.

"Tell us about it," Gohn said, with curiosity.

This time she hesitated.

"It's okay," her dad said.

"I saw pastor Gohn walking in the desert. A young lion came bounding toward him. Gohn killed the lion with his bare hands."

Gohn flexed his muscles in a joking manner, causing the entire group to burst out into laughter.

"What happened next?" Gohn asked.

"When you cut open the carcass, there was honey in it. You ate until you were full. Then you gathered more honey and took it and sat it in front of two maidens. I couldn't see their faces, but you intended to give the honey to the one who would become your wife."

The entire group laughed again. Will poked Gohn in the ribs and began to tease him.

"Look at you," Will joked. "You've got two women to choose from."

"Be quiet," Gohn said. "I want to hear this."

He felt in his spirit that this vision was from the Lord. Gohn saw both Marta and Aria squirm in their seats.

"How did I choose which maiden to marry?" Gohn asked.

"You gave them a riddle. You said that the one who could answer the riddle would be your wife."

"What was the riddle?" Gohn asked.

"When may a husband call his wife honey?" Pret said.

"When?" Marta asked.

"I don't know," Pret said. "It's a riddle. The maiden who answers it is the one who Gohn marries."

"That doesn't make any sense," Marta said.

"I'm just telling you what I saw in the dream," Pret replied.

Then her eyes narrowed, and her shoulders drooped. Pret looked down, apparently not wanting to make eye contact with anyone.

"What's wrong?" Will asked his daughter.

"I saw something else," Pret said. "Something about pastor."

"What?" Gohn asked.

"Your hair," she said.

"What about it?"

Gohn reached up and ran his head through the back of his hair which was past his shoulders. He probably should get it cut.

"A woman cut your hair. The next time you were walking in the desert, the lion attacked you. This time, he killed you. You were powerless to stop him."

"What does that mean?" Gohn asked, soberly.

"I don't know," Pret said.

"Enough of this silly talk," Will said dismissively. "We have more important things to discuss."

He was clearly skeptical of the dream.

His daughter slinked back in her chair.

"We do need to move on," Gohn said. "But it's not silly, Pret. I think the vision is from God."

A smile flashed across her face. Gohn didn't want her to get discouraged the first time she shared a dream or vision. She might not share them again.

"What does the vision mean?" Marta asked.

"I don't know," Gohn said. "We'll have to ask God to reveal it to us. Thank you, Pret. Tell us if you have any more dreams or visions."

"I will," she said.

"Okay. Let's talk about today's service," Gohn said. "I have an idea."

* * *

Before Gohn could move to the next topic on his agenda, a heated discussion broke out on another topic.

Cloyd.

He was supposed to be there but was late for some unknown reason. Cloyd was the soldier who shot and killed Will but then came back to the church to get saved later that night.

"How do we know we can trust him?" Roux argued.

Surprisingly, Will was the first to speak up in Cloyd's defense.

"I prayed with him to receive Christ," Will said. "I know we can trust him."

"He might've been pretending," Roux retorted. "To gain our trust. To spy on us. How do you know his conversion was real? The man killed you for goodness sake. I would think *you* of all people would be leery of the man."

"How do we know what's in anyone's heart?" Aria said sweetly, softening the tension in the room which she was good at doing.

"Salvation is from God," Will added. "It seemed genuine to me."

"I can tell when a man is broken," Lars chimed in. "God saved him. I'm sure of it."

"I hope you're right," Roux said. "I just wonder if it's worth the risk. Maybe he really meant it at the time, but who knows if it'll stick. Look around us. More than three-thousand people were saved and healed last week. Yet not one of them has the faith to defy the authorities and come to church."

"Roux's right," Lars said. "None of us knows that Cloyd will keep the faith. If the authorities find out about his conversion, he'll be tortured and then killed. Even if he is sincere about Christ, he'll give us up under torture."

"Who knows if any of us will stay firm in the faith under this type of persecution?" Will replied. "We all have to trust God to withstand the persecution."

"Where is Cloyd?" Aria asked, in a clear attempt to change the subject.

Gohn could see the strain on Aria's face. Her otherwise beautiful features were noticeably tense. Her jaw was clenched, shoulders raised, and her eyebrows furrowed.

"I'm worried," she added. "He's supposed to be here by now."

"I heard from him this morning," Will said. "He has several churches to check on. Don't worry, he'll be here."

In the back of his mind, Gohn wondered if soldiers might burst into the church at any time. He refused to express those doubts to the others. Hopefully, Cloyd was the only one who would check on them. If they could trust him to protect them. He felt like they could. At least, he'd give Cloyd the benefit of the doubt until proven otherwise.

"We'll pray that Cloyd stays safe," Gohn said. "Let's not waste time arguing among ourselves. The more important question is, what are we going to do about church today?" He already knew but wanted them to buy into the idea.

"We should close for the sixty days and see what happens after that," Lars said.

Gohn shook his head from side to side, firmly for emphasis and then said, "No! The Bible says we're not to forsake the assembling of ourselves together. We still need to meet once a week, even in these difficult times."

"How can we?" Lars asked. "The people are afraid to come. Does God really intend for us to open the church even if everyone will be arrested if we do?"

"That verse in the Bible actually addresses that very question," Gohn explained. "The verse says we should meet and exhort each other as we see the day approaching. It's talking about the last days which I believe we're in. I've seen it in my visions and dreams. Now, more than ever, we must meet together and exhort each other. Especially during these difficult times."

"If we're caught, we'll be arrested and killed," Roux said.

"I'm not afraid," Will said.

"Neither am I," Aria said weakly, but with a hint of resolve.

"The Bible says to hold fast in our faith," Gohn interjected, in a more sober tone. "It won't be easy. But let's exhort one another to good works and to love. It doesn't say to assemble together unless the government tells you not to. It says don't forsake meeting together. No matter what. Even if the government tells you that you can't. Even if you're arrested. But each of you has to make his own decision. I'm not telling you what to do. If I'm the only person who shows up, I'm still going to open the doors of the church every sabbath. If I die, I die."

"Me too," Marta said.

Gohn smiled at her which she returned, although he could see the concern written all over face as her forehead was furrowed so tightly, he could see lines that weren't normally there.

Aria quickly agreed.

"Kind of a moot point, don't you think?" Roux continued. "No one's here. They aren't coming even if the doors are open. I don't think it's worth the risk to open the church if no one's going to come anyway."

"We could take the church to them," Gohn said. "Like I've always said, the church is the people not the building."

"How would we do that?" Aria asked.

"Through the squares," Marta said. "Pastor and I talked about it this morning. I've got the image broadcaster already set up." She pointed to the device in front of the pulpit that captured an image and then sent it to a mechanical mind reader which broadcast it into the squares.

"I saw that," Will said. "I wondered what it was for."

"Pastor Gohn will preach his message, and we'll broadcast it through the squares to all the quadrangles."

"That's an interesting idea," Roux said, as his mood changed, and he now sounded excited.

"The church could make friendship requests in each square," Aria said excitedly. "You could create posts and reach the people that way."

"I know how to save the videos and keep them up in the square," Will said. "People can access them throughout the week. Even those who don't answer the friend requests. We can make it a public post."

"Has anyone ever done that before?" Roux asked.

"I've seen people post videos in the squares," Aria said. "Not to this extent. But it can be done."

"Will the authorities let us do that?" Pret asked. Not in a fearful way, but in a thoughtful tone. Gohn was glad she still had the boldness to interject even though her vision wasn't that well received by the group.

"I don't know how they would stop us," Will said. "Once the videos are out there, they can be shared from person to person. They can't go to every house and delete them."

The tone of the conversation had finally shifted to optimism. The group was brainstorming, and Gohn liked it.

"That would allow us to reach more people than we could ever reach within the four walls," Will said.

"How many are we talking about?" Marta asked.

"Thousands," Will responded. "Theoretically, we could reach every single person in a square. If all the churches did it, we could reach all of Mercury!"

"That's one of the signs of the last days before the second coming," Will said. "The gospel will be preached throughout the entire world. This is a way for us to fulfill the Great Commission."

"I have already prepared my first sermon," Gohn said.

"What's it about?" Marta asked.

"The Great Flood."

"That'll open a can of tuna," Will said. "I like it. That'll get the authorities fired up."

One of the protocols from years ago banned any mention of the flood. They said it never happened. The Bible said it did.

"Is it a good idea to speak about something that controversial in your first sermon?" Roux asked.

"I will refute the protocols," Gohn said. "The Proctorial authorities are saying that everything has to be closed for sixty days to fix a hole in the stratazone."

"That's a lie," Will said. "The Eliminati are the ones behind it. I'm sure of it."

"There you go with all your conspiracy theories," Roux said, chuckling. Not confrontationally but with a hint of sarcasm.

"The Eliminati exists," Will argued with resolve. Not defensively but strongly. "I'm telling you. As sure as I'm sitting here. They are the ones behind it. They're trying to control the world. We have to stop them."

Gohn waved his hand in the air in a lame attempt to keep the conversation from spiraling out of control. Soon they'd all know what he knew.

"I'm going to get into all of that in my sermon," Gohn said. "More importantly, I'm going to talk about God's promise to never destroy Mercury again with a flood. There is no hole in the stratazone. God wouldn't allow it."

"You're going to stir up a hornet's nest," Roux said.

"I like it," Will said.

"Me too," Aria chimed in.

"When you preach that sermon, all hell is going to break loose," Roux said.

"Then let's get to it," Gohn said. "The sooner we come against the gates of hell, the better."

8

Revelation Church
The Sabbath Day Message

Gohn should be nervous but wasn't.

He was about to deliver the most important sermon of his life. The ramifications were immeasurable. He intended to expose the Eliminati and reveal the secrets of the end times.

The admonition in the Bible resonated in his mind like a song that kept playing in his head. *Fear not. Don't be afraid. Be anxious for nothing. Don't let your heart be troubled. Be strong, do not fear. Fear no evil. Whom shall I fear? If God be for me, who can be against me?*

Three hundred and sixty-five times the Bible says to fear not. That's for a reason. In this world, there were a lot of things to fear. None more than the risk Gohn was taking today. The entire wrath of the Mercurian Proctor and the Eliminati was about to come down on his head. As soon as he opened his mouth and delivered his sermon.

Was he ready for the coming storm?

He had to be. It was his destiny.

The Holy Spirit kept saying to him, *What can mere mortals do to you?*

Gohn felt energized. The power of the Holy Spirit pulsed through his veins like a raging river flowed through a canyon. He almost felt drunk. Giddy. Not that he'd ever been drunk before. Alcohol had never touched his lips. This was what he imagined being drunk felt like.

He was drunk in the spirit.

Even in the euphoria, one thing did concern him. Where was Cloyd? He expected him to be there by now. Gohn hadn't had a chance to tell him his plan. He'd hear it in the squares like everyone else. In real time. What would he think?

Cloyd was going to ask his supervisors to put him in charge of monitoring the churches in the fifth quadrangle. That way he could protect Gohn and the church when they met. He was going to report back to the authorities that all the churches in the quadrangle were closed. That would put Cloyd in extreme danger. He was taking as many risks as anyone. If found out, he'd be arrested and put to death almost immediately. A risk he insisted he was willing to take.

Gohn wished he could tell him what he was about to do and warn him. After the morning broadcast, everyone would be at risk. Including Cloyd. He took comfort in knowing he was doing the right thing. Having Cloyd there for support would help.

He did have Aria. She was a tremendous comfort. All morning, she'd been right by his side almost like a helpmate. Will and Marta were hard at work setting up the connection between the image broadcaster and the screen and testing the broadcast to the squares. They'd be ready soon.

While they waited, Aria tried her best to be encouraging. Her smile was calming. She touched his hand once, sending chills down his spine. All his senses were heightened because of what he was about to do, but he didn't remember ever feeling that way before. Not for another woman.

Maybe he could see himself with her after all.

Focus!

Gohn tried to put those thoughts out of his mind. The last thing he needed to be thinking about were romantic feelings.

"We're ready," Marta said, in a matter-of-fact voice as she approached Gohn.

Ever since he'd told her about Aria, Marta had been cold and distant. This morning was no exception. She was never warm and friendly, but now she seemed even more withdrawn. Business like. Emotionless. Almost like she was angry at him.

He wished he hadn't told her about Aria. Some things were better left unsaid.

Will approached and put a microphone on the lapel of Gohn's shirt. "You'll not be able to move around," Will said. "Stand behind the pulpit and look directly into the image broadcaster."

That would be hard. Gohn was an animated preacher. He liked to roam around the stage and use his hands to make exaggerated movements. For emphasis. When he really wanted to make a point, he'd have to remember to stay stationary.

"We're ready," Marta said. "Are you okay?" she asked Gohn.

"I think I'm ready."

"You're going to be great," she said, flashing a slight smile in a rare expression of warmth.

It felt good.

Seconds later, Aria was next to him and kissed him on the cheek. Marta stormed off. Or at least it appeared that way.

"I'm so proud of you," Aria said. "You're amazing! I can't wait to hear your message."

The contrast couldn't have been starker. As always, between the two sisters, Aria was the more effusive one. If given the choice, men preferred women like Aria. Affectionate. Beautiful. Loving. Marta was about as warm as a cold fish just taken out of the freezer. Up till now, Gohn had always thought Marta was more his type.

He had to remind himself for a second time to focus.

Marta stepped behind the image broadcaster, and Will took his place behind the table with the broadcast equipment. Gohn stood behind the pulpit.

A brief moment of anxiety came over him. It suddenly became very real. When Marta motioned for him to begin, his words would go out to every household on Mercury. To every square on social media.

The task seemed daunting. They were making history today. Doing something no one had ever done before. For the first time, the gospel would be preached to every corner of the planet. A requirement before the end times could come to pass. God had chosen him to deliver the message. Would he say the right thing?

Why did God choose him for such a time as this? He wasn't worthy.

Marta gave Gohn the cue to begin. A green light appeared on the top of the image broadcaster. That meant they were live. He looked over at Will. A thumbs up sign meant they were broadcasting. Aria sat on the front pew on the edge of the seat. A broad smile was on her face and her hands were clasped together under her chin in anticipation. She looked like she could barely contain her excitement.

Gohn took a deep breath, put all distractions out of his mind, and began speaking.

"To my fellow Mercurians. I am Gohn. A fellow partaker in the kingdom of God and the perseverance of the saints who are in Christ Jesus. The Lord has come to me in visions and dreams. He has chosen to reveal to me what is happening in the end times."

His words were careful and deliberate. Almost as if he wasn't the one speaking to them. Like the Holy Spirit had taken over his thoughts.

For ten minutes, he laid the groundwork. Told them about how he was awakened in the middle of the night. During the fourth watch. Just a few hours before. God had instructed him to take the message to all of Mercury. The first of seven. Today's message today would be directed to the Church of the first quadrangle.

Gohn looked down at his notes which were sparse. Only one sentence was highlighted.

Here goes!

No turning back. Once he spoke these words, all of their lives would change forever.

"To the saints of the first quadrangle. I know your deeds. That you used to hate evil men. In former days, you didn't accept false apostles. You never drew tired of the truth. But I have this against you."

Gohn could feel the tension in the room. His words were filled with power and intensity. His entire body tensed. He turned slightly so he could raise his hand and point his finger at the image broadcaster.

"I have this against you," Gohn repeated, with even more fervor. "You tolerate the Eliminati!"

And there it was!

Gohn said it.

Now, he had to clarify his words, or the people would be confused. For years, rumors abounded of a secret society. A cabal. A counsel of evil men who were running Mercury. No one dared speak of them publicly.

Gohn just had.

The first quadrangle was where the Eliminati dwelled. The Lord had shown him that in the dream. Their seat of power was in that quadrangle. That's where all the learning centers on Mercury existed, including the schools of higher learning. The center of government was there as well. Even the theological seminaries were in the first quadrangle. Over the years, liberal ideology and thought had pervaded the schools, and most truth had been abandoned for the sake of correctness.

Gohn continued. This time with anger in his voice. "When Mercury Protocol 347 was first introduced, the saints of the first quadrangle were the first to condemn it. Rightly so. Man did not evolve from fish. Protocol 347 denied that God created the heavens and Mercury. You found the men who purported those lies to be false prophets, and you didn't endure the evil men even though you came under great persecution. That's no longer true."

Protocol 347 was now the only acceptable teaching in learning institutions. From childhood classrooms to universities. God and creationism had been removed from all classroom curriculum.

"Over the years, you've become more tolerant. More accepting of so-called 'liberation theology' that embraced Protocol 347 as proven science. Now, you accept all kinds of aberrant doctrines. You consider yourself enlightened. Open-minded. Free-thinking. But you deny the power within. You even deny God."

Gohn took a deep breath. He wanted the words to be strong but didn't want to come across as too judgmental or condemning. He softened his tone.

"Protocol 661 was introduced last week. It said that the strata-zone was in danger of rupturing. That a hole was developing because man has not taken care of the environment. The saints of the first quadrangle have embraced the protocol. You even teach that the change in the climate is real. That if we don't do something, then the world will be destroyed."

The churches of the first quadrangle were the only ones who weren't meeting in secret. They supported the lockdown. None of the other quadrangles were as defiant as Gohn, but at least they spoke against it. The First Church didn't.

"Protocol 661 is a lie!" Gohn shouted at the top of his lungs. "It's nothing more than a man-made crisis manufactured by the Elimi-nati. That's right. I said it. The Eliminati is real. I've seen them with my own eyes. Six men. They meet in a room in the first quadrangle. Herodius is the leader. He is the spirit of the antichrist. These men have been behind the protocols from the very beginning. Their pur-pose is evil. They want to close churches. Shut down free speech. Control our movement."

Gohn was on a roll. The words flowed off his tongue as easily as his breath.

"There is no hole in the stratazone! There is no climate crisis! Mercury can never be destroyed by a flood! Have you forgotten God's promises?"

Gohn moved his arms and hands in animated gestures for emphasis but remembered to stay stationary.

Will kept saying "amen" over and over again. Pumping his fist. Exuberantly. Gohn drew energy from him. Aria's face was bright with excitement. Her lips were pursed in a tight smile, and her eyes were wide as saucers.

Aria looked upon him longingly. He couldn't help but be touched.

Marta was the only one who was emotionless. She continued to monitor the image broadcaster without looking up at him. He wanted to catch her eye but couldn't. Was she looking away on purpose? He wanted so much to have her approval. One glancing look would be enough. If only she thought of him the way Aria did. Maybe things would be different.

Gohn's focus turned back to the message. Once again, he found that he was no longer in control of his words. They were coming from his spirit.

"Repent! First Church. Remember from where you have fallen. Do the same deeds you did at first. Or God will remove your place of authority and importance."

The churches of the first quadrangle were the most powerful and influential. God had shown him that he would remove their power if they didn't repent.

"Remember the Great Flood," Gohn continued. His words were coming quickly now. "God was angry at man and regretted ever creating him. Centuries ago, God decided to destroy Mercury and every living thing. He caused a flood. God opened up a hole in the strata-zone and all of Mercury was underwater. But God saved a remnant."

Gohn's tone had turned to storytelling. He wanted this section to be powerful prose. Most of Mercury was not familiar with the story of the flood. An earlier protocol forbade it being mentioned or taught in classrooms. The Protocol denied that it ever happened. Churches were forbidden to preach sermons on it. The first quad-rangle was the only one who complied. The rest continued to teach the Great Flood, but surreptitiously.

"Argo found favor with the Lord," Gohn said. "The Lord told him to build an underwater craft. There were no such crafts on Mercury. No one even knew what they were. He was mocked and ridiculed. Made fun of by his friends and family. When God told him to enter the vessel, he did so out of faith. His wife and sons and daughters were the only ones who would listen to him. Argo took two of every living species in the underwater sea vessel so they would be spared as well. God sealed the vessel, and water flooded Mercury."

Gohn stopped to catch his breath. Everyone in the room seemed to be riveted to his words. Everyone but Marta who continued to focus on the image broadcaster. He didn't know why she was acting this way.

He ignored the thoughts and kept his attention on telling the story of Argo and the great flood.

"After forty days and forty nights, the flood stopped. When the water subsided, God opened the sanctuary, and Argo and his family came out of it onto dry land. The whole world was destroyed and everyone in it. Suddenly, there appeared a great rainbow. An array of colors that formed an arch across the stratazone."

Gohn took another breath. Then paused. He was talking too fast. "God spoke to Argo. He said, 'Never again will there be a flood to destroy Mercury. The rainbow shall be a sign of my covenant with man.'"

Gohn raised the intensity of his words again. His deep bass voice resounded through the sanctuary. He had a microphone but didn't need it for those in the room. Just for those listening in the squares.

"God is not a man that he should lie. Shall he not do what he says? Will God not keep his promises?"

Gohn was practically shouting again.

"Mercury Protocol 661 is straight out of the pit of hell. Filled with the lies of the evil one. The Eliminati are nothing but pawns of Satan himself. Instruments of his diabolical plans. There is no hole in the stratazone. God will never allow Mercury to be destroyed again by a flood."

Aria burst into applause. The others joined her. They encouraged Gohn with their enthusiasm. It warmed his heart.

Gohn let the applause die down and then said, "To the saints of the first quadrangle. You know the story of the great flood. You know God's promises. Do you deny them? Repent! Or God will take away your authority."

Gohn walked down from the podium and stood in front of the image broadcaster. Marta was clearly startled as she fumbled with the machine and wasn't sure what to do. Gohn motioned for her in a way to tell her not to worry. Just keep the lens focused on him. He came and stood right in front of it.

"Resist the Eliminati! I urge the people of Mercury to rise up. Refuse the lockdown. Go to your churches. Leave your homes. There are more of us than there are of them. Trust God. He will protect you. Churches of Mercury. Open your doors. Fill your sanctuaries with singing. Preach that the day of the Lord is at hand."

Gohn's hands were raised high in the air.

He continued to exhort the people for twenty more minutes. Explaining to them more about his vision earlier that morning. That he'd be coming to them once a week for the next seven weeks.

A door opened in the back of the sanctuary.

A man entered.

Then another man.

Seconds later, an entire family entered. They all came into the sanctuary and sat down.

Gohn lifted his hands again and praised God.

More people came. Soon the sanctuary was filled.

Someone said a throng of people were outside. Gohn kept exhorting the people in the squares to come.

"That's right. Come to the house of God. Everyone within the sound of my voice, go to your local church. Let's fill God's temple with people who are not afraid of the Eliminati! Trust God. He will protect you from your enemies."

Aria stood and began to shout. So did Will. The other elders of the church stood with them.

The back door opened again.

In walked Cloyd.

9

Pastor Gohn felt a euphoria unlike any he'd ever felt before.
To see the church filled with believers who defied the Eliminati and trusted God was one of the most exciting things he'd ever witnessed in his entire life. Along with seeing the three thousand healed the week before.

This had been the best seven days of his entire ministry.

Admittedly, he didn't know what ramifications would come from the sermon and the noncompliance with Protocol 661. Gohn would know more after talking to Cloyd who had just walked in the back of the sanctuary. His furrowed brow and narrowed eyes told Gohn that Cloyd didn't share his enthusiasm. Not surprising considering his position of authority within the Proctorial Guard. He had as much to lose as anyone. Including his own life.

Would he stand firm in the faith?

They didn't know. Several of the elders had questioned Gohn's faith in Cloyd. Not so much faith in him but believing the best in a person. No one knew a person's heart but God. But they could discern the fruit. They'd soon know. Cloyd's behavior would be proof enough.

Cloyd was wearing his uniform and brandished his gun. The people in the congregation didn't seem to notice. Or if they did, they weren't afraid. They didn't seem to fear anything. They had crossed the checkpoints at considerable risks to life and limb and had already faced down soldiers with weapons. One more probably wouldn't shake their faith. They came to the house of God in defiance of the authorities, and no one could make them leave without resistance.

The bravery and determination warmed his heart and spurred him on to speak final words of encouragement to those in the sanctuary and those listening in the square. Gohn was surprised by the words that came out of his mouth.

"My fellow Mercurians. Listen to the words of Jesus. 'Do not think that I came to bring peace in the world. Rather I came to bring a sword.' He went on to say that there would be division. Father would turn against his son. A daughter against her mother. A daughter-in-law against her mother-in-law. A friend against a friend.'"

Gohn looked right at Cloyd when he said it. His expression gave nothing away.

"I say to you that you must not go in peace," Gohn said.

The crowd stood. Cheered. Applauded loudly.

Gohn let them carry on for a period of time then raised his hands in the air to silence them.

"I saw a vision of a horse. A red horse. Bright red. The rider asked permission to remove peace from the world. The request was granted. When peace was removed, men slay men."

The sermon was unlike any he'd ever expressed before. He'd always spoken of peace and love. He expected to tell the people to not violently resist the authorities. To love their enemies. Turn the other cheek. What he was doing was inciting a revolution. There was no turning back from such a blatant display of defiance.

That didn't stop him. But he needed to clarify.

"Jesus was not referring to a literal sword. He never brandished a weapon in his hand. Even when he was arrested, he lifted not a hand against his accusers. Because, friends, our battle is not against flesh and blood. It's against spiritual forces who would destroy the world.

The prince of the power of the air. It is these forces of evil that we must resist with all of our might. Greater is he that is in you than he that is in the world."

Gohn was shouting those last words.

The crowd was nearing a frenzy.

"So put on the full armor of God so that you can stand against the enemy's schemes. The belt of truth around your waist. The breastplate of righteousness. Let your feet be fitted with the gospel of peace."

Gohn's hands were balled into fists and raised in the air. He had to shout at the top of his lungs to be heard over the crowd.

"Carry with you the shield of faith! It will extinguish all the flaming darts of the evil one. Take on the helmet of salvation! And the sword of the Spirit! Which is the Word of God!"

Gohn waited for the din to die down.

When it did, he said, "Pray without ceasing. Pray also for me. That whenever I speak, words may be given me so that I will fearlessly make known the mystery of the gospel for which I am an ambassador. Soon to be in chains."

The crowd began to boo and hiss.

Gohn saw a vision of him being led out of the sanctuary in chains. Led away by Cloyd. Did that mean he was being betrayed?

He had to finish his words to the masses. "Grace to all who love our Lord Jesus Christ with an undying love. Be back here next Sunday. I will return with a message to the churches of the second quadrangle."

Was he saying that in faith?

If he were led away in chains, how would he ever return? Would he even be alive next week?

He would. God had commanded him to preach seven sermons. God wouldn't tell him to do something without giving him the opportunity to do it.

Gohn walked through the crowd, hugged everyone he could, and encouraged them. Actually, their words were as heartening to him as his were to them. One by one the crowd began to thin out as he sent them home. The only ones left in the sanctuary were Gohn's leaders and Cloyd who walked down the aisle toward him.

Their eyes met.

Gohn spoke first. "May I have a few minutes to speak with everyone before you do what I know you must."

Cloyd nodded his head.

"What's going on?" Will asked.

"Cloyd has come to arrest me," Gohn replied.

"No!" Aria cried out.

She fell into Gohn's arms.

"Traitor!" Will said to Cloyd angrily. "How could you? I defended you."

Will took several steps toward him. Gohn released Aria from his grasp and put his hand on Will's shoulder to hold him back.

"He does what he has to do," Gohn said soberly.

"Don't go with him!" Roux interjected.

"You'll have to go through me," Will said, as he put himself between Cloyd and Gohn.

"How could you do this?" Aria said to Cloyd. "After everything he's done for you. Why aren't you saying anything? Defend yourself."

Tears had formed in Cloyd's eyes. A lone tear escaped and ran down his cheek.

"I don't have any choice," Cloyd said. "I'm in charge of the churches in the fifth quadrangle. I've been ordered to arrest him. If I don't, they'll send dozens of soldiers and arrest all of you. I know you'd defy them. You'd all be killed. I'm trying to save your lives."

"Let Gohn go," Will argued. "We'll hide him. Say that you came here, and Pastor was gone."

"No!" a young girl's voice cried out from behind them.

Pret.

She stepped forward and spoke directly to Gohn. "God has allowed this. Not one hair of your head will be harmed if you stay faithful to the Word. I've seen it in a vision. I saw you in prison. You opened the prison doors with your bare hands. The ground was strewn with dead guards."

"How is that possible?" Will said. "Can one man fight against hundreds of armed men? They'll kill him."

"The source of your strength is your hair," Pret continued.

Gohn ran his hand through it. "You said that earlier this week, Pret. At the healing service. You mentioned my hair. Why?"

"Don't cut your hair. When you do, your strength will leave you."

Will took his daughter by the arm and demanded that she be quiet. "Don't listen to this silly girl. She has no idea what she's talking about."

"Her words ring true," Gohn said. "I said that in the last days your daughters would prophesy. Thank you, Pret. Your words are encouraging to me."

"It's time for us to go," Cloyd said.

"May I have a minute to change and gather my things?" Gohn asked.

"Of course."

Gohn left the sanctuary and went to his apartment. He changed clothes and then went into the washroom to splash water on his face. Then into the kitchen to eat something. He didn't know when his next meal might come.

A slight knock on the door startled him. He hadn't expected it.

"Come in," he said.

Aria entered.

She practically ran to him and threw her arms around him. "I'm so worried about you," she said.

"You don't have to worry. You heard Pret. No one can harm me unless God allows it."

"What if she's wrong?"

"Don't worry about me. God will protect me. You'll see. I'll be home soon. God has shown me that I'm to preach to the squares for seven straight weeks. This is week one. God wouldn't have told me that unless it were true."

Aria was back in his arms again.

He held her closer.

A strange feeling came over him.

What was it?

Aria's head was against his chest. He could smell her hair.

Gohn put his hands on the side of her arms and moved her so that she was away from his body.

He looked into her eyes.

So beautiful.

Loving.

For a moment, he was at a loss for words.

Gohn took his hand and brushed the tears off her cheeks.

Before he knew it, they were kissing.

Soft at first. Then harder. He didn't remember breathing.

What have I done?

Gohn pulled away.

Aria looked at him. Confused. Her eyebrows raised in puzzlement. Maybe amazement.

"I'm sorry," Gohn said.

"Don't be," Aria replied sweetly. "I've dreamed of that moment. It's okay. I love you."

"I've got to go," he said abruptly.

Aria fumbled for words.

She tried to stop him. He was resolved.

That shouldn't have happened.

It did.

He kissed Aria.

What did it mean?

He grabbed his things and walked swiftly for the door. Leaving Aria standing in the spot where they had kissed.

I can't believe that just happened.

It can never happen again.

10

Pastor Gohn was taken to the local prison and placed in a cell two floors below the ground. More of a cave with steel bars blocking the entrance than anything else. The small twelve by twelve space was dark and dank and smelled of mold and human suffering. Because the cities on Mercury were below the water, inside the bubble was naturally humid. Under the bubble, the temperature outside was a balmy seventy most of the time.

Where Gohn was, two stories below ground, the temperature had dropped by a noticeable twenty or thirty degrees.

Cloyd dropped Pastor off at the prison and had apologized profusely. "I hope you understand that I had no choice. Please forgive me."

"I understand. I do forgive you," Gohn assured him. They were in agreement that Gohn essentially turned himself in, thinking he'd save lives by doing so.

"I'll come and check on you every day," Cloyd said.

Gohn could see the tears in his eyes as Cloyd turned his head away in shame. Gohn truly didn't blame Cloyd.

Cloyd did come every day. He brought Gohn food and drink and updated him on the events happening in Mercury. The sustenance was welcomed; the bad news wasn't. All the guards gave Gohn was a small serving of rice and a piece of bread every morning. Often the bowl of food was crawling with live creatures. Gohn gave his portions to a man in a cell next to him. A thief who was sentenced to death. Someone without hope. Biding his time waiting for the authorities to carry out his sentence.

Gohn shared the gospel with him, and the man gave his heart to Jesus during one of the many long conversations the men had about life, death, and the afterlife. Cloyd was going to do what he could to get the man's sentence commuted. The man should already be dead. Cloyd explained that there was a backlog of people awaiting execution. Primarily because of the arrest of the Christians who were defying the protocols.

Thousands of Christians were inspired by Gohn's sermon the week before and had taken to the streets. Not so much in protest but living their lives. Refusing to bow a knee to the evil rulers. That part of the news had buoyed Gohn's spirits. The rest was troubling. The crackdown had been brutal. Thousands were taken away to prison. Some already executed. Given the AXX-E laced with mercury. But the sheer numbers of people defying the protocols had overwhelmed the authorities.

Many of the unbelievers had risen up in opposition as well to the point that the soldiers gave up trying to enforce them.

They turned most of their focus on persecuting the Christians and ignored trying to keep everyone locked down. Pastor Gohn would feel guilty except for the knowledge that he had spoken God's Word to the people and followed the Holy Spirit's guidance. He had to trust that God would work all things together for good to those who had the courage to stand strong in the faith.

That was his only comfort. Knowing that God loved them more than he did and was working a greater plan. The word Gohn had been given was that the end times were upon them. He knew from Scripture that evil would be unleashed in those times. It shouldn't be a surprise to see it happening.

The Eliminati was intent on destroying the rebellion and everything associated with God and Christians. If they could, they'd eliminate Christians off the face of Mercury. God wouldn't allow it. At some point, God would overcome evil and destroy it. Until then, evil was only restrained. Not fully, but the Christians had been given the authority by God to resist the evil one. The battle of the end times had begun, and even though it seemed like the good side wasn't winning, Gohn knew that wasn't true. God would win in the end. Between now and then would bring tremendous suffering.

It broke Gohn's heart, and he felt the burden. Helpless. What could he do about it if he were rotting away in that cell?

Something else was troubling him.

The kiss.

Gohn didn't know quite how he felt about it. Aria told him she loved him in his office. Then she kissed him on the lips as he was being taken away to prison. Out of the blue. Before he could react. He didn't really even remember if he kissed her back. He must have because the kiss lasted longer than it should have.

He should feel comforted by the affection of a woman like Aria. Why did he feel such remorse? She was beautiful. Kind. Loving. Any man would be crazy not to reciprocate her feelings.

But Gohn loved someone else. Marta. Aria's sister. He'd had feelings for her since the first day they met. Marta wasn't as pretty as Aria. Didn't have as good a figure. Was not as affectionate and loving. But Gohn knew from experience that feelings weren't always easy to explain. Especially when accompanied by God's will.

He'd always thought God wanted them together. That Marta was his soulmate. Over time, the feelings had grown stronger. Gohn was certain Marta felt the same way. Occasionally, she'd let her guard down, and he could see behind the wall of protection she'd put over her heart.

Why hadn't she said anything?

Why hadn't he?

For the same reason. Fear.

Now, in that lonely prison cell it seemed stupid.

How did Gohn let that happen? The days had turned to weeks. Weeks turned to months. Months turned to years. Neither of them acted on their feelings. Gohn began to wonder if they ever would.

He would die with that regret.

At one point, he thought he should ask.

Should've asked.

It was probably too late.

If he ever got out of prison and had the chance to talk to her again, he would say something.

No, he wouldn't. He was still afraid. When he saw Marta, the words wouldn't come. How was it that he could face down a dozen armed soldiers but was afraid to share his feelings with the woman he loved?

Afraid of what? Rejection. Putting his heart out there. Unrequited love. Ruining their friendship. Making Marta uncomfortable. They worked together. At the church. Unwanted advances could ruin his ministry.

Now they were complicated by Aria and her feelings. Aria would be devastated if he pursued a romantic relationship with her sister. Was that even allowed now that he had kissed Aria? If Marta resisted his advances, he'd destroy two friendships. Hurt two women. It didn't seem worth the risk.

Perhaps, he should pursue the sure thing. At least Aria had feelings for him and was ready to act on them. He should let go of his feelings for Marta and see what happened with Aria. A helpmate was just what he needed in these troubled times. He had to admit to himself that kissing her felt good. At night, when all was dark and quiet, he could almost smell her hair. Feel her soft lips against his.

He made the decision.

He'd pursue things with Aria and see where they led. That seemed like the practical thing to do. Ever since he told Marta about his talk with Aria, she had withdrawn from him. Acted like she didn't care. Dismissed her sister's feelings as nothing more than a childhood crush.

That made Gohn mad. Aria was a grown woman. Old enough to be in love and to be loved. When Marta became cold and distant, Gohn realized that nothing was ever going to happen with her. He needed to move on. Extinguish that torch he'd been carrying for months.

As each day passed in prison, the flame for Marta died slowly. By the pain he felt in his heart, he realized that he really did love Marta. But the suffering in the prison cell had given him many agonizing hours to think about it. By the end of the week, the only conclusion Gohn could come to was that Marta didn't feel the same way. He needed to get over it.

He'd pursue Aria.

That caused Gohn to laugh out loud.

How could he? He was in jail. When would he get out? Would he ever get out? Not likely. Why would the authorities release him? It'd take a miracle from God.

Another source of angst. God told Gohn to preach seven messages to the seven churches. How was he going to do that in prison? Had he missed God? The visions of last Sabbath morning seemed so real. The people responded to the Word. They left their homes. Defied the protocols at great risk of bodily harm and followed Gohn's admonition. Or what he thought was God's prophetic word for the people.

Was it all for nothing now?

He was in prison along with many other Christ followers. No telling how many were dead or awaiting execution. He kept expecting the authorities to come and take him away at any time. Lead him into the square and make him suffer a long and painful death.

He was willing to die for the cause of Christ, but what about the messages? Gohn was so sure that he was going to deliver one the next Sabbath and every week after for six more weeks.

As each day passed, and his deliverance didn't come, Gohn's faith began to wane. Not unlike his feelings for Marta. Not that they completely went away. He just no longer trusted them. No longer believed they'd come to pass.

The night before the Sabbath was the hardest. Gohn was tired. Cold. Hungry. His right arm was chained to the side of the wall. In the middle of the cell was a small hole where he could relieve himself. The stench was so bad it burned his eyes and nostrils. Gohn could feel his strength fading. His hair was matted, and his beard had grown longer and sticky from the combination of sweat, grime, and lack of water.

Gohn tried to sleep but the pain inside was too great. He could feel hope slipping away, like a cloud of smoke dissipating in the wind. He felt like he was letting God down. Letting the people down. He was supposed to deliver a sermon in the morning but wouldn't be able to. Because of his own lack of faith. What else could it be?

When he began to cry, he knew all was lost. He wouldn't deliver the sermon. And he'd never see Marta again.

Aria, he meant.

He was so confused.

* * *

Sunday morning
3:00 a.m.
The Fourth Watch of the Night

My cell began to shake.

I was startled from my sleep.

Awakened by a loud voice calling my name. "Gohn."

Whether in my body or out of my body, I didn't know.

All I knew was it felt eerily familiar. The same thing had happened on the Sabbath morning one week earlier. When God gave me a vision.

I looked up and beheld a white cloud. Sitting on the cloud was the Son of Man. In one hand was a scepter, in the other a sword.

I fell to my knees.

An angel of the Lord cried out, "Your deliverance is at hand. Blessed be the name of the Lord."

A vision appeared on the wall of the cave. Like it had in my bedroom.

I knew what I had to do to get out of that prison cell.

11

I suddenly felt alive with the power of the Holy Spirit who pulsed through my veins like a wild stallion runs through a clearing.

All around me was a cacophony of sights and sounds.

Loud cracks of thunder. Bolts of lightning filled the ceiling and sides of the cell.

I could hear the sounds of battles. Swords clanging. Men shouting. Demons fleeing. Then I could see it playing out on the walls of the cell like a movie. I stood in the center and slowly moved in a circle to see each scene and to take in the different parts of the spiritual warfare taking place in the heavenlies.

Good versus evil. Angels versus demons.

The other prisoners were asleep in their cells. How was that possible? My ears were ringing from the deafening sound.

An angel of the Lord appeared with me in the cell.

I fell to my knees.

He took my hand and lifted me back to my feet.

I beheld his beauty. The angel was in the form of a man and dressed in fine linen, with a gold belt around his waist. His body shone like diamonds. His eyes were like torches. When he spoke, it sounded like a chorus of a dozen men.

My strength suddenly left me. I could feel the blood leave my face. If I could look in a mirror, I'd expect it to be white and pale.

My hands and knees were trembling.

"Gohn," the angel said as he took my hand. "You have found favor with the Lord. Consider my words. Do not be afraid, for I have been sent to you by God."

If he weren't holding my hand, I would've fallen to the ground. I'd almost forgotten I was in a prison cell.

"God has heard your prayer and supplication."

"I was afraid God had abandoned me," I said, my voice sounding timid in my ears. I've been praying all week that God would deliver me."

"God answered your prayer on the day of your imprisonment."

"He did?"

"He sent me to respond to your prayer six days ago. I wanted to come to you, but the prince of the power of the air resisted me."

"I didn't know. I'd lost faith."

"Then Michael, the powerful archangel, came to rescue me. He guarded me the entire way. Until I was finally able to bring you the answer to your prayer."

I could barely breathe. Then I realized I was holding my breath. Waiting for the answer. Was it what I wanted to hear?

"You are to preach the Word of God to the congregation this morning as God has instructed. From the vision and dreams that you see here."

A picture appeared on the wall. My eyes were fixed to it.

A woman.

With child. Her stomach protruding out. She had her hand on it. She was crying.

I went to her and laid my hand on her shoulder.

"Why are you crying?" I asked.

She didn't respond. Like she couldn't hear me. I turned to the angel and asked him, "Can she hear me?"

"Yes."

I touched her head and hair, but she kept her head down.

A loud voice began to speak. I recognized it as the voice of the Lord. The Bible verse came to mind, *My sheep hear my voice and I know them, and they follow me.*

"The desolation is nigh," the Lord said. "In the days of vengeance, these things which are written will be fulfilled. Woe unto them who are with child. For there shall be great distress in the land, and wrath upon his people."

Then the Son of Man was gone, and I was left alone in the prison cell. I was shaking all over.

Why has God abandoned me a second time? I'm supposed to get out of there. I walked over to the prison bars and shook them. They rattled but were secure. I expected them to be loosened. I tried the door, but it was locked.

A still, small voice spoke to me in my spirit. "Remember the words I tell you and speak them to the Church of the Second Quadrangle."

I could hear the words now in an audible voice. I searched for something to write them down with, but of course, there was nothing in my cell. So, I listened intently so I wouldn't forget a single word.

For more than an hour, the voice spoke to me. Of the things to come and those things that would come to pass in the last days.

I began to weep greatly, because of the devastation and human suffering I was told was about to take place. Women with child would suffer greatly.

"Stop weeping!" the voice said. "The Lamb of God has overcome the world."

The pictures on the wall reappeared. I saw a multitude of people worshiping and praising God. I looked off at a distance and saw the temple of the tabernacle opened, ready to receive the people into it. Smoke filled the temple as the glory of God consumed it.

Then I saw the conference room.

Six men, sitting around the table.

The Eliminati.

Anger rose inside me. These were the men responsible for the protocols and all the persecution of the church.

They were talking about me.

"Gohn is in prison. He will die."

Then they started talking about a new protocol. Number 662. To be released this week.

I strained to see what was in it, but my eyes couldn't focus well enough to see the words on the paper.

The vision on the cavern wall changed, and I saw the great city in flames. A fire came down from heaven and consumed it.

Then an admonition to give to the Church of the Second Quadrangle.

"Do not fear what you are about to suffer. The evil one is about to throw some of you into prison."

I remembered the verse that our battle is not against flesh and blood but against spiritual forces. The evil one had thrown me in prison. Not the Eliminati. It seemed like the battle was against the council of six. But they were only instruments of Satan. Carrying out his wrath on earth. I needed to remind the people to focus on the real enemy.

"You may be tested," the angel continued the word for the second church. "I know you are rich."

The second quadrangle church had more money and resources than all the other churches combined. Most of the silver mines were in the second quadrangle.

"Be faithful unto death. For I have overcome the world."

My heart was full of joy.

Then the fear returned. How was I going to get out of prison? I went to the door of the cell and shook it again. Lightly. I didn't want to wake the guards.

"Go and leave your chains and make haste to your church," the angel said. "Prepare your sermon. The multitudes awake."

"Are you mocking me?" I asked.

The angel suddenly disappeared.

I began to cry.

"Wait! How will God deliver me from these chains?"

I grabbed my chains angrily and shook them.

"Will you not have mercy on me? You tell me to leave the cell but leave me chained."

I fell to my knees again and began to pray.

No answer came.

I begged and pleaded to God to deliver me.

Then I grew angry again.

Had God forsaken me? Were the angels trying to bring the answer to prayer, but they were being thwarted again? By the power of the enemy?

When I had begun to give up hope again, a vision appeared on the wall.

Pret.

Will's daughter.

She reached out and touched my hair. Stroked it. Then she was gone.

I suddenly remembered the prophecy she had spoken over me.

Not one hair on your head will be harmed.

What was the rest of it?

I saw you in prison.

You opened the prison doors with your bare hands.

I walked over to the door of my cell. I shook it. Still careful not to awaken the guards. I saw one of the two guards stir then lay still again.

The man in the cell next to me did awaken.

"What are you doing?" he asked.

"I don't know. I'm trying to get out of here, but the door is locked."

"Of course, it's locked. We're in prison."

I shook them again. Harder this time.

Nothing happened.

I heard more of Pret's words of prophecy. *The ground was strewn with dead guards.*

I looked around the corner. The guards were asleep in their chairs.

Why was I afraid of them? God said he would deliver me from them.

Then I heard Pret's final words.

The source of your strength is your hair.

I touched my head.

I felt power rush through my hands.

I jerked my arm, and the chains separated from the wall.

I ripped the chains that had bound me for six days off of my wrist.

They fell to the ground with a loud clang.

The guards jumped to their feet. Groggy at first, but then they saw me without my chains.

"How did you get out of your chains?" one of them asked roughly.

"God has delivered me."

He fumbled for his keys.

The other guard was next to him now with his gun drawn.

The prison door flew open, and they came in. Their eyes were on fire like burning pieces of logs. Hatred spewed from their mouths.

I took the chain in my hand and swung it back and forth in front of me.

They stepped back.

One of them raised his weapon to fire.

The gun jammed.

Before the other could react, I swung the chain and hit him with such force that he bounced off the side of the wall and collapsed to the floor with blood gushing from the wound on his head.

The second guard started to run away, but I swung the chain and hit him from behind. I could hear his head crack on the stone floor. I checked him. He was dead. Pret's prophecy was coming to pass before my eyes.

Where did I get such strength?

She said it was from my hair.

The man in the cell next to me pleaded with me to release him. He was the one who had gotten saved earlier that week. The thief awaiting execution.

"Get the key from the guard," he said. "Free me, as well."

"I don't need the key," I said.

I grabbed the bars on the door with my bare hands. Shook them with such might that their hinges broke, and the door was now in my hands unattached.

"You are free," I said to him as I discarded the steel door by throwing it on the floor.

He threw his arms around my neck.

"God does not condemn you," I said. "Now go and sin no more."

"Thank you. Will you come to my house so I can repay you with a meal?"

"I can't," I said. "I have a sermon to deliver."

12

Marta was practically despondent.

Pastor Gohn had been imprisoned for a week. The church members had been praying earnestly without ceasing that he'd be miraculously delivered and able to preach his sermon this morning at church. When the week ended without an answer to prayer, the supplications turned to begging God to spare Pastor Gohn's life.

Marta hoped for the best but was prepared for the worst. Cloyd had said as much. Gohn was sentenced to die. Only a matter of time before they carried out that sentence. The hope now was that the end would come quickly and that he wouldn't have to suffer.

Aria was almost inconsolable in her grief.

Marta sat on the bed next to her and tried to comfort her sister. Aria's crying had gone on most of the night, and neither of them had gotten any sleep. Soon they'd have to get ready for church.

"Gohn is in God's hands," Marta said. "If he's killed, then at least we know he'll be with Jesus in heaven."

Aria collapsed into her arms and began sobbing again. Marta felt the same pain. She was just better at hiding it. More than anything, she was trying to keep it together for her sister. And for the people of the church who were now her responsibility.

"I miss... him... so much," Aria said between sobs. "I don't know how I'm going to live without him. I love him."

Marta knew how Aria felt. She'd been in love with Gohn for as long as she could remember. The only regret was that she hadn't told him. Especially since she knew Aria had. Gohn would die never knowing how she felt about him.

Marta brushed her own tears away. Roughly. They had to pull themselves together. Members of the congregation would be arriving shortly. While the Mercurian Proctors had cracked down on the Christian insurrection started by Gohn's sermon the week before, many were still defiant. More than the authorities could control. The lockdown was for all practical purposes, unenforceable. No one followed it. The Christians moved around Mercury freely. At least those with the courage of their convictions to do so.

Marta was expecting a full house today. Probably standing room only. Most likely would overflow onto the street. The image broadcaster was already set up in the sanctuary and connected to the mechanical mindbrain which would broadcast the day's services into the squares. Most people knew Pastor Gohn had been arrested. The urgent prayer request had gone out to all of Mercury.

They had to be careful when they communicated through the squares. While they sent out updates, they also knew the authorities were monitoring their communications. Every one of them was at risk of being arrested. They kept things generic and didn't mention that the updates were coming from Cloyd who was wracked with guilt. Thinking it was his fault.

He was walking a fine line. If the authorities knew he had converted to Christianity, he'd be arrested and executed as well. The church elders met and encouraged Cloyd to continue the ruse. He was providing them with valuable information. Troop movements. Protocols. Gohn's health. God had placed him in that position of authority for a purpose, and he was wise to continue the subterfuge for as long as possible.

Something that was hard to do, considering his wife Lyla was not a convert. Cloyd was concerned that she was beginning to suspect something. They continued to pray that he'd stay safe.

Marta felt overwhelmed. Like she was being attacked from every angle. She was juggling all of the pastor's responsibilities along with maintaining the church and apartment, and now having to deal with her sister's heartache. When the broadcast started, she had no idea who was going to take up the mantle and stand in front of the image broadcaster and deliver a word to a people hungry for hope in the end times.

Maybe Marta herself would have to do it.

She shuddered at that thought.

Right now, she was trying to help Aria pull herself together long enough to help her with the details in the sanctuary. They were short handed as it was. The Bible said there was a time to mourn. Now wasn't it. They had work that needed to be done. The long nights of crying herself to sleep would come later.

"I told Gohn I love him," Aria said, bringing up a subject Marta had tried desperately to avoid. Tears stained Aria's cheeks and were wetting Marta's shirt that she had worn to bed. She used it to wipe some of Aria's tears away.

"I know," Marta said soberly. "He told me."

That stopped the flow of tears momentarily.

"He told you?" Aria said. "What did he say? Did he say that he loves me too?"

Marta considered telling Aria what she wanted to hear but couldn't bring herself to do it. Lying and saying that Gohn told Marta he loved Aria might make her feel better temporarily, but that would be short-term. It might even make things worse.

Telling her the truth didn't seem like a good idea either. Gohn seemed confused when they talked about it. He never said he loved Aria. He never said he didn't. But Marta got the impression the feelings weren't necessarily mutual. That might've been wishful thinking on her part, but she considered herself a good judge of character.

Aria wasn't Gohn's type. In her mind, he could never fall for someone as ditzy and self-centered as Aria.

So, Marta simply said, "Gohn didn't say one way or the other. It was none of my business, so I didn't ask." She tried to muster up a sympathetic tone.

"I know he loved me," Aria said. "He kissed me right before he left for prison."

Marta almost fell off the bed as her heart sank to the bottom of her chest.

"He kissed you?" Marta said, somewhat between a question and a statement of disbelief.

"Yes. In his bedroom. I mean... maybe I kissed him. But he kissed me back."

That made more sense. Aria was exaggerating. Either way, Marta felt like a dagger had been thrust deep into her heart. The man she considered her soulmate had kissed her sister. The pain was almost too much to bear. Losing Gohn was hard enough. Knowing the last thing he'd done was kiss Aria was agonizing.

She brushed away more tears that were now escaping her eyes. Tears caused by anger more than grief. Now she was mad at both of them. The sympathy she felt for Aria had now turned to disdain. Her sister had thrown herself at Gohn in a desperate attempt to win his affections. In a moment of weakness, he had reciprocated. What man wouldn't? Gohn was going off to prison. Who wouldn't want to be kissed goodbye?

It should've been me.

Marta stood to her feet. "We need to get ready for church," she said, wanting desperately to change the subject.

Aria let her head fall down onto the bed and snuggled into her pillow and began sobbing again.

"I don't want to go to church," she said in a pouty voice. "I just want to lay here and die."

A sound startled Marta.

It came from just outside their opened door which wasn't closed at night since they were alone.

Was it soldiers?

"Did somebody die and not tell me about it?" a familiar voice suddenly sounded in the doorway.

"Gohn!" Aria cried out.

She jumped out of bed, ran across the room, and flew into his arms. He hugged her tightly with one arm. Aria reached up to kiss him, but he turned his lips away at the last moment, and her kiss landed on his cheek.

Was that on purpose? Or just because I was there?

At that moment, it didn't matter. Gohn was alive! Standing in her doorway. Marta thought she was seeing a ghost. She didn't react as quickly as Aria, but as soon as the shock began to wear off, all feelings of animosity went by the wayside. A joy overwhelmed her. She barely noticed that Aria was still in his arms.

Gohn motioned for Marta to come to him. He took her in his other arm and squeezed her tightly and kissed her forehead. Aria was clutching Gohn like a hyena guarding a prey. She wasn't about to let go.

"You're alive!" Marta exclaimed, breaking the embrace and standing a few feet away from him. The coldness had returned. Especially with the new information.

"Very much so," Gohn said.

"It's a miracle," Aria said, with exuberance.

"I told you we have to trust God," Gohn said. "He delivered me from the prison. And we have work to do," he said directly to Marta. "I have a sermon to deliver."

"You're going to have to take a shower first," Aria said, putting her hand to her nose and squeezing it. "You stink."

"That prison cell didn't have a shower. It's been almost a week."

"The image broadcaster is already set up," Marta said. "All you have to do is stand in front of it and deliver your message."

"I want to speak to the squares a half hour before service time. To let them know I'm alive and to invite them to come to church."

"You must be starving," Marta said.

"Famished."

"I'll go fix you something."

"It's so good to see you," Aria said, patting Gohn on the chest.

"It's good to be seen."

"I was so worried. They said you weren't coming back," Aria said.

"God had other plans."

Aria pushed Gohn toward the door. "You have to leave so I can get dressed for church," she said excitedly.

Suddenly, Aria wanted to go to church? A few minutes ago, she wanted to lay on the bed and die.

Marta understood.

She was thrilled to see Gohn.

But determined to not let him see it.

13

Revelation Church
Sunday morning
8:30 a.m.

G ohn stood before the image broadcaster and addressed the squares exactly thirty minutes before the morning service was scheduled to start. The sanctuary was already half full, and he wanted the people of Mercury to know that he was very much alive and had an important vision to share with them.

He brought the chains with him from his prison cell. He held them up for everyone to see.

"I, Gohn, have been in chains for Christ. I count it a privilege to have been found worthy to suffer for his name's sake. The brood of vipers arrested me after the service last Sunday. Threw me in a prison cell. Left me there to die."

Gohn wished he had worded that differently. Technically, Cloyd had led him out of the church service and still felt badly about it. Cloyd was probably watching. The brood of vipers were the ones who had ordered him to do so. Cloyd and Gohn believed that God would deliver him from the authorities which was why Cloyd agreed to take him in.

Neither of them knew Gohn would have to suffer all week in that cell. Turns out, he didn't have to. All he had to do was trust God and believe the prophecy. His long hair provided him with supernatural strength. He could've left the cell at any time. A mistake he wouldn't make a second time.

Gohn continued, constantly interrupted by applause and cheering. The buzz around the church was almost like they'd seen someone raised from the dead.

"But God. My dear friends and fellow Mercurians. Remember those two words. *But God.* If you are sick today, but God has provided healing for your body through the stripes Jesus took upon his back. If you are in jail today, but God will deliver you from all evil. If God doesn't deliver you, still trust God. Do not submit to the evil rulers of the Eliminati. We will not bow our knees to their lockdowns. To their orders that are contrary to God's Word. We will not forsake the assembly together."

The crowd was on its feet. Applauding. Cheering. Worshipping God at the top of their lungs. In the short time Gohn had been speaking, the crowd had grown, and the sanctuary was nearly full. Gohn waved his arms up and down to quiet the throng.

"Come one, come all. To the house of the Lord. Ignore the protocols. Defy the checkpoints. In thirty minutes, if you can't make it in person, then tune in to the squares. I have a word for you. God appeared to me in a vision. In my prison cell. He showed me things that are yet to come. I have an important message I will be sharing to the church of the second quadrangle."

The crowd erupted in applause again.

He tried to end in a crescendo. "I'm Pastor Gohn! A bondservant of Christ! Formerly in chains! Very much alive and well! I'll speak to you at nine o'clock."

When Pastor Gohn concluded his remarks, he was immediately surrounded by a throng of people. So much so that the elders couldn't get to him. They were all well-wishers. Encouraging him. Patting him on the back. Thanking God for his deliverance.

Marta pushed through the crowd to get to him and took him by the arm. Gohn needed to eat something. He'd only had time to shower and put on clean clothes before he delivered his remarks. She had prepared him a hot meal, and he wanted to scarf it down before the nine o'clock hour which was quickly approaching.

They managed to break away from the people and went through the side door back to his apartment. Once out of the view of others, Gohn took Marta's hand and said, "I missed you while I was in prison. I thought of you often. I didn't know if I would ever see you again and my heart was breaking."

His voice cracked as he said it. Today was an emotional day. Would be for everyone. He saw a tear form in the corner of her eye.

"I missed you too," she said. "I thought for sure that you were never coming home." Her voice also cracked as she said it although she recovered more quickly. Within seconds, Marta was all business and scurried him away to the dining room area.

Gohn was certain this was the first time he'd ever seen Marta express any kind of emotion. It warmed his heart. At some point, he needed to drum up the courage to tell her how he felt. Now wasn't the time.

When they got back to the apartment, Marta scooped up a bowl of hot soup and served it to him with a piece of bread. The aroma filled his nostrils, and he took a moment to savor the contrast to the meals he'd eaten over the last week.

After taking the first bite, he said, "I missed your cooking so much."

"I missed cooking for you. It's good to have you home."

Gohn believed her. Marta's gifts were hospitality and administration. She liked serving people. His whole body was warmed by the food, and he felt energized like someone had pumped him full of vitamins. He took a long draw of the cool drink she served him and then turned his thoughts back to his sermon.

Last week, the Lord had told him in the vision to write down what he had seen and heard. This time he had to remember it. In prison, he had nothing to write with. He didn't want to forget a thing.

A loud bang at the door of the apartment startled him.

Cloyd burst in.

"We have to get you out of here," he said excitedly. "The soldiers are coming for you. Quick. Out the back way."

"I'm not leaving."

"Did you hear me? The soldiers are coming for you. They saw what you said in the squares. They have orders to arrest you. They said several guards at the prison are dead. That you killed them."

"I must preach a sermon to the people."

"They'll kill you. They aren't coming to take you back to prison. They have orders to execute you on the spot."

"God will protect me. He has told me to preach seven sermons to the seven churches of the seven quadrangles. God wouldn't tell me to do something and not give me the power or the protection to do it."

"Can you talk some sense into him?" Cloyd said to Marta.

"You heard him. We have to trust God," she exclaimed.

Cloyd pleaded, "Pastor. You know I'd die for you. But I'm just one man. I can't protect you from all the soldiers."

"You don't have to," Gohn said. Then he prayed, "God open Cloyd's eyes. Let him see what I see."

Seconds later, Cloyd stared into the ceiling. In plain view was a vision, like the ones Gohn saw earlier that morning in his prison cell. On the ceiling was a picture of the sanctuary. Full of horses and chariots. Angels with swords and mighty warriors who were already engaging demons and holding them back.

Cloyd stood there with his mouth agape.

"What are you looking at?" Marta said. Apparently, she couldn't see the vision. Only Cloyd and Gohn could see it.

"See, Cloyd," Gohn said. "You don't have to be afraid. Greater is he who is in me than he that is in the world. There are more of us than there are of them. We'll be fine my friend. Let's go deliver the sermon."

Gohn finished what was left of the soup, walked over and kissed Marta on the cheek.

She touched the spot where he had kissed her.

"What was that for?" she asked.

"I was thanking you for the soup and bread. They were delicious."

"You are welcome."

Gohn abruptly turned and immediately walked out of the apartment and back to the sanctuary. The clock showed three minutes to nine. Gohn cracked the door open and looked out to a full sanctuary.

Soldiers were already standing in the back. A group of people had blocked the aisle and were preventing them from coming forward. The soldiers had their guns drawn. It appeared to be a standoff. The men were likely afraid to use their weapons, knowing the multitude would be on them in seconds and tear them apart limb by limb.

The people were satisfied with blocking the path to the front.

Before it could get more heated, Gohn opened the door and walked out. For a few seconds, no one noticed him. All eyes were fixed on the confrontation in the back of the sanctuary.

Gohn made it all the way up on stage and stood behind the pulpit before anyone noticed him.

Where should he begin?

He had so many things to share.

When the soldiers saw Gohn they began to press forward. Against the throng.

Clearly, Gohn wasn't going to be able to say anything until the threat was dealt with.

He urged the members of his congregation to step aside. Most did so but reluctantly.

Gohn came down from the pulpit area and stood in the front. The soldiers pushed their way through the crowd and down to the front. Two of them took Gohn's arms. One on each side.

Others were in the back guarding the exits, and three more were within a few feet of them with their guns drawn.

People were yelling at the soldiers.

"Let him go!"

"We won't let you take him!"

"You won't get out of here alive!"

The soldiers were wide eyed, and their fingers were on the triggers of their guns, ready for almost anything. They were clearly petrified even though they had the weapons.

Gohn began to speak in a loud voice, so he could be heard over the din.

"Would you like to see something really amazing?" Gohn asked.

He could feel the strength enter his arms. It flowed from his hair into his shoulders and down both sides of his arms, to his fists.

Gohn flexed his biceps.

In about five seconds, these two men are going to wish they weren't holding on to my arms.

14

Later that day

M arta was exhausted and slightly irritated.

The church service was over, and the emotional roller coaster had come to an abrupt halt for the time being. First, they thought Gohn was going to die in prison. Then he showed up at their bedroom door, very much alive. Prepared to deliver his sermon that Sunday morning.

The euphoria from seeing him alive was short-lived.

Before church even started, a dozen soldiers showed up. Marta thought Gohn was going to be arrested again. Instead, he single-handedly defeated all of them with his bare hands.

The sermon to the church of the second quadrangle was emotional as well. A prophetic warning that severe persecution was on its way. Many would be thrown into prison. Many more executed.

These were trying times they lived in.

The service was over, and the crowd finally went home. Standing room only and overflow outside had attended. They couldn't even begin to guess how many people watched at home in the squares. It took more than two hours before Marta, Aria, and Gohn could finally go back to the apartment and get something to eat.

Lunch.

Marta had to cook it!

Who else was going to do it? Certainly not Aria. Marta had been up all night trying to comfort her sister. Now she was cooking lunch

117

for everyone and struggling to find the energy. To make matters worse, Aria was no help at all.

Pastor Gohn slouched on the living room couch in his own state of physical and emotional exhaustion which was to be expected considering everything he'd gone through over the last week. Aria sat at his feet.

Aria was the reason Marta's feathers were ruffled, and anger had her tied up in knots. She could use some help. Why did she always have to do all the work? She wanted to say something, but the last thing Pastor Gohn needed was to deal with another confrontation. A petty one at that, considering he stared down a band of soldiers with loaded guns and lived to talk about it.

How could she make a big deal out of cooking him lunch considering everything he'd been through? She did most of the cooking and housework anyway.

Why was that?

Because Aria was lazy!

Marta bit her lip to keep from saying anything. For Gohn's sake. She was amazed at his ability to withstand so much difficulty. Even more amazing was his supernatural strength. Pret said his strength came from his hair. Marta wasn't sure. All she knew was that she'd never seen anything like it and attributed it to God who deserved all the glory.

At the service that morning, two men held Gohn by the arms. He tossed them aside like rag dolls. One flew into the side wall and his neck was broken on contact. He slumped over dead.

Gohn picked the other one up, high over his head and threw him a good ten yards at a group of six soldiers who were charging down the aisle at him. The tossed man hit the six and knocked them to the ground like a bowling ball knocked down pins.

The other soldiers were afraid to charge Gohn and instead lifted their rifles to aim and fire. Marta had let out a scream when the men pulled the triggers. Amazingly, all their guns jammed. Gohn took one of the guns from the hands of one man, smashed it over his knee, breaking it in half. He tossed the gun aside and chased the men out of the sanctuary and told them never to return.

Two men were dead on the floor and two more injured. Gohn felt compassion for them. He laid his hands on the men, and the two were brought back to life and the other two were healed of their injuries.

Three of the men were in awe and stayed to hear the sermon and were later saved after hearing the Word. The other left in a panic. Marta was concerned that more soldiers would come, but none did.

Gohn preached the most powerful sermon Marta had ever heard. To the church of the second quadrangle. About standing firm in the faith in the midst of persecution. Gohn spoke of a second death and how Christians would not be hurt by it. Gohn warned that there were some in the church who said they were believers but were really instruments of Satan. Tares among the wheat. Wolves in sheep's clothing.

How did they know who those people were?

Gohn said they wouldn't know until God separated the wheat from the chaff after the end times were over.

According to Gohn, a new protocol was coming. The worst yet. One that would bring great suffering to Mercury. Somehow it affected pregnant women. Gohn didn't say what was in the protocol, but each new directive from the Eliminati was increasingly evil and devastating to Mercury. Particularly to the Christians who seemed to be the target of the Eliminati's wrath.

Marta felt guilty. With all the troubles in the world, she was bothered by her sister's behavior. Angry because she had to prepare the meal alone. Her complaints sounded so petty in her head. She wanted to say something but couldn't find the words.

If they were alone, she would say something. But not in front of Gohn.

Still!

Couldn't Aria at least set the table? Prepare the drinks? Set out the napkins? Why did Marta have to do it all?

Marta would love nothing more than to sit at Gohn's feet and stroke his hair. Was that the source of her anger? Was she jealous of her sister? Marta tried to tamp those feelings down, but they weren't so easily controlled. Maybe she was jealous. Seeing Gohn and Aria together was twisting her heart into knots of resentment. She pictured them kissing. No matter how hard she tried, she couldn't get the images of them locked in an embrace out of her head and it drove her crazy.

Why was she so angry at her sister? Didn't she want her to be happy? Wouldn't Gohn be the perfect husband for her?

No! He wouldn't. Aria wasn't even willing to lift a finger around the house. All she wanted to do was laugh and have fun. Life wasn't always fun. Especially in these incredibly difficult times. The threat of the soldiers wasn't going away anytime soon. If ever.

Marta glared at Aria. Of course, her sister was oblivious to it.

Which only made Marta angrier.

How could Aria be so insensitive? She didn't mind cooking lunch for Gohn, but why did she have to cook for Aria as well? She was a grown woman. Their mother taught them both how to cook. Aria was lazy. Actually, she was selfish. And Marta let her sister get away with it by not confronting her.

When Marta burned her hand slightly stirring the potatoes, she let out a yelp as the hot pan seared into the side of her hand.

Gohn looked up.

"Are you okay?" he asked.

Aria didn't say anything.

Marta took the pan off the burner and marched into the living room. She'd had enough.

"Why have you left me alone to do all the work?" she asked Aria. "Can you not lift a finger to help me?"

"I didn't know you needed my help," Aria said innocently. Which only made Marta angrier. "You always cook lunch on Sundays," Aria added.

Marta wiped her brow with her arm. Then clutched her hand. It still stung from the burn.

Gohn sat up on the couch. He was clearly still weak from his ordeal in prison. "I'll help you," he said, as he rubbed his eyes to try and wake up. He'd clearly been sleeping. It only made Marta feel guiltier.

"No, sweetie, you lay back down. I'll go help her," Aria said to Gohn.

"Thank you," Gohn said, and laid his head back down.

Marta wished she hadn't said anything.

Aria stood to her feet and glared at Marta who gave her back the same look. Both girls walked into the kitchen. Marta was fuming and began clanging the pans angrily together which made a loud sound that echoed through the small room.

"What do you want me to do?" Aria asked snottily.

"Help me! Set the table. Pour the drinks. Slice the bread. There's a thousand things to do."

Marta went back to her potatoes which had been off the stove for too long. Trying to time it so everything was finished at the same time was a chore anyway. Because she took the pan off the stove, it caused the potatoes to not cook properly. Marta had to turn her efforts to salvaging that part of the meal. She blamed her sister for distracting her.

Aria went to the cabinet and pulled out the plates. Two minutes later, the table was set. Aria was back at Gohn's feet. Stroking his hair. The bread wasn't cut. The drinks weren't poured. The only thing her sister did was take the plates out of the cabinet and put them on the table along with the silverware. She didn't even do that right. The knives, forks, and spoons weren't in the proper order. They go on the left side, not the right. That and Aria had forgotten to set out the salad bowls.

If she could, she'd wring her sister's neck.

15

SCOTE
Secret Council of the Eliminati

"I don't think the protocol goes far enough," Herodius, leader of the Eliminati said.

The Eliminati was the council of six men who ruled all of Mercury as a secret cabal and had for more than ten thousand years. They maintained their control of the people by issuing protocols. The council was working on protocol 663.

Number 662 had been a disaster. The Christians defied the lockdowns and were meeting every Sunday—the day they called the Sabbath. The protocol forbade it. All non-essential citizens were to remain in their homes for sixty days, and all churches were ordered closed. The actions of the Disorderlies, a name they gave to the Christians, was an affront to the council's power and had to be dealt with swiftly and ruthlessly.

A man named Gohn led the rebellion. A self-professed prophet. He was publicly preaching in the squares. Urging the citizens of Mercury to defy the protocols. Even arguing that there was no hole in the stratazone. The fact that there wasn't, was beside the point. The council was the sole authority on Mercury, and the Eliminati was determined to maintain its control.

They'd get to the problem with Gohn after they finalized the newest protocol. Herodius had concerns about it, which he was voicing for the first time.

"What is it that you don't agree with?" Incubus asked. He was the Prime Minister of Health and Medicine and had written the protocol. Mercury Protocol 663 dealt with when life should be considered viable.

"The basic premise is good," Herodius said pensively. He rubbed his chin for effect like he was thinking about it, even though he already knew what he wanted the council to do. "The thinking is sound. You say in the protocol that life begins at the point when the baby is viable. We've always defined that to be at birth. As soon as it's outside the mother's womb."

Produced years ago, the first protocol on the subject said life began when the baby's heart began to beat. The next protocol said it began after the first trimester once the lungs and organs began to form. This newest one said that life began when the fetus could live outside the womb. Viability was defined as the baby's ability to breath on its own.

The ultimate purpose of this intellectual exercise was population control. Prior protocols had not had the desired effect. The purpose of the recent protocols was to eliminate those in the population who were unproductive. The population who were a drain on society. The infirmed. The elderly. The disabled. The protocols called for designated people to be injected with an AXX-E shot filled with mercury. Enough mercury to be lethal. The estimate was that they would thin out the population by five to seven percent. Two thirds was the ultimate goal.

That hadn't happened. The problem was the Disorderlies. The Christians began healing many of those people, so they no longer qualified for elimination. While some were given the AXX-E, and a few thousand died, it had little to no effect on the overall population.

The newest protocol was designed to attack the problem from a different angle. The plan was to terminate babies in the womb by proactively preventing the population from growing any further. Called scrubbing. They already allowed women to scrub their babies. Even encouraged it. They estimated that more than three hundred thousand babies had been eliminated in the womb over the years. That at least helped stunt the rate of population growth. More needed to be done.

"This protocol will slow population growth, but doesn't do anything about our current population," Herodius said.

The protocol called for all babies still in the womb to be terminated if the parents already had one or more children. The babies would be delivered from the womb, given the AXX-E shot and their fetuses used for scientific research and production of various products such as cosmetics.

Zagan raised his hand to speak even though it wasn't necessary. Every member of the council was considered equal to the others. Herodius was the leader because he had risen to the position and was an effective administrator. He now had so much power that the members couldn't oust him from that role even if they wanted to. That didn't mean they weren't treated equally when in the council conference room.

"Yes. Zagan. What say you?" Herodius said.

Zagan was in charge of the religious institutions. Herodius wasn't happy with him at the moment. The churches were out of control, and he blamed Zagan to some extent.

"What does *viable* really mean?" Zagan asked.

"Do you mean in a religious or a practical sense?" Herodius answered. "The Disorderlies say life begins at conception, and if left alone the fetus will grow into viability."

"That's my point," Zagan said. "If someday, the fetus would become viable, does that make it viable today?"

"No!" several people answered.

TERRY TOLER

Herodius wasn't sure where Zagan was going with this. They'd had this discussion many times. Viability was the justification for eliminating babies in the womb. Had been for many years. The policy was working well. Many women liked it because they could end unwanted pregnancies. Men liked it as well for obvious reasons. Regardless of whether men or women liked the protocol, the fact remained that it was the council's right to choose when a life was viable.

"If you follow that logic," Saleos said, "technically, life is not viable until it's self-sustaining."

Saleos was over the educational system. A scholar, he was the most learned of the group.

"Explain what you mean," Herodius said.

"Can a one-year-old baby sustain life without help?" Saleos asked.

Herodius thought he knew where he was going with this and liked it.

"Of course not," Incubus said. "The baby needs its mother to breastfeed him, watch over him, change his diaper... you know. All of those things."

"What would happen to the baby if no one was around to take care of it?" Saleos asked.

"The baby would die," Zagan said.

"Exactly! So, is that baby actually viable under the definition offered earlier by Zagan? While the Disorderlies would argue that a baby will grow into viability and someday be able to sustain life on its own, I would argue that until it can, that baby is not viable. I think we should expand the protocol to state that life doesn't begin until a child can sustain life on its own without any help."

"Here! Here!" several of the others said in agreement. "If I hear what you're saying, we should inject the AXX-E into all babies inside and outside the womb who are unable to sustain life without help."

"That's exactly what I'm saying," Saleos said.

"Brilliant," Herodius responded, and began to cross through certain provisions in the protocol. He made several notes next to the provision regarding viability.

"Does everyone agree?" Herodius asked. "Let's vote."

Everyone was unanimous, so there was no need to take a formal vote.

Saleos spoke up again. "What we must decide then is, what age is a child viable and able to sustain life? Two years old? Three?"

"I have a three-year-old," Zagan said, and he can't find his rear end without my help. "I say older than three."

The protocols didn't apply to members of the council. They were exempt from them. Zagan didn't have to worry about his child being AXX-E-nated.

"We must be careful," Incubus replied. "If the protocol is too far reaching, the people will rebel."

"The Disorderlies will already oppose any protocol," Zagan said. "They oppose scrubbing, but people have begun to accept it as mainstream and normal. Most protocols are resisted at first. Eventually, they become accepted because the people don't know any better."

"What percentage of the population are under two-years-old?" Herodius asked.

Lechies would be the one with that information. He was in charge of the governmental institutions. He was already scrolling through his micro-mechanical minibrain.

"I don't have it broken down that precisely," Lechies said. "I can tell you that thirty percent of the population is under seventeen and five percent is under six."

"Perfect. Let's make the age six. Five percent is a good start."

The actual goal of the council was to eliminate two thirds of the population. They had to take these steps incrementally.

"I make a motion that we give the AXX-E to all kids under six," Incubus said.

"Under six or six and under?" Lechies asked.

"Six and under," Incubus said.

"Not all kids six and under. Only the families with more than one child," Zagan added.

"Correct," Herodius said. "That won't reduce the entire population by five percent, but it'll make a dent. Let's change the protocol to state that all babies in the womb will be given AXX-E and the pregnancy terminated immediately, if the woman already has kids. If she doesn't have kids, then she may keep the child. All kids six or under who aren't the first born will be given AXX-E."

"Keep in mind," Incubus interjected, "children do not consume as many resources as adults. Even though we will be eliminating five percent of our population, we won't see the same percentage reduction in our resources. Food supply. Water. Medicines."

"Understood," Herodius said. "But we have to start somewhere. The scrubbing has already helped. We have fewer people alive today because of it. Thousands of babies have been scrubbed, and that's a good thing. This mandatory scrubbing will help stunt the future drain on our resources and help in the short-term as well as we'll have fewer brats to deal with."

"I agree," somebody said.

"What if the mother is pregnant with twins?" Saleos asked.

Herodius was glad to have a scholar on the council. He thought of things they didn't think of.

"Let the mother choose which baby should live," Herodius said.

"The mother or the father?" Zagan asked. He believed that men were superior to women. As the religious authority on the council, he often touted that the gods preferred men over women, and the council should as well.

"The father, of course," Saleos said.

A protocol had settled that argument years before.

"My mistake," Herodius said. "I misspoke. I agree that the father should decide which baby should live."

"Then we are agreed," Zagan said.

"Let's vote on Mercury Protocol 663. All in favor say aye," Herodius said.

A chorus of ayes resonated through the room.

"Any opposed?"

No opposition was expressed.

Herodius made more notes on his paper. "The protocol carries. It will be issued this week. On to new business. What are we going to do about this Pastor Gohn?"

16

Aria didn't understand why Marta was being so mean to her. All she was doing was spending time with her boyfriend, and Marta had practically bitten her head off.

Didn't she understand that Gohn needed her? He'd been through a trying week in prison, and none of them had been sure he'd even make it out alive. When he showed up that morning at their bedroom door, Aria had been ecstatic. Marta was ruining it with her attitude.

The three of them sat around the table eating the meal Aria helped prepare. After Marta made a big deal about it a second time, Aria sliced the bread, and stirred the potatoes. Even helped put the salad into bowls and placed them on the table.

Gohn seemed genuinely appreciative of their efforts. He devoured the meal like a starving coyote who'd come across prey. He refused to tell them what he ate while in prison. It sounded like it wasn't good.

"Where do you think this sudden strength is coming from?" Marta asked Gohn.

For whatever reason, Marta wouldn't look Aria in the eye. Even when spoken to. She must be jealous because Aria has found true love before her even though Aria was younger.

"I don't know," Gohn said. "I mean... obviously it's from God. Pret's prophecy said the strength comes from my hair."

"What is a prophecy?" Aria asked.

"It's an utterance inspired by God," Gohn answered. "Most people think it's foretelling or predicting what is to come. Like when the prophets predicted the coming of Christ in the Old Testament. Even though Christ was born hundreds of years later, the prophecies accurately predicted it. But a prophecy is more than a prognostication. Any word given by God and spoken for someone's benefit could be considered a prophecy."

Aria nodded her head, so he'd know she understood it. She didn't fully understand but didn't want to come across as stupid. "What did Pret prophesy?"

Gohn took a big, long sip of his drink before answering. "She saw me in prison. Guards were strewn dead on the floor. God told her my strength came from my hair. That actually happened. I killed two guards who tried to stop me from leaving the prison."

"I remember Pret saying that, but I didn't understand it," Aria said.

"Don't feel bad," Gohn said. "I didn't understand it either until after it happened. That's how it was with the prophecies of Christ's coming. No one fully understood them until afterward. There are many prophecies in the Bible about the end times. Now that we're seeing them come to pass, I'm beginning to understand them better."

Marta was being surprisingly quiet.

"Prophecies seem scary to me," Aria said. Then regretted it. She was hoping she wasn't coming off as too immature. She was ten years younger than Gohn. Another reason Marta probably objected to them dating.

"I understand how you feel," Gohn said. "Sometimes prophecies foretell that something bad is about to happen. They aren't always predictions that good things are going to happen. In fact, most of the time, they are a warning of bad things to come."

Aria felt her heart suddenly race.

"Did Pret say that something bad is going to happen to you?"

A bolt of fear ran through her body. She knew Gohn wasn't safe. He was out of prison for now, but the soldiers could come back at any time. How were they going to marry with all this uncertainty?

"She prophesied that I'm going to be married," Gohn said. "Although some people consider that a bad thing." He laughed.

Marta looked up from eating for the first time since the conversation started.

"What did Pret say about who you were going to marry?" Aria asked.

"She said that I was going to marry a maiden."

"What's a maiden?"

"A virgin," Marta answered, while giving Aria a vicious glare. She turned her head to the side and furrowed her forehead and her eyes narrowed, and her lips formed a scowl.

If looks could kill, Aria would be dead ten times over. Why the hostility? Aria was just asking Gohn a question. As soon as Gohn brought up marriage, Marta started glaring at Aria like she was an enemy.

They'd always been close as sisters. Inseparable even. They were different in personalities, but Marta had always been protective of Aria. Took on the role of big sister and did it well. Aria loved Marta. Since they moved into the church's apartment, Marta had been different. Cold. Aloof. Belligerent even. Aria didn't know why and was afraid to ask. The only thing she could think of was that Marta was jealous of her relationship with Gohn.

"Pret said that I was going to marry the woman who could solve a riddle," Gohn said with a sly grin on his face.

Gohn looked over at Marta. She looked at him and their eyes met. *What was that about?*

"Do you remember the riddle?" Aria asked.

"Not word for word," Gohn said. "Do you remember it, Marta?"

She nodded her head yes.

"What is it?" Aria asked.

"I don't know," Marta mumbled.

"You just said you did know!" Aria exclaimed. "What is it?"

Marta didn't say anything. She took another bite of bread and looked away from both of them. Was she keeping the riddle from Aria until she could figure it out for herself? Did Marta want to marry Gohn? That would explain the hostility.

"Why won't you tell me?" Aria asked angrily.

"It's something like... when does a man call his wife honey?" Gohn said.

"I don't understand," Aria said. "When does a man call his wife honey?"

"I don't know," Gohn replied. He still had a smug grin on his face. The whole conversation seemed to be amusing him.

"According to Pret," Gohn continued, "I will marry the woman who solves the riddle."

"I want to solve it," Aria blurted, then immediately regretted it. She and Gohn hadn't talked about marriage.

Gohn's face turned red. His cheeks flushed. He suddenly looked down and moved the rest of the food around on his plate. Like he was embarrassed.

Marta kept her stoic, blank stare. Fixated on her own food. She refused to make eye contact with Aria or with Gohn.

I am going to marry Gohn!

Aria wanted to press the issue further but thought better of it. Then she had an idea.

"Can you excuse me?" Aria said.

"Where are you going?" Marta asked.

Not that it was any of her business.

"I remembered that I needed to do something," Aria said. "I'm going out."

"Be careful," Gohn said. "The soldiers are still out in force. Trust me. You don't want to get thrown into prison."

"I'll be careful," Aria said, as she practically ran out of the room and into her bedroom to change her shoes. She also threw on a different shirt and shorts. Didn't even bother looking in the mirror to fix her hair. She was in a hurry.

Aria was going to see Pret. She had to find out the answer to the riddle. Hopefully, Pret would know it since she was the one who spoke the riddle to Gohn. Aria didn't understand how all these prophecies worked, but she did know that if this one was true, she had to be the one to answer the riddle.

The walk to Pret's house was less than a mile. Aria made it there in less than fifteen minutes. She practically ran.

When she arrived at the house, Aria banged on the door several times. Loudly.

Will opened the door. He appeared to have been taking a nap.

"Is something wrong?" he asked. "Is Pastor okay?"

"He's fine," Aria said. "I cooked him a big meal, and he's probably laying down for a nap right now. Can I come in?"

"Of course," Will said.

"I need to talk to Pret."

"She's upstairs in her room."

Aria bolted down the hall and up the stairs and burst into Pret's room without knocking.

Pret was on the bed, listening to music which was playing softly in the background. Aria startled her, and she sat up straight in her bed.

Aria closed the door behind her and went and sat next to Pret. "You have to tell me the answer to the riddle," Aria implored.

"What riddle?" Pret asked.

"You know. The prophecy. The one you told to Pastor Gohn. About who he's going to marry."

"Oh, that riddle."

Aria clasped Pret's hands. "I have to know. You have to tell me the answer to the riddle."

"I don't know it. God didn't give me the answer."

Aria threw her hands in the air. "How am I supposed to figure it out?"

"I don't know. Why do you want to know?"

Aria grabbed Pret's hands again. "Tell me the riddle. Word for word. Exactly like God told it to you."

"I don't know if I can remember it word for word, but I'll try."

"Pret! Think hard. It's important."

"When may a husband call his wife honey?" Pret said hesitantly, like she wasn't sure.

Gohn had said the same thing at lunch. That must be it.

"What does it mean?" Aria asked.

"I have no idea."

"Help me figure it out," Aria said. "I'm not leaving here until we know the answer to that riddle."

"It could mean anything. I don't know. Why is it so important to you?" Pret's eyes suddenly widened. Her mouth gaped open. "Do you want to marry Pastor Gohn?"

"Yes. And he wants to marry me. So, I need to know the answer to the riddle. Gohn won't marry me unless I can answer it. He thinks it's a prophecy from God."

"It might have something to do with a bee," Pret said. "Bees make honey."

"Bee something... A husband calls his wife honey when she has a bee in her bonnet."

"That's not it. Something to do with bees though. I think."

135

"Honey is sweet," Aria said. "A husband can call his wife honey if he thinks she's sweet."

"I don't think that's it."

"That's it! I'm sure of it." Aria grabbed Pret's hand and practically jerked her off the bed.

"Let's go tell Gohn that I have answered the riddle."

"I don't know if that's the right answer."

"It has to be. When can a man call his wife honey? When he thinks she's sweet. That makes perfect sense."

"It might not be right."

"It has to be. Tell Gohn it's the answer to the riddle. Do it for me?"

They were standing now.

"Hurry. Get your shoes on," Aria said. "We have to go see Gohn."

Pret reluctantly agreed.

They raced back to Gohn's apartment and burst through the door.

Gohn and Marta were in the kitchen. Marta was cleaning up and Gohn was helping.

"I've solved the riddle," Aria said. She was out of breath from rushing over there. Also, from having solved the riddle.

"Marta already solved it," Gohn said.

Aria's heart sunk to the bottom of her chest.

"But I solved it first," Aria said. "Pret can tell you."

"What is the answer to the riddle?" Pret asked.

"When may a husband call his wife honey?" Marta said. "When he has a comb in his hair."

"That's it!" Pret said. "That's the answer to the riddle. God just confirmed it."

Aria could not believe what she was hearing. This can't be right. Gohn can't marry Marta.

He's supposed to marry me!

17

The Secret Council of the Eliminati had moved on to new business. The Disorderlies. Old business, actually. The Christians had been a thorn in the side of the Eliminati since Jesus was killed. No matter how hard they tried, they'd not been able to develop a protocol that would end the threat altogether.

A new threat had emerged. The pastor from Revelation Church. Gohn. He wasn't new either. Men like Gohn had been around for centuries, resisting the Eliminati and every effort they made to make life better for the people of Mercury. They'd executed hundreds of men like Gohn. Every time they did, another one emerged.

Herodius didn't remember one ever being as big a threat as Gohn. This time things were different. They weren't able to kill him. He had supernatural strength. Every time a soldier pointed their guns at him and fired, the gun jammed. When they tried to take him by force, he had the strength to fight off a hundred men.

"We have to find out the source of his strength," Herodius said to the Council.

"He must have a weakness," Zagan said. "Something that will tempt him to give away his secret."

"What is the one thing that men can never resist?" Herodius said, with a devilish grin.

"A pretty woman," Incubus said. "Let's hire a woman to go in and tempt him. A prostitute."

"I don't know," Zagan replied. "I think it has to be someone close to him. Someone he trusts. A woman Gohn is willing to confide in. I don't think he'll fall for a prostitute. Do we know of anyone?"

Herodius opened a file in front of him. "There's a man in his inner circle. One of our soldiers. His name is Cloyd. The spies in his church tell us that Cloyd is secretly a Disorderly. And that he is working with them. Giving them secrets. Troop movements. Warning Gohn when we are getting close."

"I'll have him arrested at once!" Zagan said.

Zagan was in charge of the religious institutions. He oversaw the churches and was called upon to tamp down any threats. His job might be the hardest of all the council members.

Herodius raised his hand to silence Zagan.

"Not so fast. I agree the man is a traitor and must be put to death. Just not yet. If he's in the inner circle, perhaps he might be of use to us."

"If he is truly a Disorderly, he'll never betray one of his own," Zagan said.

"Let's offer him a large sum of money to betray Gohn. Every man has a price."

"I don't think we have to offer him money," Herodius said. "I have a different idea. I'm told that this man, Cloyd, has a beautiful wife."

Herodius pulled a picture out of the file and passed it around.

A number of oohs and aahs and catcalls went up as the picture circulated to each person. The woman had brown hair. Hazel eyes. High cheekbones. Dark and heavy eyebrows that accentuated her eyes. If there was a more beautiful woman on Mercury, Herodius hadn't met her.

"I'd like to get my hands on that woman," Incubus said, laughing.

"Zagan, when you kill her husband, let me know," Lechies said. "She'll need comforting. I'll be there for her."

"She'll need a *real* man to comfort her," Botis spoke up for the first time. He was the richest man in the group. If anyone had a chance with the man's wife, Botis would be the one Herodius would be most worried about. "I have a good feeling about that woman. She's going to be my next ex-wife."

The room roared with laughter as the men continued the banter for a good two or three minutes.

Herodius wouldn't mind an afternoon with the woman himself. He'd try to figure out a way to make it happen after her husband was out of the way.

"Why would she betray her husband?" Zagan asked, after the din settled down.

"I believe she already has," Herodius said. "I'm told she despises the Disorderlies. She made a call to the local authorities and said she suspects her husband is working with them."

"Interesting," Zagan said. "The woman is not only beautiful but cunning. Mischievous. She'll turn in her own husband. I like her already. Maybe I *will* give her a call."

"Nobody's going to call her," Herodius said, impatiently. "Focus, men. We need information. I want to use this woman to find out Gohn's weakness. Where does his strength come from? I propose that I call her and discuss it with her."

"That's a good idea," Zagan said. "Once you find out, let me know, and I'll send my men to capture Gohn. And Cloyd. We'll kill them both."

Herodius went over a few more details and then left the meeting to call the woman. Because very few people knew the identities of the members of the Eliminati, Herodius had to remain anonymous. He wouldn't tell her his name or title. The woman didn't know that he had the power to snuff out her life in an instant. Or have her brought to his house where he could hold her as his slave and have his way with her for as long as he desired.

According to the file, her name was Lyla. She answered on the second ring. "Lyla, I'm calling from the Proctorial Guard. I'm your husband's supervisor."

Thankfully she didn't ask his name.

"Okay," she said in a sweet voice. "How may I help you?

He already desired her. She sounded educated as well.

"I've been expecting your call. Someone told me you'd be calling," Lyla added.

"I wanted to talk to you about your husband."

"Cloyd?"

"Yes. Is he home? Are you free to talk?"

"He's at work. I'm alone. So, I'm free to talk."

Since she was alone, Herodius wanted to visit her in person but had to dismiss that thought and image out of his mind. Women had always been his weakness. Even though he could have as many women as he wanted, he gravitated toward those he couldn't have. Those who resisted his advances. Those who he could take against their will. Lyla qualified simply because she was another man's wife.

"We have confirmed your suspicions," Herodius stated. "Your husband is a Disorderly."

"I know. He has spoken to me about it. He's tried to get me to go to church with him. I refuse."

The woman's voice was raspy and sensual. It sent chills down Herodius's spine. He needed to focus, or he'd say the wrong thing.

"Good girl. But I don't want you to refuse."

"You don't?"

"No. I want you to play along with him. Go to the church."

"Why?"

"I need for you to be our eyes and ears. Have you met the pastor of the church? Gohn?"

"My husband has mentioned him."

"Gohn is a threat to the future of Mercury. He incites revolution. Encourages the Disorderlies to defy the protocols."

"I know. Men like that are pure evil. I can't believe the Disorderlies have taken to the streets and defied the protocols. I've seen them everywhere. Don't they know they are endangering the stratazone? We should all stay in our houses."

"You are so right. The threat is real, and the Disorderlies are putting us all in danger."

"What can I do to help you?"

"Get close to Pastor Gohn. Find out the source of his strength. We need to know what makes him strong and what will make him weak."

"I don't know if he'll trust me."

"You are a very beautiful woman. I'm told he can't resist beautiful women. Use all of your womanly wiles to seduce him."

"I'm a married woman."

"Your husband is a traitor. We will pay you three and seven pieces of silver if you are successful."

Silver coins were the most valuable currency on Mercury. Called mercs. Only the very elite owned them.

The other end of the phone was silent for a good ten seconds. The silver was more mercs than Cloyd would make in ten lifetimes. Lyla would become a very wealthy woman. Herodius knew they lived in a modest house and on a soldier's salary. She was probably willing to do it for free, but Herodius wanted to make sure that he owned her.

"I'll do it," she said emphatically.

"Write down this number." Herodius gave her a direct line that only he answered. "When you know Gohn's weakness, call me."

"I will."

"Don't let your husband know what you're doing."

"I won't. You can count on me."

They hung up the phone. The call went well. Herodius liked what he heard from the woman. Maybe when all this was said and done and her husband was dead, he could have her over. Probably just once. She was damaged goods. A low-level soldier's wife. Herodius did have standards. Which he would be willing to violate one time for a woman as pretty as Lyla.

* * *

Later that night

Lyla and Cloyd were in bed. The lights were out, and they were about to go to sleep. A debate raged in her head as she wondered if now was the best time to talk to Cloyd about going to church with him. She somehow needed to get close to Gohn.

"Honey, I've been thinking," Lyla said, finally drumming up the courage.

"About what?" Cloyd asked.

"I think I'd like to go to church with you."

Cloyd sat up in the bed and turned on the light.

"Are you serious?" he asked.

"I am. I'd like to meet your friends."

"You don't know how happy you've made me."

"I'd really like to meet your pastor. Gohn. He sounds like an interesting man."

"I'm sure he'd like to meet you as well."

"How soon can we go?"

"This Sunday. You can go to church with me."

That wasn't soon enough. And she wouldn't be able to meet Gohn without there being a crowd around him. She'd rather meet him alone. That wasn't possible, but perhaps Cloyd could arrange a meeting with the three of them.

"I want to meet him sooner than that," she said.

Lyla was thinking about the mercs. The sooner she got the answers, the sooner she'd get the money. While she cared for her husband somewhat, she had no remorse about betraying him. He'd betrayed her. Since he met Gohn and became a Christian, all he talked about was God and the church. He'd even tried to convince her to become a Christian. The Proctorial authorities were rounding up Christians and killing them. She wasn't willing to die for a false God.

"We'll go see him tomorrow," Cloyd said. "He'll be home."

"Wonderful."

Lyla kissed Cloyd on the cheek and then turned over to go to sleep. She couldn't wait to meet this Gohn.

Lyla fell asleep with visions of silver fairies dancing around in her head.

18

G ohn wasn't sure exactly how to handle the situation between Aria and Marta other than to tackle it head on. He'd always been the kind to resolve conflict immediately. In this instance, he wasn't sure how that was possible. Aria thought she was the one who had solved the riddle and clearly wasn't going to drop it.

"A comb in your hair? What does that even mean?" Aria cried out, practically in tears.

"When can a husband call his wife honey?" Gohn said. Repeating the riddle. "Marta guessed that it's when he has a comb in his hair. A comb is a honeycomb. Something bees make."

"I know what a honeycomb is. But that's stupid. It doesn't even make sense. I said it's because she's sweet," Aria argued. "Honey is sweet. So is a man's wife."

Aria was making the case that her guess was the correct answer to the riddle. Gohn wasn't even sure what all this meant either. When Pret first mentioned the riddle a couple of weeks ago, Gohn had dismissed it. Now it seemed like the riddle might actually be from God.

"Pret said Marta gave the correct answer," Gohn replied softly, trying not to inflame the already tense situation.

Pret had already left, and the three of them—Gohn, Aria, and Marta—were left to sort it all out. Marta was surprisingly quiet.

"What does Pret know?" Aria said. "She's only seventeen. You should get to decide who you want to marry."

Gohn had decided. He wanted to marry Marta. If she'd have him. It seemed like it was God's will. Would she see it that way? By Marta's stoic demeanor, he wasn't sure. The distance between them still seemed as big as a canyon. Then he remembered the kiss with Aria. Had he blown it with Marta? Would she ever forgive him? As soon as he convinced Aria, he'd have to deal with Marta.

The only option was to be honest with her. Tell her about the kiss. Hopefully, she'd understand. He was confused. Taken in by the moment. On his way to jail. It happened so fast he wasn't even thinking clearly.

"I want to marry you," Aria added.

"According to the prophecy, God wants me to marry the maiden who solves the riddle," Gohn said.

Aria was standing over Gohn now. Trying to put her arms around his neck.

He was trying to keep them off of him.

By the look on her face, Aria was hurt. "That's not fair! I'm the one in love with you. I told you how I feel. I know you love me too. I could tell when you kissed me."

Gohn saw Marta wince and turn her head away. He needed to cut off this conversation but wasn't sure how to do it. What he really needed to do was talk to Marta alone. Gohn had to forcibly remove Aria's hands from around him. A knock on the door startled all of them and caused a momentary pause in the conversation.

"Come in," Gohn said.

Will walked in with a piece of paper in his hand.

"We'll talk about this later," Gohn said to Aria. He saw Marta nod. Still refusing to look him in the eye.

Aria let out a huff and stormed out of the room, brushing past Will on the way, who looked at Gohn with a puzzled twist of the lips.

Gohn waved his hand dismissively. Like... don't ask.

"Hello, Will," Gohn said. "What brings you out on this Sunday afternoon? I figured you'd be taking a nap."

Something Gohn wished he were doing at that moment.

"I was. First, Aria woke me up. Then Pret came home a few minutes ago and woke me up. I'd barely gotten back to sleep when I got another knock on the door. Someone brought me this."

Will handed a paper to Gohn.

"What is it?" Gohn asked.

"A new protocol."

Gohn was still sitting at the kitchen table. Marta next to him. Will sat down next to Gohn across from Marta.

"Can I get you something to drink?" Marta asked Will.

He mumbled a no. By the strained look on his face, he was deeply troubled. Probably by the protocol.

Gohn began reading it to himself

Mercury Protocol 663
Viability of Life and Policy of Birth Planning

WHEREAS a state of emergency has been declared on Mercury and excessive population growth is an extremely difficult problem facing the contemporary world, and

WHEREAS Mercury's population now exceeds 732,000 persons. The annual births have averaged 21,000 per year. Annual deaths have averaged 11,200. Such massive total population and annual population growth constitutes a heavy burden on Mercury, and

WHEREAS, due to the strain on food and water resources, the ability of the governmental agencies to adequately support the current population has been impacted and with associated impacts due to lack of adherences to previous protocols, and

WHEREAS family planning will control the population to an appropriate size and will make the speed of population growth lower than the growth of resources, and WHEREAS family planning will relieve women of frequent births further liberating them from the heavy family burden, thus greatly improving their socioeconomic and personal well-being, and

WHEREAS consistent with the protection of public health and safety, it is determined that parents do not have the right to decide the number and spacing of their children when it puts at risk the population at large, therefore,

The Mercurial Proctor declares the following:

Viability of life is defined as the moment when a child is able to sustain life on its own. As such, it has been determined by the Department of Health that life begins at age seven. It is further determined that one child for one couple is a necessary choice to alleviate the grim population situation.

Therefore, it is hereby ordered:

1. Children under seven who are not first-born, must report to the Department of Health immediately. Compliance is mandatory.

2. Induced scrubbing under safe and reliable conditions shall be authorized as a method of compliance for an expectant mother who already has a living child.

3. Fertile married couples with a living child must select contraceptive methods of their own accord per the guidelines of the Department of Health. Failure to do so will result in a fine up to one year's salary and imprisonment of up to five years.

4. Fertile married couples without a living child must obtain a birth permit from the Department of Health before discontinuing the use of contraception.

5. As to those couples who are unwilling to accept such measures, family planning workers are authorized to assume custody of children, and parents will be segregated. IT IS FURTHER ORDERED that, as soon as possible, these protocols will be widely publicized to the general population.

Signed by Chief Proctor of Mercury:
Joseph Osinim Yukov

Gohn stared at the protocol in stunned disbelief. He read it a second time. Then handed it to Marta.

"I can't believe it," Gohn said soberly.

"The Eliminati is behind it," Will said.

Gohn stood and began pacing the floor. The extreme exhaustion he felt was overridden by the seriousness of the protocol. This was more than lockdowns. The Eliminati was proposing mass genocide.

Gohn agreed with Will. "Of course, the Eliminati's behind it. What's worse is that they actually think they can get away with it."

"They will unless we do something about it," Will said.

"Is the image broadcaster still set up in the church?" Gohn asked.

"No," Will answered. "But it wouldn't take long to set it back up."

Marta looked up from reading the protocol with her mouth agape. She laid it on the table, having finished reading it.

"Does this mean what I think it means?" Marta asked. "Do they really intend to murder all children under seven?"

"All except the first born," Will said. All Will's kids were older than seven, so he wouldn't be affected.

"They also intend to kill all the babies in the womb," Gohn added.

"What's this so-called population crisis?" Marta asked. "I went to the store yesterday. There was plenty of food to go around."

"It's a made-up crisis," Will said. "The Eliminati is trying to gain control over everything. The way to do that is to instill fear in the people. They tried that with the climate crisis, but it didn't work."

"Yeah. Whatever happened to that?" Marta asked. "Apparently, there's no hole in the stratazone anymore. It must've magically fixed itself."

"There never was a climate crisis. Or a hole in the stratazone," Will said. "They made it up. To try and force the churches into lockdown. The Christians refused. We stood up to them, and they backed down. Now they're raising the stakes. We have to fight back."

"These are the end times," Gohn said. "This is what I saw in my vision. A pregnant woman crying. Jesus said, 'Woe to those with child and nursing mothers in the last days.' Now we know why. We're seeing it play out right before our eyes."

"What's the end goal of the Eliminati?" Will asked.

"God hasn't revealed that to me yet," Gohn said.

"Is Herodius behind this?" Will asked. "You said he was the leader of the Eliminati."

"I don't think so. Herodius is the spirit of the antichrist. A messenger of Satan. Things are going to get much worse."

"How does it get worse than this?" Marta asked.

"It will," Gohn said soberly. "Remember that two thirds of all the people on Mercury will die in the end times. I think this is a trial run for that. The Eliminati is trying to gain control over the churches. And rule the people by instilling fear in them. We're the ones who restrain evil. We're their biggest threat to power."

"What do you want to do with the image broadcaster?" Marta asked. "Do you want to address the people in the squares?"

"I did. But I changed my mind. I want to but not yet," Gohn said. "I need to pray about it. Seek the Lord and find out what I should say."

"You need to get some rest," Marta said. "You must be exhausted."

"I am," Gohn said. "It's all hitting me at once."

He'd had quite an eventful week. Spent the week in jail, chained to a wall. Threatened by soldiers. Then he had the visions and dreams in his prison cell and the message to the church. God delivered him. He killed the guards. Then preached a message to the masses. Fought more guards with weapons in the sanctuary. Now this. The protocol.

Add Aria and Marta on top of all that, and he felt the emotional overload. That made him think of Aria. Perhaps he should go talk to her. *What do I say?*

As if she read his mind, Marta said. "I'll be right back. I'm going to go check on Aria."

She stood and left the room.

"I don't envy you," Will said to Gohn. "You're going to need wisdom. The Bible says to ask for it, and God will give it to you freely and without judgment."

"If we don't figure out how to stop this protocol, a lot of people are going to die, and the suffering will be indescribable."

"Remember, my friend. The battle belongs to the Lord. We don't have to figure out anything. The Lord will show us what to do if we are humble."

Marta returned. Her brow was furrowed with a look of deep concern.

"Aria's gone," she said.

Gohn bolted from his chair.

"Where did she go? Is she coming back?"

"I don't think so. All her stuff's gone. I think she left for good."

Everything hit Gohn at once. He slumped down onto the edge of the couch.

The exhaustion. The burden he felt for the people. Now he realized that he'd hurt Aria. Unintentionally. Perhaps he should've handled it differently. Talked to her privately. He never promised her anything. Aria had been right. He should be free to marry who he wanted to marry.

Marta.

Would she even want him now?

Could he even think about marriage when the weight of all of Mercury was on his shoulders?

19

Gohn stood in front of the image broadcaster in the sanctuary, having finished preparing his message to the people concerning Mercury Protocol 663. A barbaric edict even by Eliminati standards.

Writing the message had been relatively easy as the Holy Spirit gave Gohn the words to say. He even felt the strength to deliver it. A miracle in and of itself considering he'd barely slept for a week, and the hardship of the prison had taken a toll on his body which he would no doubt feel later that night.

For now, he had to deliver one of the most important sermons of his life and was excited. Powered by waning adrenaline fumes which had been taxed to the max over the last few weeks. He felt unworthy as he always did with the weight of the world seemingly on his shoulders.

To whom much has been given, much is expected.

Will motioned for him to begin. Marta was behind the broadcaster. No one knew where Aria was, which still weighed heavily on his heart. He put that out of his mind for now.

Word had spread through the squares that he was going to speak. Most people probably didn't know why. The protocol hadn't yet made its way to all the quadrangles of Mercury. So Gohn began his remarks by reading it to them.

When he finished, he said, "This protocol is an abomination to the Lord. There are several things which God hates. Hands who shed innocent blood is one of them."

Gohn waved the protocol in the air. He raised his voice. "These are wicked plans, straight from the pit of hell. Created by the Eliminati, who are messengers of Satan. They intend to shed innocent blood. The blood of our most vulnerable. Our children."

He wished he'd had a full sanctuary to draw strength from. A booing and hissing crowd would add to the effect. He glanced down at his notes, even though it wasn't necessary. He knew this first part by heart.

"The Bible says that man was created in the image of God. Every child was formed in the womb by his hand. The Scripture says that we were beautifully and wonderfully made."

He raised the protocol again. Rather than raising his voice, he softened it. Gohn felt a tear form in his eye and escape down his cheek.

"What the Eliminati proposes is murder. They want to kill our children. Scrub them out of the womb for a lie. Do you remember how Jesus called the little children to himself on more than one occasion? He even said, 'suffer not the little children to come unto me.'"

Gohn wiped the tear away with his sleeve.

"Then Jesus said a remarkable thing. 'Such is the kingdom of heaven.' Children are the essence of the kingdom of God. They are precious in the eyes of God. He said if any man harms a child, a millstone tied around his neck and him drowned in the sea would be a better fate for him."

He raised the protocol again and shook it violently.

"This protocol says that life begins at age seven. How ridiculous is that? Life begins the moment God begins to form it in the womb!"

He paused as if a crowd was there. Like he was waiting for the cheer to die down. Even though there wasn't a cheer, the silence was effective. Gohn could feel it.

"When you tuck your children into bed tonight, look at them, touch them. Tell me they don't have life. Even the newest of newborns can respond to your touch. They can breathe. The child's heart beats, and life flows through their veins just like it does all of us—regardless of age. Those of you with child, put your hand on your stomach and feel your baby move. Feel him or her kick. You no doubt feel them change positions. That baby has a heartbeat. Even in the womb, that baby has life."

Gohn could hardly believe he had to make these arguments. They seemed so obvious to him. Yet the line of depravity had been continually moving. At first, the Eliminati allowed scrubbing in the first three months of pregnancy. Then they moved the line to include up to six months. The next protocol allowed scrubbing all the way up to the point when the baby was born. Several years ago, a protocol allowed the baby to be partially born. Just enough to where his or her head was visible. The physician was then allowed to sever the baby's spinal cord at the neck, so the baby would die on its own. A partial-birth scrubbing they called it.

Gohn had preached many sermons against that. Incredibly, the church in the first quadrangle had endorsed the practice. Claimed that it was better than the delivery of an unwanted baby.

"Remember when the Eliminati tried to kill Jesus," Gohn said, letting the vitriol into his words. "Remember that decree that all first-born children were to be killed. By Herodius I. His descendant several times removed is now the one in charge of the Eliminati. His name is also Herodius. He is still trying to kill Christians. He still wants to murder babies. We must not let him!"

Gohn had to take a deep breath. He was talking so fast he'd lost his breath for a second. So much to say. He had to get it all in. They were always concerned that the Eliminati would find a way to cut off the feed to the squares. So far, they hadn't been able to. The simple way was to shut off the power grid. The Eliminati apparently hadn't thought of that yet.

Gohn felt the need to continue on with haste.

"Why would the Eliminati kill our children? They say it's because the population is out of control, and they don't have the resources to feed everyone. I tell you it's all lies! There is no food shortage."

Gohn could feel the anger rising inside of him. He wanted that righteous indignation to come out in his words.

"God told Adam and Eve in the garden of Eden to be fruitful and multiply. Meaning they were to fill Mercury with children. To my knowledge, God has not rescinded that command. We're still called to fill the world with children and take dominion over all of Mercury."

Gohn flipped the pages on his notes. Time to move on. He'd made that point.

"So, we have *permission* from God to continue to produce children. Permission is my first point."

He had to mention that because he had three points of alliteration. Gohn liked to begin all his points in his sermons with the same letter. In this case, all three points of this message would begin with the letter P.

"If God has given us permission to continue to procreate, then he is bound to his own word to give us provision. Provision is my second point. In fact, God has bound himself. The Almighty is not a man that he should lie. Look at the birds of the air. They don't sow or reap or store food in barns. Yet our heavenly father feeds them. Are you not more valuable than they?"

Gohn paused to let that sink in. Also took a second to look at Marta who smiled at him, which gave him new energy to continue.

"We don't get our provision of food from the Eliminati. They say they don't have the resources to feed all of us. I say that God does! Trust in the Lord. He will provide everything you will ever need. Food. Clothing. Shelter. If our population increases, God will make additional provision."

Gohn flipped the page on his notes again.

Point three: *Protection*.

The red light on the broadcaster flickered. Gohn could see Will frantically typing away on the mechanical brain. Apparently, he was temporarily off the air. The green light would come on when he could continue. He was getting to the best part.

Gohn had fallen asleep that afternoon while preparing the message. Right in his desk chair. His head had slumped on the desk without even realizing it. God woke him with a loud voice, and another vision on his bedroom wall.

He saw dozens of children being given a shot with a deadly poison. A silvery colored liquid was in the vile. Mercury. Gohn wasn't sure how he knew but was certain the children were being given a heavy dose of mercury poisoning. Through a shot in the arm. He saw thousands of children dead and strewn around a large field.

The label on the syringe read AXX-E.

Then Gohn saw another child.

Six years old. Nearly seven. Not old enough to meet the criteria of when life began, according to the protocol. Four more months and she would've been able to live.

Gohn recognized that the child belonged to a couple in his congregation. Berra.

She refused to take the AXX-E.

Folded her arms in defiance.

The medical personnel grabbed her by the arm and threw her to the ground. Another one of them sat on top of her, even though she wasn't resisting.

Berra was calm.

A woman stuck the needle in her arm and injected the mercury into her veins.

Then they went to the next child in line. Berra was left to die. Gohn felt the pain in his heart and wanted to turn away but couldn't make himself.

He watched the girl closely. Several minutes passed. She didn't die. Berra sat in the corner singing to herself.

The medical personnel noticed her. They were confused and assumed the shot was defective. So, they gave her another dose.

Then left her alone.

Several more minutes passed. The same thing happened. The girl didn't die.

When they weren't watching, she stood and walked out of the Department of Health facility. Walked all the way home.

The vision changed to a picture of the family's living room. Berra's parents were sitting on the couch, crying. When the girl walked in, they thought they'd seen a ghost.

The mother screamed.

Berra ran into her arms.

The entire house was filled with joy.

The girl showed them her arm. The red mark where she'd been given the AXX-E was still visible. Twice.

She seemed perfectly normal. God had protected her.

The vision ended. Gohn remembered Jesus's words to his disciples. *You will drink deadly poison, and it won't hurt you. You can be bitten by a snake, and you will not die.*

The green light came back on.

Gohn began to relate the entire vision to the people in the squares.

Then he said, "Don't be afraid of the AXX-E. It won't harm you if you trust God. Pray over your children. Lay hands on them. Refuse to believe the lies of the Eliminati. God will protect us."

Gohn ended the sermon with that vision. Marta shut off the broadcaster, and he felt the relief fall off his shoulders. He still felt strong but knew the exhaustion would hit him soon.

Before anyone could say anything, the doors in the back opened.

In walked Cloyd. With a beautiful woman on his arm. Someone Gohn had never seen before, but he assumed she was Cloyd's wife.

Cloyd walked forward and hugged Gohn enthusiastically while the woman stood to the side.

"I want you to meet someone," Cloyd said. "This is my wife, Lyla."

Gohn was confused. Cloyd had said his wife wasn't interested in the church or the things of God. He was actually concerned that she might turn him in to the authorities.

Lyla held out her hand and smiled widely.

Gohn took her hand and felt something immediately. A chill went down his spine.

Her hand was ice cold.

Like he was touching evil.

He tried to tamp it down. This was his friend's wife.

He looked into her eyes.

Could see the deception.

Red alarm bells sounded in Gohn's head like a dozen fire trucks racing to the scene.

Discernment. The Holy Spirit was sending him a message.

Be careful.

Be very careful.

20

After everyone left the church and went home, the emotional upheaval of the week hit Gohn all at once. He went back to his apartment and crashed on the couch. Not even able to garner the strength to warm up the meal Marta had left for him. In a few minutes, he'd drum up the energy, pull himself up off the couch, scarf down dinner, and then fall into bed. He'd feel a lot better tomorrow.

So many things would consume his mind if he let it. Aria. Marta. The riddle. The protocol. The encounter with Cloyd's wife. He wouldn't let his mind go there. It'd take too much of his mental energy. If he thought about it too long, he wouldn't be able to go to sleep. He'd think about that later.

He was about to doze off when Marta suddenly appeared out of her bedroom. Carrying her clothes cases. That caused Gohn to sit up, suddenly fully awake.

"What are you doing?" he asked.

"I left you meals for the entire week," Marta said soberly. In a tone like someone had recently died.

"Sounds like you're leaving."

"I can't stay here with Aria gone."

Gohn hadn't really thought about that fact. The elders of the church wouldn't be happy to know that Gohn and Marta were living alone in the church apartment.

"I guess you're right. Will you be back tomorrow for work?"

"I'll continue to work until you find someone else."

"I don't understand. Why don't you want to work with me anymore?"

Gohn saw a rare bit of emotion cross Marta's face as her eyes began to water.

"How can I now? With things the way they are with Aria. I think it'd be best if I backed out of the picture."

Gohn got up from the couch and walked over to her. He wanted to put his arm around her shoulder but thought better of it.

"There's nothing between me and your sister," Gohn said softly.

Marta bit her lip. Like she wanted to say something but was trying not to.

She hesitated, then said with her voice cracking, "She told me the two of you kissed. Right here in this room."

Gohn was stunned. He didn't know Marta knew about that. At some point, he planned on telling her. Certainly not now, with things so fragile between them. He was surprised Aria had told her sister about it. That made him angry. As much at himself as at Aria. He should've known better.

"It was one kiss. It didn't mean anything. I mean..."

He wasn't prepared to explain it to anyone. Certainly not Aria's sister.

"It meant something to her," Marta said with more anger in her tone. "She told you she was in love with you. Then you kissed her. What's she supposed to think? What am I supposed to think?"

"I don't love Aria. I love you."

Marta's eyes widened in complete surprise. Then she quickly gained control over her reaction and returned to her cool demeanor.

"Then why were you kissing Aria?"

"I don't know. It just happened. Before I even realized it."

"Kisses don't just happen. You must've felt something."

"I did feel something. But not what you think. I was sad. And confused. I was going off to prison. I didn't know if I was going to ever come back. Your sister is beautiful. I just got caught up in the moment."

"Yeah, well. I don't know how to get past it."

Gohn took Marta by the hand, but she pulled it away.

"When I was in prison, all I could think about was you," Gohn said sincerely. "That's the only thing that got me through it. I knew at that moment that nothing was ever going to happen with Aria."

"You broke her heart."

"I know. And I'm sorry. I'll talk to her about it when I get the chance."

"You should."

"What about us?"

"I don't know. There is no *us*. Never has been. I don't know that there ever will be. I can't hurt my sister."

"Will you be able to forgive me?"

"I don't... of course, I forgive you."

"Where are you going to go?" Gohn asked.

"Back home to our apartment. Hopefully, Aria is there. I have to talk to her. I can't hurt her. She's my sister. I'll tell her that there's nothing between us."

"That would be a lie, though. I know you have feelings for me."

"I don't. I mean... feelings come and go. They'll pass over time."

"Then why did you answer the riddle?" Gohn asked, in a more accusing tone than he'd intended.

Marta hesitated again, telling Gohn she hadn't considered that fact. Or didn't have an answer. He knew why she solved the riddle and told her why.

"God said I was going to marry the maiden who correctly answered the riddle," Gohn argued. More forcefully this time. "That was you. You answered it because you want the same thing. You know it's God's will. Are we just going to ignore the prophecy?"

"Are you saying you want to marry me?" Marta asked.

"Yes. I've always had feelings for you."

"I'm sorry, but I can't," she said.

Then ran out of the room.

* * *

Cloyd was asleep, and Lyla was in a different room of the house making preparations.

She had a plan. Tomorrow she'd pay Pastor Gohn a visit. If things went well, she'd be on her way to collecting the three and seven mercs from the Mercurial Proctor. Or whoever it was who'd called her and offered her the mercs if she'd betray Gohn and her husband. Which she was willing to do for the good of Mercury. And for the mercs.

Gohn would be arrested. So would Cloyd. The rebellion would be stifled. She'd be a rich woman.

Lyla felt a twinge of guilt about betraying her husband. None whatsoever about scheming to bring Gohn down. He deserved it. She'd heard his sermon earlier that evening. About the children. It made her angry. She had scrubbed two of her pregnancies. Those were before she met Cloyd, but they were still a sore point with her. The sermon reminded her of the pain of having never had kids.

The pregnancies before were inconvenient at the time. Lyla was unmarried, and the men were losers. Unfit to be the father of her children. Her father was abusive. If he'd known she was pregnant out of wedlock, he would've disowned her. Probably killed the two boys who had gotten her pregnant. She was only a teenager with her whole life ahead of her. The babies would have ruined her future. Scrubbing seemed like the best option.

When she married Cloyd, the plan was to have two kids. That never happened. They tried, but she could never get pregnant. The doctors couldn't pinpoint why. Maybe complications from her scrubbings. More than likely the problem lay with Cloyd since she was able to get pregnant so easily before.

This was her ticket out. If she stayed with Cloyd, she'd never have kids. With him out of the way and her being a grieving widow with money, she'd be able to marry someone of means. Someone in the elite class. One to whom the protocols didn't apply. She'd be able to have those two kids after all. Lyla had the looks and would have the money to have the pick of the most eligible bachelors on Mercury.

First, she had to execute her plan.

Tomorrow.

She'd call Pastor Gohn. Make up some excuse to meet with him. Of course, he wouldn't refuse. She had a way of making men do whatever she wanted them to do.

Lyla snuck back into the bedroom, being careful not to wake Cloyd. She went into her closet and picked out an outfit. What she wore to her meeting with Gohn had to be perfect. Not too sexy but enough to get his attention. Getting a man to notice her had never been a problem. Although, she'd never seduced a preacher before. This was uncharted territory. Still, men were men. With the same desires. Easily manipulated.

A loud snore came from the bed. Another annoyance that she'd soon be rid of. When was the last night of restful sleep she'd had? She looked over at Cloyd with mixed emotions.

He was a good man and was madly in love with her. He treated her well. It's just that she could do better. Now that he'd become a Christian, there's no way they could stay together. Actually, she should've never married him.

At the time, she thought she was in love. More than anything, she resented her father, which was why she made the rash decision. When he forbade her from dating Cloyd, that pushed her even further away and into a serious relationship with him.

Certainly, she could've done worse. A soldier was just below the rich society types on Mercury. Cloyd was a good provider, a hard worker, and good to her. That's how she justified staying with him all these years.

Didn't matter. Her decision was made. Whatever guilt she felt was inconsequential. Cloyd would die. That was a reality whether she betrayed him or not. When he decided to become a Christian and commit treason by breaking the protocols, he sealed his fate. She'd only move the time frame up by a few days.

Once Cloyd and Gohn were dead, and she got the three and seven mercs, she could make a new life for herself. She went into the bathroom, turned on the light, and looked in the mirror. Lyla liked what she saw. The mercs couldn't have come at a better time. While she still had her looks. A husband in the upper crest shouldn't be that hard to find. Then she'd have everything she'd always wanted.

Lyla went through the plan again in her mind.

Somehow, she had to find out the source of Gohn's strength. Hopefully, he'd confide in her and tell her the source h. Once they knew, the soldiers could arrest him, and he'd be unable to resist.

If that didn't work, then all she had to do was find a way to discredit him. So he'd lose his influence. Create such a scandal that the people in the squares would quit listening to him. She knew just what to do.

The man on the phone said either plan would work. It didn't matter to her as long as she got paid.

Lyla went back to her closet and pulled a sweater off the hanger. She took it into the kitchen and got a knife out of the drawer. She sat the sweater on the counter and made a small nick in the arm. Then carefully ripped the hole further so that the material began to unravel.

She left the sweater on the counter and went to sleep in the guest bedroom. The best night's sleep she'd had in days.

The next morning, she prepared breakfast for Cloyd and sent him off to work.

Once she was certain he wasn't coming back, she picked up the phone and called the number for the church.

A man answered with a friendly hello. She recognized the voice.

"Pastor Gohn," Lyla said, matching his friendly tone.

"This is Pastor Gohn."

"Hello Pastor, this is Lyla. Cloyd's wife. I met you last night."

"Of course. What can I do for you?"

He sounded cold over the phone. She wasn't sure why.

"I need to meet with you," Lyla said. "To discuss something urgent. About Cloyd."

"Is everything okay?"

"I don't think so. I think his life may be in danger. Can I please come by and see you as soon as possible? This morning, perhaps?"

Gohn didn't answer right away.

"I'm busy this morning. I was in jail all last week and have a lot of things to do."

"It won't take ten minutes."

"Is Cloyd coming with you?"

She had to be careful. According to Cloyd, Pastor Gohn never met with women alone. She had a way around that.

"He's at work. But I'll contact him and get him to come as well. Can we stop by at ten?"

"Ten will be fine. I look forward to it."

"Thank you. I'll see you then."

Lyla hung up the phone. That's all she needed.

Her plan was in motion.

21

Revelation Church

Pastor Gohn hung up the phone. Confused. Leery. Not sure what to make of it. Cloyd's wife had called. Said it was urgent. Something about Cloyd. He got a weird feeling the night before when he met her. After thinking about it, he'd dismissed the trepidation. After delivering his sermon, he was hardly in the frame of mind to be thinking clearly. While he wasn't sure what the red flags were about, he decided to ignore them for now.

Cloyd was his friend. A man he now knew he could trust. At first, he wasn't sure about Cloyd either. Cloyd was a soldier in the Mercurian Guard. Even the elders of his church had questioned his conversion. Over time, Cloyd had proven himself trustworthy and would give his life for Gohn if necessary.

In these uncertain times, it'd be easy to question everyone's motives. Gohn had warned the elders of the church about being suspicious of people, and he was reminding himself of the admonition. Whatever concerns he had about Cloyd's wife, he needed to put them aside. He'd give Lyla the benefit of the doubt until she proved she didn't deserve it.

Then the confusion returned. Cloyd had said that Lyla wasn't interested in church. Why the sudden change of heart? He quickly dismissed the thought. God could change anyone's heart. The fact that she was suddenly open to coming to church was a good thing for Cloyd.

Of greater concern at the moment was Marta. She hadn't come in to work that morning, and Gohn hadn't heard from her. He wondered if he had totally misread that situation. He thought she felt the same way about him that he felt toward her. Her words last night echoed in his mind.

"I can't marry you," she had said.

Was it because of Aria or because she really didn't want to marry him? What about the riddle? Was it really a prophecy? If God was behind it, would it be this hard?

Could it be because Marta wasn't in love with him? That wasn't it. He could see it in her eyes when he told her he loved her. They brightened, and she smiled. Her face turned red. If only for a second. Marta definitely had feelings for him.

It had to be because of Aria. A sadness filled his heart as he remembered the kiss. He still needed to talk to Marta's sister. He intended to do so, but now was too soon. He could see why Marta might be unwilling to pursue a romantic relationship with him because of it. It certainly complicated things for everyone. Now was not the time to talk to Aria because, frankly, he didn't know what he'd say.

Gohn tried to concentrate on his work, but too many things occupied his thoughts. He kept listening for the door. Hoping and praying Marta would walk in. When ten o'clock came around, she hadn't. When he did hear the door to the church offices open, he figured Cloyd and Lyla were there. A welcomed respite. It'd get his mind off Marta and Aria. If only for a few minutes.

To his surprise, Lyla showed up alone.

She stood at the open door of his office.

Gohn stood to greet her. He looked away to keep from doing a double take. Lyla was wearing white, form-fitting shorts and a red, sleeveless blouse with a plunging neckline. Her cleavage was covered only by a thin, silver cross necklace.

The sight almost took his breath away. Lyla was stunningly beautiful.

"Thank you for meeting with me," she said sweetly.

"Cloyd's not here yet," Gohn said, putting on his most professional demeanor.

He didn't remember ever feeling this uncomfortable around another person. Even Aria, who was beautiful but innocent. Not as beautiful as Lyla, but attractive in a school-girl kind of way.

Unlike Lyla, who was clearly a woman of the world. Lyla had on makeup, and her eyelashes were long and flowing. Dark. Seductive. Gohn wondered if they were natural or fake.

"Cloyd is at work," Lyla said. "I tried to call him but couldn't reach him. Things are in such chaos at work that it demands most of his time. I hardly ever see him."

Gohn stayed behind his desk to keep his distance. He considered calling Cloyd but decided against it. Lyla was right. Cloyd was knee-deep in problems. Complicated by his relationship with the church. A while back, Gohn and Cloyd agreed that their phone communications should be limited. Only in the event of an emergency. Cloyd couldn't be linked to Gohn in any way or his life would be in danger. This didn't seem like one of those times where Cloyd should be bothered.

"What can I help you with?" Gohn asked, as he extended his hand to offer Lyla a chair.

She sat down in one of the two across from his desk and crossed her legs. Then uncrossed them and crossed her other leg over the one. She wiggled around in the chair to get comfortable. Gohn stared past her at a picture on the wall, so he wouldn't be tempted to look at her long and sexy legs.

Lyla seemed nervous.

Gohn was beyond nervous. He was petrified.

He tried hard to keep his focus on her eyes and nothing below them. Then he realized how creepy that might seem. So, he tried to relax his demeanor and just treat her like any other woman he might be meeting with.

"I'm worried about Cloyd," Lyla said.

That helped distract Gohn. For twenty minutes they discussed it. She was concerned about his job and the affiliation with the church. She was afraid they might find out that her husband was a Christian. He'd likely be killed. She might be killed as well, considering she was his wife.

Lyla was simply voicing the same concerns Gohn felt. Those feelings were to be expected. He wondered if he had misjudged her. She seemed sincere.

"Cloyd felt so bad when you were arrested," Lyla said. "He felt like he was to blame."

"I understood he was only doing his job," Gohn replied. "Turned out, God rescued me anyway."

"Cloyd told me about that," Lyla said with a grin. Her smile was mesmerizing. "My husband said God has given you superhuman strength."

"I suppose. It does come in handy during these dangerous times."

He told her about his ability to take the prison door off its hinges. Then regretted it. It sounded like he was bragging. She might think he was trying to impress her.

"What is the source of your strength?" Lyla asked. "Cloyd didn't know."

Red sirens went off in Gohn's head again. Like they had the night before. The Holy Spirit had previously told him to keep the source of his strength a secret. Very few people knew that the power came from his hair. If the Eliminati learned that fact, they could cut his hair, and he'd be powerless to stop them. Even if he could trust Lyla, he wasn't going to share that information with her.

He evaded the subject.

For another ten minutes, Lyla grilled Gohn about the source of his strength. He lied and said he didn't know where it came from. She kept pressing until finally she gave up.

"I guess I'd better be going," she said, almost like she was disappointed. Then she stood to her feet.

Gohn breathed a sigh of relief.

He walked out of the office with her.

"What's back here?" Lyla asked, as they came to the closed door to his apartment which was on the hallway leading to the exit.

"That's where I live," Gohn answered. "The church graciously provides it for me."

"Can I see it?" Lyla asked.

Before he could answer, she opened the door to his apartment and walked through it.

Gohn followed her and had to quicken his pace to keep up. They walked into the open area which was the living room, dining room, and kitchen.

"This is cozy," she said. "Small but quaint. Do you live here alone?"

"Yes."

The ugly scene with Marta from the night before played out in Gohn's head. They were standing at the exact same spot where Marta bolted out of the room. Not far from where he and Aria had kissed. A twinge of regret reared its ugly head and shot through him like a knife cutting through a piece of meat.

"Is this your bedroom?" Lyla asked, as she suddenly walked straight toward it. The door was open, and Gohn could see the bed from the living area.

He hesitated. He didn't know if he should follow her or not. Then he remembered the notes from his visions were on the desk. He might've written something about his hair being the source of his strength.

Did he not trust her?

The thought occurred to him that Lyla might've been sent by the Eliminati. As a spy. To find out the source of his strength. Gohn walked into his bedroom and put himself between his desk and Lyla.

"You really shouldn't be in here," Gohn said. "These are my private quarters."

She ignored him. "It's so nice in here. Plain and understated. That's refreshing."

Lyla sat down on the bed, which was made, thankfully.

Then she laid down on it.

Gohn felt his mouth gape open.

Lyla motioned for Gohn to come and lay down with her. At least that's what he thought she meant when she patted a spot on the bedspread next to her.

Confirmed when she said, "Come to bed with me!"

Gohn felt his knees wobble.

Then he felt temptation.

A weird lust of the flesh came on him.

He fought it off.

Resist the devil.

She said it again. "Come lie with me." This time seductively. Making her intentions perfectly clear. Gohn could not believe what he was hearing. He'd just met this lady, and she wanted him to have an affair with her.

Gohn refused.

"Cloyd has been a good friend to me. You are his wife. No one is more grateful for our friendship than I am."

"Cloyd will never know. Don't you find me attractive?"

"You are very attractive."

The wrong thing to say.

"Then come and be with me. I find you very handsome."

The temptation returned with a fury. Burning lusts of desire.

Gohn bowed his back and strengthened his resolve. He wouldn't even let his mind go there.

"How could I do something so wicked and sin against God?" Gohn asked, as much to himself as to her.

Lyla sat up in the bed. She had a sweater in her hand. She threw it on the ground. Then stood up from the bed and was next to Gohn within seconds. Before he could react, she had her hands on his chest and their lips were only inches apart.

Gohn took two steps back. If he hadn't, she would've kissed him.

A noise came from out in the living room. Like a door closing. Someone was there.

Suddenly, Lyla let out a scream!

A loud, shrill scream.

What was happening?

Lyla took off running out of the room.

Gohn was stunned. Then followed her.

When he came out of the bedroom, Marta was standing there.

Lyla ran into her arms.

"Help me!" Lyla said. She was sobbing now.

"What's going on?" Marta asked.

"That man attacked me," Lyla said, pointing at Gohn. "He tried to get me to have sex with him in his bed. I fought him off. Thank God you were here."

Gohn was so stunned, he didn't even know what to say. He was being set up and knew it. Lyla was lying to Marta. Telling her things that never happened. Gohn realized that it didn't look good for him.

How could he explain why she was in his bedroom?

Or why she screamed?

How could I have been so stupid?

22

Gohn had known Lyla couldn't be trusted. He just didn't know why. Now he knew. The Holy Spirit had tried to warn him. He should've listened. He'd walked right into her trap. What seemed like a thousand questions were processing through his mind.

Did the Eliminati send her? Would she betray her husband as well? Were both their lives in danger? Would the elders of his church believe him? What about Marta? Aria? Would the kiss come up? Would the two situations be linked?

It looked bad for him.

"He asked me to lay on the bed with him," Lyla said to Marta. "I refused. He was going to force himself on me." She said it between sobs, which Gohn knew were fake.

"That's why I screamed and ran out of the room," she added. "Thank God you were here."

Marta had her arms around Lyla and was trying to comfort her.

"That's a lie!" Gohn said, angrily. He wasn't sure what would be the proper tone. If he sounded too angry, Marta might become scared of him.

Lyla pulled away from Marta. Then stood behind her. Like she was afraid of Gohn and hoped Marta would protect her.

Gohn saw right through the ruse. She was pretending to be frightened. For effect. It was working.

Marta glared at Gohn.

Did she believe her?

"What do you have to say for yourself?" Marta demanded, confirming Gohn's worst fears.

He tried to explain. "Lyla called me and wanted to meet. I suggested that we meet with her husband there. She showed up without him."

"That's not true! Pastor Gohn called me," Lyla exclaimed. "He told me he needed to talk to me about Cloyd."

"She called me!"

"Let her finish," Marta said sternly.

"I told him my husband was at work," Lyla continued. "Pastor said he wanted to meet with me. To talk about my husband. I wasn't sure what to do. He's a pastor. So, I agreed. I had no idea my life would be in danger."

Oh please! The woman sure had a flair for the dramatic. Even if it was all a lie.

"That's not what happened," Gohn said calmly.

"I thought you didn't meet with women alone?" Marta said accusingly.

That raised his ire again. He needed to show some righteous indignation.

"She said Cloyd was coming with her!"

"Why would I say that?" Lyla retorted. "My husband's at work."

"I just met the woman last night. Why would I invite her to the church if I intended to make a pass at her? As far as I knew, you'd come into work at any time. Am I going to risk attacking a woman in my apartment knowing you could walk in at any time?"

"Why was she in your bedroom?" Marta asked, like an investigator questioning a suspect.

Before Gohn could answer, Lyla said, "When I got here, we talked in his office. Then he said he wanted to show me something. In this back area. I didn't know this was his living area. When we got back here, he said there was something in that room he wanted to show me."

Lyla pointed at the bedroom.

"I didn't know it was his bedroom or I'd never gone in there," she added. "That's when he attacked me."

"She walked into the bedroom," Gohn retorted. "Before I could stop her. She sat down on my bed and wanted to lay with me. But I refused. I said I'd never sin against God in that way. Or against Cloyd. He's my friend."

"I trusted you!" Lyla screamed. "You're a monster."

"I never laid a finger on you," Gohn said roughly. This time he was pointing his finger at her. "You are a Jelez!"

A Jelez was a seductress. A temptress. Marta would be familiar with that term from the Bible.

"I swear I never touched her, Marta," Gohn said. "You have to believe me."

"I don't know what to believe. I heard her scream and run out of your room," Marta said. "What am I supposed to think?"

"I'm calling my husband!" Lyla said, as she pulled a phone out of her back pocket.

She dialed a number. He must've answered because she said, "Honey. I'm at the church." Lyla was sobbing again.

Gohn looked at Marta and pleaded with her to believe him with his eyes. She must've known what he was trying to communicate because she shrugged her shoulders and then looked away in disgust.

Lyla was good. She was playing the part of the victim perfectly. Even Marta believed her.

"You have to come right away," Lyla said to Cloyd. "Something terrible has happened. I can't even tell you over the phone. Please hurry!"

"Oh, for goodness sake," Gohn said. "You're such a liar."

"Gohn!" Marta said. "Don't you think you've done enough to this woman? First Aria. Now Lyla. I don't even know you anymore."

"I can't believe you're taking her side. After everything we've been through. You know I could never do such a thing."

"I don't know what to believe."

Gohn could see Marta's eyes begin to water.

She did believe her. That much was becoming clear. Gohn decided to keep his mouth shut. Cloyd would believe his wife as well. Of course, he would. It was his word against hers, and they would all believe her. The poor innocent woman. Taken advantage of by the man.

He had to expect the worst. It looked bad.

Gohn walked over to the kitchen table and calmly sat down. Marta and Lyla kept their distance and stayed on the other side of the room.

Cloyd arrived within ten minutes. He must've been in the neighborhood.

As soon as Lyla saw him, she ran into his arms and burst into tears. Cloyd seemed confused. His eyes were narrowed, and his lips pursed. He looked at Gohn with more of a questioning glance than accusatory. The scene probably wasn't making sense to him.

Why was his wife even at the church? Much less in Gohn's living quarters. Gohn didn't know how to convince him that his wife was dangerous. A threat to both of them.

Lyla began trying to tell Cloyd her pack of lies. It sounded more like gibberish between the sobs.

"Calm down," Cloyd said to Lyla. "I don't understand a word you're saying."

She took a deep breath and then composed herself. Or at least she was able to start speaking more clearly. Gohn was convinced the whole thing was an act, and she wasn't distressed at all.

Gohn decided to stay on the other side of the room. He didn't know how Cloyd would react once he heard the whole sordid tale. Gohn's strength was superior to Cloyd's because of his hair, but he didn't want a physical confrontation with him and would avoid one at all cost. Any fight would make things worse when the elders confronted Gohn. Which they would do soon enough.

Lyla began again. Slower this time. She told Cloyd the whole story from the lies she had concocted in her head. Even spouting out new lies. Gohn wondered if Marta caught the inconsistencies in her story.

Cloyd was surprisingly calm.

When she finished, Cloyd asked Gohn, "How could you do this to me?"

Fortunately, he didn't make any move toward Gohn. He seemed more hurt than angry. Gohn tried to be understanding. He was being duped in the same way Gohn was.

"I didn't."

"Are you calling my wife a liar?" he said, with more vitriol in his voice.

"She is lying. What she said didn't happen."

"Why would she lie?" Marta asked, interjecting herself back into the conversation.

Gohn knew why. Lyla was sent by the Eliminati. To discover the source of his strength. That's why she had grilled him so hard in his office. They'd probably offered her a lot of money to betray him. He wanted to accuse her but knew how it sounded. No one in the room would believe him. Cloyd clearly had no idea that his wife worked for the Eliminati and would be offended by any suggestion that she was.

Jesus said not to answer your accusers. Let your yeas be yea and your nays be nay. That seemed like good advice. Anything Gohn said in his defense would only make things worse.

"I want to press charges," Lyla blurted out.

"Are you sure?" Cloyd said. "I'll have to take him to jail."

"Take him! That's where he belongs."

"It's your word against his," Cloyd said to his wife.

"Ask her. She saw it." Lyla pointed at Marta.

"What did you see, Marta?" Cloyd asked.

Marta didn't answer at first. She rocked from side to side, like the question had made her uncomfortable. Which she clearly was. Whatever she said would probably make things worse for Gohn.

"I didn't see anything," Marta finally said. "I never saw Pastor Gohn touch her."

"She's lying!" Lyla said. "She saw the whole thing."

Marta seemed offended by Lyla's outburst, because her tone changed. "What I was going to say was that I heard your wife scream, and she came running out of the bedroom. Then Pastor Gohn came out right behind her. But I can't confirm that he actually touched her. I didn't see it."

"Obviously, he did. Otherwise, why would I scream?"

"Because you were trying to frame me," Gohn answered. No longer able to remain silent.

"My sweater," Lyla said. "When Gohn grabbed my arm on the bed, he ripped my sweater. It's in his bedroom on the floor. I left it there when I was trying to get away from him. Go get it. You'll see the tear. That'll prove I'm telling the truth."

Cloyd walked into Gohn's bedroom. Moments later he came out with the sweater in his hands.

"It's clearly torn," Cloyd said. He showed it to Gohn and then to Marta. Then gave the sweater to Lyla.

"That's right! He tore it as I was running out of the room."

Seconds before she had said Gohn tore it when she was on the bed. Gohn really wanted to make his case.

"Look at your wife's arm," Gohn said to Cloyd. "I don't see any bruises. If I tore her sweater, I think there'd be a red mark."

"I didn't say he grabbed my arm. I said he grabbed my sweater."

She actually did say he grabbed her arm.

"I'm going to have to arrest you, Gohn. It'll be up to the authorities to decide what to do with you. Are you going to go peacefully?"

Cloyd was clearly concerned about Gohn's superior strength.

"Be careful," Lyla said. "He could hurt you."

Gohn stood to his feet. Held out his wrists. Like he was going willingly.

When Cloyd got near Gohn, he grabbed Cloyd's arm. Surprising him. Cloyd tried to pull away. He couldn't. Gohn's grip was too strong. Then Gohn released it.

"Interesting that your wife said I grabbed her arm, but she pulled away. She weighs half what you weigh, Cloyd. How was she able to pull away from me when you couldn't? I'm sorry, my friend. Your wife is a liar. She will be the downfall of all of us."

"He grabbed my sweater!" Lyla exclaimed. "Not my arm. That's why it ripped."

Gohn held out his wrists again. Cloyd wasn't going to listen to reason.

He had supernatural strength but wasn't going to resist.

Cloyd led Gohn away to prison. For the second time in a week.

23

Even though it had been less than twelve hours, getting away from Pastor Gohn's house had given Aria a new perspective on things. Not that the feelings for Gohn had gone away; she simply understood them better.

Marta was right. Hers was an infatuation. She was more in love with the idea of being in love than she was actually in love with Pastor. It'd been a hard reality to face. She probably still didn't fully understand how or why it happened. Regardless, she wasn't going to ruin the relationship with her sister over it. No man was worth that.

That became clear when Marta came home later that night having moved out of Pastor Gohn's apartment as well. After several hours of a heated discussion, Aria finally realized that her sister was in love with Gohn. Had been for a while. She finally admitted it late into the night.

What shifted Aria's feelings was when Marta said she wasn't going to act on her feelings.

"Why not?" Aria had asked.

"Because you're in love with Gohn. I don't want to hurt you."

"He's clearly not in love with me. He wants to marry you."

"Doesn't matter. You're my sister. You're my flesh and blood. I can't put a man over our relationship."

That Marta would give up her relationship with Gohn because of her had changed her whole perspective. She no longer felt the animosity toward Marta. It also made her realize how selfish she was being. Why hadn't that been her first reaction? She had become angry at Marta and stormed out of Gohn's house like a spoiled brat.

When she really thought about it, Gohn and Marta were better suited for each other anyway. They were the same age. Had the same obsessive attention to detail. Both loved the church and dedicated their whole lives to working at it.

Add to the fact that Marta had answered the riddle correctly, and Aria had no other choice but to accept the fact that Gohn and Marta were meant to be together. That was the main thing that had given her pause. She wanted God's will for her life. More than anything else in the world. If she were to marry a man who wasn't her soulmate, the relationship would be a disaster.

What Marta said next nearly sent Aria into a panic.

"I'm going to quit tomorrow," Marta said. "I'm going to give Pastor Gohn my notice."

"You can't do that!" Aria exclaimed. "You love working at the church."

"It'll be too awkward."

"You're quitting because of me. I won't let you. You have to go back to work tomorrow and tell Pastor how you feel."

It took some convincing, but Marta finally agreed.

When her sister pulled up in the driveway before lunchtime, Aria assumed the worst. Their conversation must not have gone well. When she saw the distressed look on Marta's face, it appeared things might be even worse than she had anticipated.

They were.

"Pastor Gohn's been arrested," Marta said, soberly as Aria ran to the door to greet her.

"What happened?" Aria asked. "Did the soldiers come for him again?"

Marta hesitated. "You won't even believe it."

"We knew they eventually would. His sermons yesterday struck at the heart of the Eliminati's authority. Don't worry. Gohn has strength in his hair. He'll break out of the prison in no time."

"It's not what you think," Marta said. "Pastor Gohn isn't who we think he is."

"I don't understand what you mean."

Marta seemed hesitant to tell Aria. She set her things on the kitchen counter and got something to drink out of the cabinet. When she walked out of the kitchen and sat down on the living room couch, Aria was beside herself with curiosity.

"Marta! Tell me what's going on," Aria said strongly.

"Gohn tried to force himself on Lyla."

"Who's Lyla?"

"Cloyd's wife. Remember? We met her at church last night."

"Oh... Yeah..." Aria said as she remembered the beautiful and extremely sexy lady who'd come to church with Cloyd the night before. Everybody noticed the woman when she walked in. Especially the men.

"I didn't like that lady," Aria said. "I didn't trust her the moment I met her. What do you mean Pastor Gohn tried to force himself on her?"

"I thought the same thing about her," Marta said. "I didn't trust her either. But I saw it. Pastor Gohn attacked Lyla."

"Pastor attacked her in front of you?"

"Not exactly."

"You're not making sense. Tell me what happened."

"I was trying to spare your feelings."

"Well don't! I want to know what happened. I'm not a little girl anymore."

They'd made a lot of gains in their relationship the night before. Today, Aria felt like they were taking two steps backwards.

Aria sat down beside Marta. She wasn't moving until Marta told her everything.

"I got to church and saw a strange car in the parking lot," Marta said. "I went inside, and no one was there. The door was opened to Pastor Gohn's office, but he wasn't anywhere to be found. I went in the sanctuary. All the lights were off."

"Where was he?"

"I'm getting to that."

Aria's heart was skipping around her chest in circles. She wished Marta would get to the point.

"The door to Pastor Gohn's apartment was open. I called out his name, but no one responded. So, I went inside. I figured... it's ten thirty. Pastor Gohn has to be awake. When I walked in the living room, I heard a scream. Lyla came running out of Pastor Gohn's bedroom."

"Out of his bedroom?" Aria asked, hardly believing what she was hearing. Neither Aria nor Marta ever went in his bedroom, even when they were living in the apartment.

"I know!" Marta exclaimed.

"There has to be some explanation."

Aria couldn't think of one.

"She said Gohn tricked her into going there," Marta said. "According to Lyla, Pastor Gohn threw her down on the bed and tried to have sex with her."

"What! I don't believe it! Gohn would never do such a thing."

"That's what I thought. But I saw what I saw."

"You saw Gohn trying to have sex with her?"

"No. I heard the scream. Then I saw her face when she ran out of the room. She seemed genuinely scared of him."

"What did Pastor Gohn say happened?"

There had to be two sides to the story.

"He said he never laid a finger on her."

"I believe him."

"What was she doing in his bedroom then?" Marta argued.

"I don't know. That's strange. Did you ask him? What did Pastor Gohn say?"

"I'm trying to remember."

"Why was Lyla even at the church? Without you being there. Pastor Gohn doesn't meet with women alone. That's been his policy ever since he came to Revelation Church."

"Lyla said that Pastor Gohn called her and asked her to come to the church to talk about Cloyd."

"Why would he want to talk to her about her husband?"

"Gohn said she called him."

"His word against hers. Like I said. I believe Gohn over that woman. She's married to Cloyd. Cloyd is his friend. Why would Gohn risk everything for that woman? He would have to know someone would find out about it."

"Maybe not. Maybe Pastor Gohn thought he could get away with it. Or couldn't control himself. I mean... he kissed you in his apartment."

"I can't believe you're bringing that up. It's not the same thing at all. I practically threw myself at Pastor Gohn. He's always been the perfect gentleman with me."

"I'm sorry. I shouldn't have brought it up. He's always been that way with me too. He's always concerned with appearances."

Aria decided to change the subject back to the woman even though she was still angry Marta had mentioned the kiss. Maybe she still had some resentment over it.

"We don't even know the lady," Aria said. "Like I said, I had a bad feeling about her the moment I met her. She seemed suspicious to me. Like... why is she all of a sudden interested in coming to church? I honestly didn't even know Cloyd was married."

"I knew he was married, but from what I'd heard, his wife wasn't interested in becoming a Christian. Something that weighed heavy on him. I was surprised when she showed up at church last night."

Aria let out a huge sigh. "I'm sorry, but I don't believe her. If Gohn... Pastor Gohn said he didn't touch her, then I believe him over her."

"I would too, but... there's a sweater."

"What about a sweater?"

"Lyla was wearing a sweater. It had a tear in it. She said Gohn ripped it off her when she tried to get away. That's pretty damning evidence."

"There could be any number of reasons why the sweater was torn. Maybe it was torn before she ever came to church. Maybe she tore it."

"Why would she do that?"

"I don't know why, but I'm going to find out."

Aria stood abruptly, left the room, and went into her bedroom. She got her shoes out of the closet and put them on. Marta followed her in there. Then followed her back out into the kitchen where Aria began to gather her things.

"Where are you going?" Marta asked.

"I'm going to go talk to Pastor Gohn."

* * *

Aria stopped by the store to pick up a couple of food items to use to bribe the guards. It worked. They let her in to see Gohn without much resistance.

Aria had never been in the prison before, so the guard led her into the bowels of what was a large cave. She walked down two flights of steps. The stench hit her immediately. Stopped her in her tracks. She had to breathe through her mouth to even stand it.

Gohn was in the last cell on the right. Chained to a wall. His eyes widened in surprise when he saw her.

"Aria. What are you doing here?" he asked.

"I heard what happened. I needed to see you."

He walked toward the cell door. As far as the chain allowed.

"Nothing happened," Gohn said. "I promise you. I didn't do what she accused me of."

"I believe you."

He seemed relieved as his shoulders sagged.

"Why is Lyla lying?" Aria asked.

"She's framing me. I think she's working for the Eliminati. They're probably paying her a lot of mercs to set me up."

"It's your word against hers. She can't prove anything happened."

"There's the sweater."

"Marta told me about the sweater. What else was Lyla wearing?"

"I don't remember."

"Think about it. It's important."

"Shorts and a skimpy blouse. Sleeveless."

"Exactly. That's what I thought. She was wearing shorts. Yesterday, it was hot outside. Why was she wearing a sweater? No one wears a sweater on Mercury except at night. She had on shorts and a sleeveless shirt? Who wears a sweater with shorts? When I heard she was wearing a sweater, I knew Lyla was lying."

"I'm so glad you believe me. After what happened between us, I thought you'd be angry at me."

"I'm not. I believe you. I also know now the kiss was a mistake. You should marry Marta."

Gohn chuckled nervously. "I don't think she'd have me now. Not after what happened. I'm afraid she believes Lyla."

"Well... we're going to have to prove to everyone that she's lying."

"I've been thinking about that," Gohn said. "Will you help me? I can't do anything here in prison to prove my innocence."

"Your strength is in your hair. You can get out of here anytime you want."

"Not if I want to prove my innocence. I have a plan. But I need help. It involves me staying in prison for a couple more days."

"I'll help you. What's the plan?"

"I need you to talk to Lyla."

"Okay. Why would I do that?"

"So we can frame her."

"I like the sound of that."

It took Gohn nearly ten minutes, but he explained his plan to Aria.

When he was finished, Aria left the prison and went straight to Lyla's house.

24

The next day

An emergency meeting of the Eliminati was called. Everyone was present and accounted for. All six of them. Generally, a meeting could be called at any time with little notice, and they'd all drop everything to be there. The Mercury bubble was small enough that a person could travel from the first quadrangle to the seventh in less than three hours. Especially for men such as these with this much wealth and resources at their beck and call.

While the meeting was called an emergency session, a better description would be a nuisance discussion rather than a real emergency. None of the protocols had had the desired results and Herodius wasn't happy. Primarily because of the Disorderly Pastor. Gohn. From the church in the fifth quadrangle. A continued and ongoing threat. A clear and present danger to the very existence of the Eliminati.

Maybe it was a real emergency after all. He hadn't thought so because the Disorderly Pastor was under arrest. The Lyla woman had sufficiently discredited him at his church, and his days there were numbered. She'd called him the day before and told him the whole story. The plan she'd hatched. The sweater. The whole thing had been ingenious. That's why he hired her. He expected she'd be able to get close enough to the man to destroy him.

He was even more pleased to learn that the members of the man's church had bought her story. She said the church elders were meeting tomorrow to discuss his termination.

The problem was that she hadn't discovered the source of the man's strength. At any time, Herodius expected a call from the guards, informing him that the Disorderly Pastor had escaped. Killed the guards. Fled into hiding.

He wasn't that worried about it. Even if he did escape, the man would never show his face at that church again. The messages to the squares would end, and things might get back to normal. He'd even promised the woman her payment. While technically, she hadn't delivered the source of his strength, she'd performed a great service to him and the Eliminati.

With one problem seemingly under control, another had arisen. Herodius called the meeting of SCOTE, the Secret Council of the Eliminati, to address it. He gave Incubus, the Prime Minister of Health, the floor to bring everyone up to date on the problem.

"The AXX-E only works on certain people," Incubus said. "Some children seem to have an immune tolerance to the shot. It has no effect on them whatsoever. They don't die when it's administered."

"To be more specific," Zagan said. "The AXX-E doesn't work on the Disorderlies. It works on everyone else."

"How is that possible?" Botis asked. "I thought the level of mercury was such in the AXX-E that it'd kill a mule."

"It is," Incubus said. "For whatever reason, it doesn't work on the Disorderlies. Their children anyway. We've rounded up several hundred and gave them the AXX-E. Nothing happened. No side effects whatsoever."

"The Disorderly Pastor, Gohn, from the fifth quadrangle said that would happen," Zagan said. "In his message Sunday, he said that the Disorderly children could take the AXX-E, and they wouldn't die."

Herodius thought about saying that the pastor was in jail, but everyone already knew that fact.

"But it does work on the rest of the population?" Botis asked.

"Yes," Incubus answered. "We have successfully eliminated more than two hundred children under seven. We've scrubbed several dozen more. We started with the children who are institutionalized and under government care. Or they were already in the hospital. We've not had time to round up the children from the general population."

"What about the Disorderly women who are pregnant?" Botis asked. "The Protocol calls for their babies to be scrubbed. If they already have children."

"To my knowledge, none have come in," Incubus answered. "Neither have our citizens. The only ones who have come in for scrubbing are those who wanted to terminate their pregnancies anyway. Our numbers have not increased over what we usually see in our clinics on any given day."

"We expected as much," Herodius said. "The protocol has only been in existence for a few days. These things take time to enforce."

"You called an emergency meeting," Botis said. "You obviously need the council's vote for something. What did you have in mind to combat this insurrection?"

Herodius waved his hand dismissively. "I wouldn't call it an insurrection as such. Just a minor setback. Incubus has a plan for the Disorderly children. Why don't you explain it?"

"According to a previous protocol, scrubbing is allowed up until the baby is born," Incubus said. "Even seconds before. At that point, Unfinished Scrubbing, as we call it, is allowed. In that procedure, the baby is delivered by its feet. The physician uses a pair of surgical scissors to make a puncture behind the baby's neck. That severs the spinal cord, so the baby doesn't feel pain. The brains are then sucked out which collapses the skull and allows the baby to be delivered in its scrubbed state. Dead."

"I think everyone already knows this, Incubus," Herodius said roughly. "Get on with what you propose for the Disorderly children who are already born. Those up to the age of seven who we can't kill with the AXX-E."

"I simply suggest we perform the same procedure. The Unfinished Scrubbing. On those children who survive AXX-E."

"So, you want to sever their spinal cords while they're still alive?" Zagan asked.

"Yes," Incubus responded.

"Will they feel any pain?" Botis asked.

"Does it matter to you?" Herodius said, somewhat angrily. He wasn't sure if Botis was raising an objection or asking because he really wanted to know. Either way, he was wasting the council's time.

Herodius was in a hurry to get the meeting over with. Right before it started, the soldier's wife, Lyla, had called him and confirmed that she could meet with him later that afternoon. To receive her payment. They planned to meet at a home in the fifth quadrangle. One of Botis's many houses. He hadn't asked why Herodius needed to use the house, and Herodius didn't offer an explanation. These men could never know about the clandestine meeting.

"I don't care," Botis answered. "I just wondered how you were going to get the little brats to sit still long enough to cut their spinal cords."

Herodius almost laughed out loud. A few did snicker. The meeting wouldn't last much longer.

"We'll put them to sleep," Incubus answered, "with a shot."

"You already said the shots didn't work on them," Botis argued.

Herodius would let it continue for a few more minutes, but he was going to cut it off soon.

"Then they'll suffer for about ten seconds," Incubus retorted. "Once their spinal cords are cut, they won't feel a thing. They might be awake for a while. Until the suction machine is attached. But that can't be helped."

"It's their own fault," Herodius said. "If they simply died when they were given the AXX-E, then they wouldn't have to go through the procedure."

Herodius paused for a moment and looked at his notes. He started to bring up another issue but thought better of it. Instead, he abruptly said, "All in favor of passing Protocol 664 and giving physicians authority to perform the procedure on children under seven who survive AXX-E, say *aye*."

The room filled with a disinterred chorus of ayes.

"All opposed?" Herodius asked.

No opposition.

***

Fifth Quadrangle

When Herodius left the meeting, he got in his private car and drove straight to Botis's home in the fifth quadrangle. One of the many homes he had in all the quadrangles. Botis was the richest man on Mercury. His family had owned all the silver mines for as long as those records were kept.

The soldier's wife was to be picked up at her house and brought there within the hour. Herodius arrived early to make the preparations. He used the private house, so she'd never know his identity or his real address. She wouldn't even know his real name.

When she arrived and stepped out of the vehicle, he was practically giddy with excitement. If a more beautiful woman existed on Mercury, he'd never met her.

He came out of the house and greeted her as soon as she got out of the car. He kissed her on both cheeks and welcomed her warmly. Her face couldn't contain the excitement she was clearly feeling as her eyes were wide and her mouth agape as they walked into the mansion. The house was a nice touch. Herodius was rich as well but not like Botis. Very few women in Mercury had ever seen such extravagance.

Lyla was provocatively dressed which told Herodius everything he needed to know. She was there expecting the same thing he was anticipating. A payment. Then her appreciation.

Herodius wouldn't waste time on small talk. He was surprised when she took control of the conversation.

"Shall we discuss business before pleasure?" Lyla asked.

They had barely entered the house and were still in the foyer.

"To me, they are one in the same," Herodius quipped. "I draw tremendous pleasure from business."

"I have good news for you," Lyla said.

His heart was already pounding in his chest. He couldn't imagine what news she might have to add to the excitement.

"I love good news," he said.

Then took her hand and led her into the living area. She let out an affirming moan that sent chills down his spine. Either from touching her hand or hearing her moan. Maybe both.

He turned toward her and prepared to give her a deep kiss.

"I know the source of the Pastor's strength," Lyla said.

He hadn't expected it to be that good. The thought of the kiss completely left his mind.

"What is it?" Herodius asked.

He wondered if he needed to write it down. Then thought better of it. He had a photographic memory. He'd have to go to the other room to get paper and pen. He didn't want to spend one second outside of her presence.

Lyla explained. "You take seven strands of rope. Seven inches long. Soak them in goat's milk. Then braid them into his hair. Tighten them with a pin. He'll be as weak as any other man."

Herodius practically laughed in her face. He was skeptical. That's the strangest thing he'd ever heard. He didn't see how that would give a man strength, so he said as much in his tone. "Are you sure that's the source?"

If she was offended, she didn't show it. One thing the woman didn't lack was confidence.

"I heard it from a very reliable source," Lyla said, batting her long eyelashes and flashing a seductive smile.

"Can you trust this person?"

For the moment, Herodius was more focused on the conversation than the woman's beauty. If what she said was true, she could alleviate a lot of his problems.

"Oh yes," Lyla said, smiling broadly. "She's a scorned lover. A woman from his church. The pastor made advances toward her. Then dumped her. She came to my house and told me everything. She wants him dead as much as I do."

"Excellent. Will you excuse me for a second?" Herodius said.

He was convinced. As much as he hated to leave the room, he needed to call the prison and inform the guards.

The guard who answered seemed skeptical as well, but submissive.

"With all due respect, sir," the guard said, after Herodius gave him the instructions. "What if the prisoner is uncooperative?"

"Put something in his food and drink to put him to sleep," Herodius answered.

"He doesn't eat the prison food. I hardly blame him."

"Then prepare him a decent meal. Put a sedative in his food. When he goes to sleep, braid his hair. Follow the instructions, perfectly. I don't want any screw ups."

"Of course, sir."

Herodius hung up the phone and walked back into the main living area. Lyla wasn't there. He went through several rooms until he found her in the bedroom. Lying on the bed. Shy most of her clothes.

"Where were we?" Herodius asked, as he began to unbutton his shirt.

"We were going to discuss business. My payment," Lyla said with a wide grin.

"Oh yes. Business and pleasure. As I said, two of my favorite things."

Herodius took three and seven pieces of silver out of his pants pocket and threw them on the bed.

Lyla squealed with delight.

She picked up the mercs and threw them in the air. They landed back on the bed. She gathered them up and sat them next to her clothes.

Then invited him to join her.

Herodius didn't remember a time when business was this pleasurable.

25

Revelation Church

Lyla didn't want to meet with the elders of the church to rehash her made up story about Pastor Gohn attacking her, but Herodius thought it'd be a good idea. And he was paying her well. Something he reminded her of several times during their tryst. If she had her preference, she would've left Cloyd already and moved to a different quadrangle, purchased a nice home, and started a new life with her abundance of riches.

She just had to get through tonight. Hopefully, she could keep the story straight and not slip up. Aria had been a big encouragement. Fed her the inside information on what gave Pastor Gohn supernatural strength. According to Herodius, the soldiers had already entered Gohn's prison cell while he was sleeping. Braided his hair with strands of rope soaked in goat's milk and secured the braids with a pin. So far, it was working. Gohn didn't appear to have any more strength than the average man.

"You've done a great service to all of Mercury," Herodius had said. "And you've given me great pleasure."

The money had given her great pleasure. Her tryst with Herodius; not so much. He wasn't that skillful a lover. She found most men with the ego of Herodius thought more of themselves than others did. He was only interested in his own pleasure. One thing she would miss about Cloyd. He was ruggedly handsome with strong powerful hands. He genuinely adored her. Worshipped the ground she walked on.

Every once in a while, she felt a twinge of guilt when she thought about how hurt he would be when she left him. Couldn't be helped.

That's why she wanted to get this night over with and put this part of her life behind her. Cloyd would be stunned but eventually would get over it. They'd all know she had lied and betrayed the Pastor, but he'd be dead and there was nothing anyone could do about it.

More than likely, Gohn was already dead. Herodius didn't want the word to get out until the leaders of the church had met. He didn't want Gohn to somehow be considered a martyr or become a sympathetic figure.

Lyla sat in a chair in the sanctuary. At the front. The elders of the church sat in the pews in front of her. A man named Will seemed to be the one in charge. Cloyd sat next to Lyla for moral support, clasping her left hand. Aria was on the second row. She smiled at Lyla which helped calm her nerves some.

"Thank you for being here," Will said. "I know this has been a difficult time for you."

Not really.

It had actually been kind of fun. The scheming. The tryst. The three and six mercs of silver coins. The whole thing had been mysterious and exciting. Much different than her humdrum, boring life as a house-wife. Lyla reminded herself not to let that sentiment show in her face.

She clutched a tissue in her right hand. Cloyd tightened his grip on her left hand. She wanted to pull it away. He was hurting her. Unintentionally, but his fingernails were digging into her hand.

Lyla dabbed at her eye with the tissue for effect.

"I'm sorry you had to go through this horrible ordeal," Will said. "We'll try to make this brief. I hope you understand it's necessary. We're meeting to consider terminating Pastor Gohn as the senior pastor of Revelation Church. As you can imagine, it's important for us to have all the facts. So we can make an informed decision."

"I'm happy to help," Lyla said softly. She'd practiced in front of a mirror to get the right look and strike the right tone.

More than happy.

Actually, everyone in the room would be dead soon. According to Herodius. They were a menace to society who had to be dealt with. Harshly. She was helping rid the world of an existential threat. Herodius had called them Disorderlies. The only one she hoped survived was Aria. She'd been brainwashed, but now saw the error of her ways. Perhaps Lyla could put in a good word with Herodius, and Aria's life could be spared.

"Please tell us in your own words what happened that morning," Will said to Lyla. Then he addressed the elders. "Members of the church council, feel free to ask questions as you think of them."

Lyla began. Slowly. Deliberately. Seemingly choosing her words carefully even though she had rehearsed them a hundred times. "I was home, doing some housework, when the phone rang. Pastor Gohn was on the other line. I figured he was calling for my husband."

Lyla looked over toward Cloyd but didn't want to make eye contact.

"Where was Cloyd?" Will asked.

"He was already at work."

Will nodded his head.

Lyla continued. "Pastor Gohn said he wanted to talk to me. Not Cloyd. I was shocked. I'd only met Pastor the night before, so I couldn't imagine why he'd be calling me."

"Did he say why?" one of the men asked.

"Yes. He said he'd like to meet with me. At the church. At ten o'clock. I said, 'Alone? Shouldn't my husband be there?'"

"Why didn't you wait for your husband?" Will asked.

"I wanted to, but Gohn insisted. He said he was concerned about Cloyd's safety and wanted to discuss it with me. Without Cloyd there."

"Pastor Gohn said that you called him," Will said. "That the meeting was your idea."

"Why would I call him? I didn't even know him. No. He definitely called me."

"Do you have your phone with you?" Aria's sister said. Lyla remembered her name was Marta. "The phones record each call. It will show who called who."

Lyla had anticipated that suggestion. Actually, Herodius had. He suggested she destroy that phone and get a new one.

"I'm sorry. I didn't bring it with me."

By the tone of the questions, Lyla realized that some on the council were skeptical. She needed to stick to her story. The whole exercise was moot anyway. Gohn was certainly dead by now. It didn't really matter if they did believe her.

For ten minutes she was largely uninterrupted. Things were going better when she wasn't interrupted with questions. The group seemed mesmerized by her every word. Perhaps she was winning them over.

Lyla was almost finished. She'd gotten to the part about the sweater.

Aria raised her hand to ask Lyla a question. Which surprised her. Aria had been silent up to that point.

"Why were you wearing a sweater?" Aria asked. Somewhat accusingly. Lyla didn't understand the sudden shift in tone. She didn't know exactly how to answer her.

"I don't know. It went with my outfit."

"It was hot outside," Aria said. "Why would you wear a sweater?"

What are you doing?

Lyla wanted to glare at Aria but tried to maintain her composure.

"I actually wasn't wearing it. I carried it."

"When you came running out of Pastor Gohn's bedroom, my sister said that you told her Pastor Gohn ripped it off of you. That's how it was torn."

"That's right! I was carrying it at first. Pastor Gohn's office was cold. So, I put it on. In there. It's hard for me to remember all the details."

What is she doing?

"Try to remember. These are important facts," Will said. "A man's livelihood and reputation are at stake."

"He attacked me! That's all you need to know. He's a monster."

"You said he threw you on the bed and got on top of you," Aria said. "How did you get him off of you?"

"I fought him off."

"How come the bed isn't mussed?" Aria asked. This time her tone was even more accusatory.

"What?" Lyla asked.

"We all went into Pastor Gohn's bedroom, right before we came here to meet with you," Aria said. "The bed is perfectly made. Pastor Gohn was arrested immediately after the attack. No one has been in his bedroom. How do you explain that?"

"How would I know? Maybe you made it. To cover up for him. You told me you were in love with him. Did you all know that?" Lyla said, pointing her finger at Aria. Then to everyone in the room.

Cloyd was no longer holding her left hand.

Anger was boiling up inside of her like a witch's cauldron.

"That's right," Lyla said, no longer able to contain the vitriol she had for everyone. "Sweet little Aria was having her own little fling with your Pastor. I'm not the first person he tried to get into bed with."

"Let's stick with your story," Will said. "Do you want to change any of it? Are you sure that Pastor Gohn threw you down on the bed?"

"Yes. He grabbed my arm. Ripped my sweater. Then threw me on the bed. He got on top of me, and I fought him off."

"I thought you said that he grabbed your arm as you were running out of the room," Marta said. "That's what you told me the night of the so-called attack."

"He did. That's what I meant."

Fear was pulsing through her veins and had replaced the anger. Lyla wanted to bolt out of there. She didn't have to put up with this. Gohn was dead. She had her money. What did she care what these people thought? It didn't matter whether they believed her or not.

"You and I met two days ago," Aria said. "At your home."

Cloyd looked at Lyla. She hadn't told Cloyd about her meeting with Aria. It seemed like he was beginning to doubt her story. His face and eyes were racked with confusion as his brow was furrowed and eyes narrowed.

"Of course, I remember," Lyla said. "That's when you told me about your own affair with Gohn. What's your point?"

"Do you remember what I told you?" Aria asked, ignoring the snide remark.

Aria had not actually told her about an affair. Just that she'd had feelings for Gohn and that he'd dumped her. Now she wondered if it had all been a lie to gain her trust.

"You told me the source of Pastor Gohn's strength," Lyla said.

It didn't seem necessary to lie anymore. She'd stick with the story that he attacked her. The rest seemed unimportant. The council would be mad at Aria for revealing Gohn's secret. Especially when they learned Gohn was dead.

"What did I tell you?" Aria insisted.

"I don't remember. Why would I care how the man gets his strength?"

"I told you that if you take seven strands of rope, soak them in goat's milk, braid them into Gohn's hair, and secure the braids with a pin, then he would have no more strength than the average man. Does that ring a bell to you?"

"Like I said, I don't remember."

A door opened.

In the back of the sanctuary.

Everyone turned their heads.

Lyla didn't have to. She was already facing that direction.

She couldn't believe what she was seeing.

Pastor Gohn stood in the doorway.

Braids in his hair.

Very much alive.

26

Gohn timed his entrance into the sanctuary for maximum dramatic effect. He could hear everything from the foyer of the church and waited until Lyla had backed herself into a corner she couldn't get out of. Then he opened the door and was elated by the look of utter disbelief on her face.

The scenario had played out perfectly. Aria fed Lyla the disinformation about the source of his strength. He didn't know if Lyla would fall for it or if she was even working for the Eliminati. When the soldiers came to braid his hair, his suspicions were confirmed, and he was certain he would be able to prove his innocence.

His entire ministry had rested on the plot. His future with Marta was on the line. He could hardly stand that he'd become the laughingstock of Mercury. Word had spread through the churches, and preachers were condemning Gohn as a false prophet. So much had been riding on the messages to the seven churches. If the Eliminati succeeded in destroying his reputation, he would never be able to tell everyone his visions from God and have them believe him.

While Gohn still had his strength and wasn't worrying about the Eliminati killing him, what good would his strength do him if everyone believed Lyla's lies? He could get out of prison, but then he'd be on the run. No church on Mercury would listen to a word he said or take him in. He'd be destitute. His own council of elders had set a meeting to decide his fate. According to Aria, the vote would be unanimous. Even Marta was against him.

When the soldiers hadn't come to braid his hair right away, Gohn was worried. He needed them to come before the meeting with the council of elders. They finally came the night before with the strands of sticky and stinky rope. Gohn pretended to be asleep. He didn't resist their efforts even though having his hair braided with the ropes was uncomfortable. They managed to accomplish the deed although Gohn had to fix it after the men were gone so the ropes would stay in place.

Then he had to wait for the right moment to escape. Too soon, and word would get out. Cloyd would hear about it, and he wouldn't be able to confront Lyla at the council meeting. Turned out the timing was near perfect. Shortly before the meeting was to commence, the soldiers came to take Gohn out to the square to execute him with the AXX-E. The power of God came over Gohn, and he slew the six soldiers with his bare hands.

He broke out of the prison and ran all the way to the church, getting there just as the meeting was scheduled to start. He waited patiently, hiding in the foyer, and threw open the doors right after Aria revealed she had told Lyla about the source of his strength. It'd been hard to listen to Lyla's lies without interrupting sooner, but he'd managed to exercise patience.

It turned out to be the best possible time to make his entrance.

The elders stared in amazement.

Gohn heard several of them gasp.

Marta's mouth flew open in amazement.

Aria hadn't told her the plan. Gohn wanted her to learn of it at the same time as everyone else. It almost broke his heart that Marta didn't believe in him. He had to prove his innocence to win back her trust. Almost as important to him as his ministry. She was the woman God had chosen for him to marry. Better for her to learn the truth from Lyla's own words and actions. Gohn was certain she'd be the one exposed as the liar.

For now, he had to focus on a greater threat. As Gohn expected, Cloyd bolted out of his chair and practically ran up the aisle toward him, ready for a fight. Gohn didn't retreat. Instead, he braced himself for whatever Cloyd would try in his fury. When he got close, Cloyd reared back and threw a right hand directed at Gohn's head. He caught Cloyd's fist in midair and squeezed it hard. Careful not to exert too much pressure. He could break Cloyd's hand if he wasn't careful. The power of God was flowing through him like a torrent of water.

Cloyd fell to his knees and cried out in pain. Gohn maintained his steel grip.

Lyla let out a scream.

"You still have your strength!" she cried out.

"Don't try to fight me," Gohn said to Cloyd. "It's no use. I don't want to hurt you. But I will if you force me to. Your wife has lied to you as well. You must know that by now."

Gohn let go of Cloyd's fist, and he clutched it and doubled over in pain. Gohn helped him to his feet.

Lyla was standing now. As was everyone. All looking his way, except Aria, who appeared to be staring straight ahead at Lyla.

She stared back at Aria. Her eyes were filled with hate. Blazed with fire like burning embers of coal. Lyla could no longer hide her hatred for all of them and the proceedings.

"You lied to me!" she shouted at Aria. "You told me the braids would zap him of his strength. All of you will pay for this. The council will kill every one of you!"

Lyla's own words condemned her.

The group of elders could see it for themselves. Gohn had barely spoken a word. Her vitriol and the vicious, evil words did more to prove Gohn's innocence than anything he could've said in his defense.

For a moment, it looked like Lyla was going to charge at Aria.

Gohn walked down the aisle toward the front to stand between them.

Lyla retreated and cowered back against the stage.

Gohn stopped when he got within ten feet of Lyla and blocked her exit. He didn't want her running out of the sanctuary. Not until he had a chance to confront her and get her to admit her lies. The council of elders were likely already persuaded, but Gohn wanted to be sure.

He stared into her eyes and suddenly felt compassion for her. He couldn't help but feel sorry for her. Realizing that the battle was against the spiritual forces that had entered her heart. The evil that deceived her as much as she tried to deceive others. While he felt bad for her, the righteous indignation was strong. He still had to defend himself and reveal her real intentions to everyone present.

"This woman is not the innocent victim she portrays herself to be," Gohn said in a softer tone than how he felt inside. "She is cunning. I told you she wasn't telling the truth. She's working for the Eliminati. My hair is proof."

"That's not true," Lyla said, still defiant with her words. "He's the liar. He's coming to kill me. Somebody stop him. Cloyd. Do something!"

"Gohn's right," Aria said. "Cloyd, your wife is a traitor. I went to the jail to see Gohn two days ago. We developed a plan. I went to see Lyla at your house. I told her that Gohn's strength was in his hair. If his hair was braided with seven strands of rope that had been soaked in goat's milk, then his strength would abate."

"The soldier's showed up at my prison cell last night," Gohn explained. "With the ropes. They braided my hair. In the same way Aria told Lyla they should. No one else knew about it but her. She's the one who told the Mercurian authorities."

"How do we know that you didn't braid them yourself?" Lyla said. "You're trying to fool us all."

Cloyd was standing behind Gohn. But he walked past him, so he was standing next to his wife.

"Pastor Gohn's telling the truth," Cloyd said. "I heard about the braiding. I didn't know where it came from. I knew about the soldiers coming to Gohn's cell to braid his hair. Aria's right. It had to come from you, Lyla."

Cloyd began to cry.

Gohn put his hand on his friend's shoulder.

"I'm so sorry, Gohn," Cloyd said. "This is my fault. I should've known."

"There's no way you could've known," Gohn answered. "I don't blame you."

The door to the offices opened. The door that led to the offices and the children's area. Pret walked through it. Her father had relegated her to watching the children during the meeting. Gohn heard the elders arguing about it before the meeting started. Will didn't think his daughter should be an elder or part of the meeting since she was so young. It had been Gohn's idea, Will argued. Not his. Others thought Pret should be allowed to stay.

Pret protested, but her father had insisted. Aria had said Pret supported Gohn and didn't believe Lyla and wanted her in the meeting.

"What's all the yelling about?" Pret asked.

"Everything's under control," Will said. "Go back and stay with the children."

A huge smile came on Pret's face when she saw Gohn. She walked over to him and hugged him from the side.

"What have you done to your hair?" Pret asked him. Then bounced the braids up and down with her hands. The pins made a clanging sound.

"Do you like the new look?" Gohn said jokingly.

"Not particularly," Pret said. "It makes you look like a young kid.

That's how the boys in my school wear their hair. Seriously. Why is your hair braided?"

"Because I told Lyla that Pastor Gohn's strength would leave him if his hair was braided," Aria said.

Pret laughed.

"His strength comes from his hair. But the weakness comes if it's cut. Not braided. That's the prophecy God gave me."

Lyla let out a squeal and then a huge smile formed on her face.

Pret suddenly put her hand over her mouth, obviously realizing her mistake.

Aria shrieked.

In a flash, Lyla began to run away. Brushed past Gohn. Before anyone could react, she was down the aisle, through the double doors, and out of the sanctuary.

Cloyd chased after her.

Will started to go after them as well.

"Let her go," Gohn said to him.

"She'll go to the Eliminati," Will said. "She knows the truth about your hair now."

"There's nothing we can do about it now," Gohn said.

27

Later that night

The church elders voted unanimously to keep Pastor Gohn as senior pastor of Revelation Church. Along with giving him a vote of confidence for the job he was doing.

Marta and Aria moved back into the apartment.

Things were looking up.

"If only I could get these dang braids out of my hair!" Gohn said, with exasperation.

"Hold still!" Marta commanded.

She and her sister, Aria, were trying to get the braids out, but they were stuck to his head and neither of them were sure how to do it without cutting them out. Gohn wasn't making it easier with his constant squirming and complaining. He couldn't help it. The braids hurt.

"Why couldn't I have come up with a simpler plan?" Gohn said. "Like... if anyone ties my wrists with seven fresh bowstrings that have not been dried. Then I'd lose my strength. I could've snapped those strings in two with no problem."

Marta jerked on one of the braids.

Gohn let out a yelp.

"All you had to do was say if anyone ties me securely with new ropes that have never been used," Aria said. "That would've worked, and new ropes wouldn't have been nearly as messy."

"Now you think of it, Aria," Gohn said sarcastically.

Marta tugged on one of the braids sending a sharp pain through his already tender scalp.

"Ow!" Gohn said. "What are you doing?

"Hold still. I'm trying to get these braids out of your hair. They're stuck."

"We're going to have to cut it," Aria said in exasperation. She wanted to help, but Marta wouldn't let her.

Everyone's tone got serious after Aria's remark sunk in.

"What will that mean for my strength?" Gohn asked.

"You can't cut his hair," Marta said. "The prophecy is that he'll lose his strength if his hair is cut."

"We don't have a choice," Aria answered. "He'll either have to live with these braids or we have to cut them out."

"I'm not walking around with these braids on my head!" Gohn said strongly. "That's for sure. Cut them out."

"Isn't that dangerous?" Marta asked. "What if the soldiers come back?"

"My strength comes from the Lord," Gohn answered. "God will protect me."

"Let me try to get them out," Aria said, pushing Marta slightly aside. This time she let her. Aria began pulling on one of the braids.

Gohn was almost in tears.

"It's no use," Aria finally said, letting out a deep sigh.

"I told you," Marta said. She walked into the kitchen and came back with a pair of cutting shears.

"Should you shave it instead of cutting it?" Gohn asked. "Wouldn't that be easier?"

"It would. But I was thinking that if we keep some of your hair, you'll still have some of your strength. Maybe not as much, but some. If we shave your head, you might lose all your strength. It'd take a few months for it to grow back."

"Good thinking, sis," Aria said.

Gohn agreed.

"Besides... I love your hair," Marta said, lovingly. Things were different between them. Marta was warming to him, and it felt good.

His head didn't. But his heart did.

Marta let out a moan as she cut the first strand of hair. Gohn had braced for the pain that never came. Cutting the rest went fairly quickly.

When Marta was finished, she stepped back to look at it.

Gohn could see both Aria and Marta fighting back grins. "What? Do I look hideous?" he asked.

When they both put their hands over their mouths to stifle their grins, Gohn said, "I'm going to look in a mirror. It can't be that bad."

He started to stand, but Marta pushed him back in the chair. Gohn couldn't help but notice that he didn't have the strength to resist.

"Let me trim it first," Marta said. "Maybe I can fix it."

"Maybe?" Gohn exclaimed.

"It's not that bad," Aria said, giggling.

"Why are you laughing then?" Gohn said roughly. The whole thing didn't seem funny anymore.

"Remind me to never braid my hair with rope dipped in goat's milk," Aria said. She tried to stifle a laugh but couldn't contain it. Instead, she let it out in a loud bellow.

Her comment reminded Gohn how bad it smelled in the room. The stench of the goat's milk was overwhelming. They had the door opened to try to air out the room. The gentle breeze of the night felt good but hadn't yet made a dent in the smell.

"Where did you even come up with something so silly?" Marta asked.

"I don't know," Gohn said. "It was the first thing that popped in my head. Stupid. In retrospect."

"I'm done," Marta said, seemingly proud of her work.

"How does it look?" Gohn asked.

"Different. It looks different," Marta said.

"That doesn't sound encouraging."

Gohn bolted up from the chair and went into the bathroom in his room. He looked in the mirror. He did look hideous. His eyes had deep bags under them from lack of sleep. He'd lost at least ten pounds from the days in the prison, and he could see it in his face. His once-long black, flowing hair looked like stumps in a forest where the trees had been cut.

He ran his hand through it. Marta hadn't been able to get all the stickiness out of his hair.

Gohn stripped off his clothes and got in the shower and scrubbed his head for a good ten minutes trying to get the remnants of the goat's milk out of his hair. Satisfied he'd done all he could, he got dressed in shorts and a shirt and went out to see what the girls were doing.

"Aria went to bed," Marta said. "She's exhausted."

"I'm going to crash soon as well," Gohn said.

Marta was sitting on the couch, and Gohn sat down next to her. She made no attempt to move. They were more comfortable with each other than at any time in their relationship. The tension was gone. So was the pretense. Gohn was pretty sure Marta was no longer holding back her feelings for him. The kiss, the incident with Lyla, the accusations—all of that seemed to be behind him.

Confirmed when Marta laid her head on his shoulder and clasped his arm with both of her hands. He lifted his right arm and put it around her, and she snuggled in closer. He rested his hand on her shoulder.

"This feels good," Gohn said. "I thought I'd lost you."

"Well, you didn't," Marta said.

"It means so much to me that you believe me."

"Can we not talk about it?" Marta said, suddenly sitting up.

They were now facing each other. Marta ran her hands through what was left of his hair.

"It doesn't look that bad," Marta said. "I love it. Everyone should change their look every now and then."

"I won't be going back to braids anytime soon. I don't know how you girls wear those things anyway."

"We don't dip them in goat's milk," Marta said laughing.

Gohn could feel the tension leaving the room. Another breeze kicked up and rushed through the opened door. It felt good. So did having Marta close to him.

"Should we close the door tonight?" Marta asked.

"I think we need to let the room air out," Gohn answered. "It still stinks."

"What if Lyla and the soldier's come back?" Marta asked nervously.

"Like you said, let's not talk about that now."

Before he even realized what he was doing, Gohn's lips were pressed against Marta's. She pulled back slightly, then pressed in. It wasn't like he imagined their first kiss would be like. He envisioned it being soft. Passionate. Short. This was deep. Powerful. Intense. Like a horse had been let out of the stable and was unleashed to newfound freedom.

Not entirely appropriate, Gohn realized. But he'd waited so long for this moment, he didn't want it to end.

Marta as well. She didn't stop.

Their embrace became tighter. Gohn felt his heart pounding in his ears. He couldn't hold her close enough. It seemed like time had stood still. Like it had lasted for minutes not seconds.

As quickly as it started, it ended.

Marta's face suddenly flushed.

Gohn took a series of deep breaths for the ones he'd lost in the moment.

The connection needed to go deeper. Emotionally. Not physically.

"I love you so much," Gohn said to Marta. "I've loved you for a long time. I need you to know that."

"I love you too," Marta said, staring into his eyes. "Almost since I met you. I was always afraid..."

Gohn put his finger on her lips to shush her.

"You don't have to be afraid anymore. Nothing's going to separate us. Not ever again. God brought us together. No man will ever be able to tear us apart."

Tears welled up in Marta's eyes. He felt his own become watery.

"We can't let it," she said.

Gohn wiped the tears off her cheeks with his hands. Gently.

This time the second kiss was like what he had expected the first one to be. Soft. Gentle. Tender. Short. Their lips were unfamiliar. His lips were shaking. Maybe hers as well. They were nervous. Like two young kids. Kissing for the first time.

"I'd better go to my room," Marta said, when she stopped after the kissing became more passionate again.

"I think that's a good idea," Gohn said. "Soon we'll be married, and we'll never have to be apart."

"Married! I don't remember you asking me to marry you."

"I just assumed," Gohn said.

"Don't assume anything. If you want to marry me, you need to get down on one knee and ask."

"I don't have a ring."

"Ask anyway," Marta said, with a grin on her face even though she was trying to sound stern in her tone.

Gohn got down on one knee next to the couch. He took her hand and looked deep into her eyes.

"Marta. Will you make me the happiest man on Mercury?"

He waited for an answer.

"Are you done?" she said with a sly grin. "I didn't hear a marriage proposal."

"That was a proposal. If you marry me, that'll make me the happiest man on Mercury."

"Then ask me!"

"You're making this very difficult."

She smiled broadly so he'd know she was kidding.

"Okay. How's this? Marta, will you cut my hair for me for the rest of our lives?"

Marta pulled her hand out of his and slapped him on the shoulder.

"Are you going to be this impossible when we're married?" she quipped.

"Does that mean your answer is yes? You will marry me?"

"Yes. Absolutely, yes."

Marta threw her arms around Gohn's neck.

"Even though you didn't exactly propose," Marta said. "Not in so many words."

"Will you marry me?" Gohn asked.

"Yes. Yes. Yes. Yes."

They kissed again. Longer than they should've, but not as long as either of them wanted.

When they finally said goodnight, Gohn went to his bedroom and fell into bed. Satisfied. He fell asleep almost as soon as his head hit the pillow. His last thought was Marta. And how good he felt.

He couldn't remember a time when he'd gone to sleep feeling this content.

* * *

Lyla answered her phone on the first ring. She already knew who was calling.

The man she'd had the tryst with. He never would tell her his real name.

He was fuming mad. "I want my silver coins back," he said roughly.

She had anticipated that reaction. Her response was already prepared. He didn't give her a chance to use it.

"You tricked me," he said, practically shouting. "I've got soldiers on the way to arrest you. I'm a powerful person. You'll regret lying to me."

"I can explain."

"What you told us to do to his hair didn't work. He killed six of my men. You're going to pay for this. I want my mercs back."

Lyla tried to interrupt him again, but he wouldn't give her the chance. When he finally did quit yelling at her, Lyla said, "I was duped. The pastor tricked me. But I know his secret now. The secret's in his hair. If it's shaved, Pastor Gohn will have no more strength than the average man."

"Why should I believe you?"

"One of the girls at the church blurted it out. By accident. I could tell from their reaction that she was telling the truth. Gohn's strength is definitely in his hair. Send your soldiers. I know where he lives. I know which bedroom he sleeps in. We'll sneak in while he's sleeping and cut his hair. Then you can do with him whatever you want."

"If you trick me again, I swear to you that you'll die a slow and painful death."

"I'm not tricking you. Send your soldiers. The man will be in your custody before the morning."

He told Lyla where to meet the soldiers. She went directly there. The man sent twelve of them. Lyla stopped at the store and got a razor. She didn't dare go home in case Cloyd was there. She also stayed mostly in the shadows in case he was out looking for her.

When Lyla and the soldiers got to the church, she led them around to the back of the building. Lyla was prepared to break in. To her surprise, the back door was wide open.

She motioned for all but two of the soldiers to stay outside and guard the entrance. She told the other two to follow her and keep quiet.

Lyla went in first. No sign of anyone.

She tiptoed over to the bedroom door. She opened it carefully.

Gohn was in the bed. Snoring softly.

The razor was in her right hand. She'd have to act quickly.

When she got next to him, she was surprised to find his hair was already gone.

That caused her to pause. She touched it to be sure.

Gohn stirred.

Then woke up.

The two soldiers jumped on top of him.

For some reason, he wasn't able to resist.

They easily dragged him out of the house and off to prison for the third time.

28

Marta woke up the next day practically euphoric. Giddy even. She couldn't believe the sudden turn of events. The roller coaster that had become her life. It had been a whirlwind few weeks. The night before, Gohn asked her to marry him. She said yes. When she came to bed, she woke Aria and told her. She seemed genuinely happy for Marta. Although, she was tired and went right back to sleep.

Marta only slept for a few hours. Too much excitement. Today would be the day she got married. On Mercury, a couple was married as soon as they consummated the union. The church didn't have any formal ceremony or exchange of vows. The act of becoming one flesh made a couple married in the eyes of God which was the most important thing.

Of course, both the man and woman had to consent to the union as a marriage and a lifelong commitment. Otherwise, the act was simply fornication. Or adultery if one of the parties was already married. Neither Gohn nor Marta had ever been intimate with another person, so their marriage would be as God intended it to be. Marta couldn't wait.

They'd talked about consummating the marriage the night before. It didn't seem right. They were both tired, and the events of the day had been draining. They'd both feel better the next day, and they wanted it to be special.

Marta quickly showered, dressed, and went to see if Gohn was awake. He wasn't in the living room, but his bedroom door was open.

The back door was still open, so Marta went and closed it. The smell in the room seemed better. Either that or she was getting used to it.

She stuck her head in Gohn's bedroom and knocked lightly.

Strange.

His bed was unmade. Gohn was a stickler about making his bed the first thing in the morning. Before he did anything else. She listened carefully for the shower running but didn't hear anything. Didn't hear any sounds at all.

He must've gone to the office already.

Then she noticed dirt on the floor in a few places. Footprints. She traced them to the back door. She opened it and saw numerous footprints on the ground outside the back entrance.

A bolt of panic shot through her like a speeding bullet.

Marta practically ran back to Gohn's bedroom. She called out his name. No answer. She decided to go into the room. He wasn't in his bathroom. She went back out to the main living area. There were no signs that he'd been in the kitchen. No dirty dishes. Empty glasses. No indication that Gohn had been in the kitchen since last night. Normally, he made a pot of coffee. The pot was untouched from yesterday.

Tears filled her eyes. She tried to calm the fears but couldn't shake the ominous feeling.

Marta walked quickly into the office area. Gohn wasn't there. No indication he had been there. She raced into the sanctuary. The lights were off. She called out his name. Maybe he was praying in the back.

No response.

Marta practically ran back to the living room. She went into her bedroom and shook Aria awake.

"I can't find Gohn," she said. "He's gone. I think the soldiers came and took him away during the night."

Aria rubbed her eyes and sat up in the bed.

"I'm sure he's okay. Did you check the office?"

"Yes! I looked everywhere. He's not here."

"He probably went out to get some breakfast or some coffee."

"I'm telling you, Gohn is gone! They came and got him. That's what I was afraid of. We cut his hair, and he lost his strength."

They searched the entire building again. Gohn was nowhere to be found.

Three months later, they still hadn't seen nor heard from him.

He wasn't in prison.

They assumed he was dead.

* * *

Isle of Desolation
Three months later

When Gohn was awakened by Lyla and the soldiers and dragged from his bed, he'd tried to resist but didn't know the Lord had left him. Not left him in the sense that God had forsaken him. As a believer, he had the Holy Spirit living inside of him always. But the spirit had come upon him with supernatural strength. More specifically, in his hair. After it was cut, his strength was no more than any man's.

As the soldiers were leading him away, he started to call out to Marta and Aria for help but thought better of it. He would lead them right into a trap. There was nothing they could've done to fight off the more than a dozen soldiers who'd come for him.

They didn't take Gohn to prison. The soldiers drove him to a private residence. A man came out of the extravagant home. Gohn recognized him. Herodius. The leader of the Eliminati was the man behind his capture.

When Gohn called out Herodius by name, the man erupted in fury. Hit him across the face. When Gohn derided him as an instrument of the devil, Herodius ordered the soldiers to gouge out Gohn's eyes. Then he had Gohn bound with shackles.

Gohn was led away and taken to a boat. Herodius exiled him to the Isle of Desolation. The only island on all of Mercury. Reserved for the worst prisoners. There Gohn was forced to grind grain from sunlight to sundown. Seven days a week. It had gone on for more than three months.

Eventually, Gohn's hair grew back, and his strength returned. He didn't have his sight, but he'd grown familiar with his surroundings.

When the soldiers came for him one morning, Gohn slew them with his bare hands. Things were like before. He had superior strength. The soldiers were no match against his powerful arms and legs. More soldiers came with their guns, but they jammed and were useless against him. After a fierce battle, he'd killed many more of them. The remaining soldiers fled. They got on the only boats on the island and left.

Mercury had only one body of water. A spring which had formed a lake which provided all of the water supply for the entire planet. In the middle of the lake was the island. Gohn was brought there because Herodius thought death was too good for him. He wanted Gohn to suffer for the rest of his life. Daily labor. Blind. The soldiers could treat him as inhumanely as they wanted to as long as they kept him alive to suffer.

Before they fled, the soldiers killed the rest of the prisoners, and Gohn was left on the island alone. So far, none of the soldiers had returned. The visions and dreams came back though. Gohn could no longer deliver his messages to the seven quadrangles, so he wrote them letters. One to each church. Giving them the words God had for them.

The church of the fourth quadrangle was where he had left off on his messages to the squares, so he wrote the church a longer letter.

221

God wasn't pleased that they tolerated Jezel. The evil adulterous. Now they tolerated Lyla. He saw in a vision that they still believed her story. They were led astray by her words. She was living in the quadrangle among them.

Many false prophets had risen up within the church of the fourth quadrangle. Immorality existed there such as didn't even exist among the heathen. The pastor had taken his father's wife. A wealthy man in the church had taken Lyla as his wife even though she was still married to Cloyd.

Gohn wrote in his letter:

Though absent in body but present in the spirit, I have already judged them who have committed such a grievous sin against the Lord. I have decided to deliver such men to Satan for the destruction of their flesh so that their spirits will be saved in the day of the Lord, Jesus.

When he was finished with the letter, he wrote one to the church of the fifth quadrangle. The area where his church was located. Gohn wrote about the second coming of the Lord to his church. The words were loving and kind. He missed them. But he gave them an admonition. Jesus would come like a thief in the night. No man knew the hour that he would come.

Be alert. Wake up. Your deeds are not complete.

See what large letters I write to you in my own hand.

He wanted them to know he was having trouble with his sight.

To the church of the sixth quadrangle.

When you come together, I see that divisions exist among you.

Gohn laughed when he wrote that line. *I see.*

He could not see. Not with physical eyes. But when the visions came, Gohn could see them clearly. On the wall of his makeshift bedroom that used to belong to one of the guards. The walls became alive with an array of colors. He could see people. Hear voices. Like he was right there with them.

When the visions ended, the darkness returned. He wished the visions never ended. Those moments were the most pleasurable. Although, Gohn had learned to be content. He wrote as much to the church of the seventh quadrangle.

> *I am weak when present but bold toward you when absent. I do not boast in my strength. I boast in my weakness. I must decrease, and he must increase. For I can do all things through Christ who strengthens me.*
>
> *I have been rich. I have been poor. I've suffered much for the gospel. I've been beaten. Chained. My eyes were gouged out. I've gone days without food or water. I've toiled from sun-up to sundown with a guard's whip on my back. I've been separated from the touch of the one I love. I've learned to be content in all things.*

Gohn spent most of his days writing letters. God kept giving him one vision after another. He couldn't read them, so he had to hope he'd recorded things accurately. He had no idea what the letters looked like. If they could even read his writing. He could only trust the Lord that the words made sense.

Not that he knew they'd ever even be read by anyone. He could only hope that someday, someone would discover him on the abandoned island. He'd be dead or alive. If alive, then he could relate his visions and dreams. If dead, these words would have meaning for future generations. If they didn't get into the wrong hands and were destroyed.

He furiously wrote everything God showed him. Teaching the churches everything he could about the ways of God.

Then the visions turned violent. Dark. Ominous.

He saw battles. Horsemen. The end of Mercury. Seven seals.

One particular vision frightened him to his core. A plague.

A prophecy.

Two thirds of the people would die. Only one third would remain.

Gohn saw the Eliminati sitting in the conference room. Scheming. Writing the next protocol.

666.

The conversation was chilling.

"We need to eliminate two thirds of the population," Herodius said.

Gohn could see it all in vivid color even though he was blind.

"AXX-E 666 is ready," Incubus said. He was the Minister of Health. If you could call someone who wanted to kill two thirds of the population a minister or someone concerned about health.

"How will we make it mandatory?" Botis asked. "You know the Disorderlies will refuse to take it."

"I'm not so sure," Zagan retorted. He was in charge of the religious institutions. "Now that the Disorderly Pastor Gohn is out of the picture, they are like sheep without a shepherd. They have no organized leadership."

"The simple solution is that you can't buy or sell without proof of AXX-E-ination," Botis said.

He was the richest man on Mercury. He also stood to lose the most by the elimination of two thirds of the population. He made his money by owning all the silver mines. From that, his empire had expanded to a number of other products his companies distributed. His businesses would take a hit from the decreased demand. He'd make up for it by charging more to those they let live. The riches from the dead were to be distributed among the living. They'd written that in Protocol 665. Botis would get a large portion of it for his sacrifice.

The AXX-E would be given to everyone. One-third of the people chosen by the Eliminati would be given an injection of saline solution.

"How will we enforce the AXX-E mandate?" Herodius asked.

"The AXX-E injection leaves a mark on the shoulder," Incubus said. "No one can buy or sell without that mark."

The devil's mark.

Gohn knew all about it. He'd seen it in his visions. He'd documented it in his writings. People would not be able to buy a loaf of bread without the mark. They really were living in the end times. The prophecies were coming to pass.

"Let's vote," Herodius said.

The council of the Eliminati voted unanimously to adopt Mercury Protocol 666.

"How long will it take to distribute the AXX-E?" he asked.

"Days," Incubus said. "No more than a few weeks."

"Timing is important," Herodius said. "We have to make enough AXX-E to cover the entire population at once. The deadly mercury has to be time-released. When people start dying, the masses will be reluctant to get the AXX-E. We have to make sure everyone gets it at the same time."

"If it's mandatory, that shouldn't be a problem," Incubus said. "We'll tell everyone that a deadly plague is spreading through our population. We'll post pictures. They'll be believable. We'll put the fear of God in people. They'll rush to get the AXX-E."

"Excellent!" Herodius said. "Let's put the plan in motion."

The vision ended, and Gohn was in total darkness again.

I've got to figure out how to get off this island!

29

Several weeks later

Gohn almost felt like God was teasing him with the dreams and visions. Every night he was awakened from a deep sleep by vivid prophecies of events that were to take place on Mercury. Many of the visions had specific instructions for him. Which was why he felt like he was being mocked. What was he supposed to do about them?

He was stuck on the island. Miles from land. Gohn was blind. He had no way to get back to the mainland to warn the people about the Eliminati and the events that were to come. In his vision, two thirds of the population were going to die by taking the AXX-E. It might already be too late. If Mercury Protocol 666 was released, then the AXX-E-nations were well under way. People would be dying soon if they weren't already.

Gohn tried everything he could think of to get off the island. He constructed a raft. With his strength, he was able to fell trees with his bare hands. From tools left behind by the soldiers, Gohn was able to shape the logs into a makeshift raft. The problem was that he didn't have sufficient rope to bind them together. Every time he launched the raft into the water, it broke apart.

Probably just as well. Without the ability to see where he was going, how would he navigate anyway? He could end up going around in circles. Or worse. End up somewhere without the food, water, and resources he had at his disposal now.

He considered swimming the distance. Would his strength hold? He estimated the distance to be about three miles. That's if he swam in a straight line. Without his sight, how could he possibly know if he was going in the right direction? Once in the water, he could swim around for hours and never reach land.

The instructions were clear, though. God told Gohn to go home and warn the people. He was supposed to round up eighty-four hundred believers who were still alive and bring them back to the island. He assumed that was how many Christians were left on Mercury. In the vision, those who remained had not taken the AXX-E and didn't have the mark of the beast on their arm. According to Protocol 666, no one could buy or sell without the mark. Gohn wasn't sure how the Christians would survive unless God performed a miracle for them.

Fourteen hundred from each quadrangle. That was the number.

Except the first quadrangle.

Surprisingly missing from the instructions.

They would be left behind. If any believers were still alive there. He assumed there were none.

Gohn didn't know why they were excluded other than he knew that the first quadrangle was where the evil one dwelled. Also where the Eliminati was headquartered. Perhaps the first church had embraced the AXX-E and had given in to it. Conceivably, there might not be fourteen hundred believers left in the first quadrangle who hadn't taken the mark of the beast on their arms. Might not be any.

God called the 8400 a remnant. *The elect* was another term God used to describe them in the vision. They were the ones who would be saved from the coming wrath and destruction. Were Marta and Aria included in the fourteen hundred from the fifth quadrangle? Were they still alive? What about Will and Pret? The other elders?

Did Cloyd repent and see the evil inside Lyla? Or did he still want to kill Gohn? It gave him hope believing that Marta and Aria had somehow managed to survive. That's what would motivate him to get off the island.

But how?

So many unanswered questions haunted Gohn at night. Sometimes he cried himself to sleep thinking about it. The visions and dreams were the only respite from the constant frustration. He'd be awakened and feel energized. Hope would spring eternal. Then dawn would come, and he'd spend one more day on the island. Frustrated. Knowing what he needed to do but unable to do it.

Work kept his mind off his plight. Gohn familiarized himself with the entire island. He found weapons the soldiers had left behind. Even learned how to use them. Although he wasn't sure what good the guns would do him if he couldn't see who or what he was shooting at.

He stored food. Hunted wild animals on the north side of the island. Caught fish from the stream that lived in the spring that fed the lake.

Under any other circumstances, his life would be bearable. Pleasant almost. Certainly compared to the horror the Christians in the quadrangles were experiencing. Gohn lived in a tropical paradise which almost made him feel guilty. The cool breeze off the water was refreshing and made his work easier. The discontent came from not knowing what was happening on the other side of Mercury. He could imagine the pain and suffering. He desperately wanted to do something.

His discontent eventually turned to anger. Toward God. He wanted to curse the visions and dreams. As days turned to weeks, his anger came to a boiling point. The weeks turned into another month, and rage burned inside of him.

He finally laid down under a tree and told God he just wanted to die.

Suddenly that night, a vision strengthened his resolve and gave him new hope.

He was awakened at 3:00 a.m. The fourth watch. He saw a sign from heaven. And a rainbow. The colors were spectacular. A sea of glass mixed with fire. Those who had come off victorious against the beast and from the mark of the AXX-E were together worshipping the Lord. Gohn assumed it was the eighty-four hundred. Those who had not taken the AXX-E and were still alive.

He saw them come out of their hiding. Led by Gohn. They sang a song.

"Great and marvelous are thy works. O Lord God. The Almighty. Righteous and true are thy ways, thou King. For your righteousness has been revealed to all the nations."

The vision turned dark as terror was unleashed on Mercury.

Gohn saw the destruction of every person except the remnant. He wept as he stood over the first quadrangle and watched as fire rained down on the entire city where those who were left behind had gathered.

"They deserve it," the angel said to Gohn. "They have shed the blood of the righteous. God's judgments are against those who blaspheme the name of God and who did not repent of their deeds."

The Lamb of God appeared.

"I am coming like a thief," the one in the white robe said.

Lightning flashed and peals of thunder tore through the air. A great earthquake shook Mercury. The great city of the first quadrangle was split into three parts. Hailstones rained down from heaven. The inhabitants were seared with fire.

Gohn warned the remnant not to look back. They kept walking to safety. Somehow on dry land where the lake once was.

Then the Lamb of God said, "Blessed is Gohn who stays awake and has not soiled his garments. He is not ashamed. Rise up and kill your donkey. The beast of burden."

Gohn could not believe what he'd just heard. The donkey was the only companion he had on the island. He'd been a godsend. The beast helped him with his work. He used it to plow fields to grow grain. To move heavy objects.

Mostly the creature made him feel like he wasn't alone. Almost like he had a companion.

Now God told him to take a knife, plunge it into the donkey's heart, and end its life.

For days, Gohn resisted.

He had the same vision every night.

Finally, he did it.

Gohn wept bitterly.

The Holy Spirit gave Gohn instructions. "Cut out the jawbone," the still small voice said.

Gohn did as he was instructed.

"Then take it down to the lake and wash it."

At the water, Gohn knelt down and washed it carefully. Tears still rushed down his cheeks, but he ignored them. When he was done, an angel of the Lord said, "Look up Gohn, for your deliverance is at hand."

That's when Gohn heard them. It sounded like dozens of boats. Hundreds of men were shouting at him. Soldiers were rapidly coming toward the island. Hurling insults at Gohn. He couldn't see them but could imagine the throng.

"Do not be afraid," the angel said.

Gohn didn't run. Where could he go? The island was small enough that they could track him down in a matter of minutes.

At this point, Gohn preferred to die rather than spend another day on the island, alone. So, he stood with his chest out. His head up. If he died, he'd die defiant. Standing against the Eliminati until the very end. In one of his dreams, he'd seen the martyr's rewards in heaven. If the Lord didn't deliver him, then he'd get such a reward if he stood and fought. Maybe not, if he turned and ran like a coward.

They neared the island. Their guns must've jammed, because they were close enough to shoot Gohn but hadn't. Gohn took several steps back to give them room to depart their boats. They quickly disembarked and had him surrounded.

The hoard of soldiers were silenced. Presumably by a leader who approached Gohn. Gohn could feel his presence less than ten feet away.

"Prepare to die," the man said. "On this day, we will give your flesh to the birds."

"How many are you?" Gohn asked.

"One thousand," the leader said confidently.

Gohn laughed.

"I am but one man," Gohn exclaimed. "I'm blind. Does it take a thousand soldiers to kill one man? Is that how weak you are?"

Gohn's hands were hot.

Almost on fire.

He could feel the strength in his arms and legs.

His tongue was also on fire. The words were not his own. The Lord was giving him what to speak as he faced his enemies.

Gohn didn't realize until that moment that he still held in his hands the jawbone of the donkey.

"Make him entertain us," the leader said to the other soldiers.

The men picked up stones and threw them at Gohn. They were toying with him. One would come up from behind and hit him. Not hard enough to hurt him, but in a mocking way. They intended to make his death slow and painful.

The Lord was with Gohn.

The stones bounced off of him. He barely felt the blows. The soldiers were like gnats landing on his arms. He sensed that he could swat them away any time he wanted.

"It is God who has delivered you into my hands," Gohn cried out in a loud voice.

That infuriated the leader who began to curse Gohn and curse God.

Gohn gripped the jawbone.

He remembered how sharp the teeth of the donkey were. He'd been cut by them before when his hands ended up in the wrong place.

Gohn said a quick thank you to the donkey. He had cared for the beast and kept him strong. Even given him some of his food. Not knowing it'd come to this purpose.

Gohn planted both feet in the sand on the beach and prepared for an assault. Because of the confined space, the soldiers couldn't attack at once. They had to rush him in groups. Gohn sensed their movements.

The sharp teeth of the donkey sliced through the flesh like a knife through butter. As one after another of the soldiers fell, some began to run toward the boats to get away. Gohn chased them and killed them. He pictured the blood mixing with water. The carnage of dead bodies littered the shoreline.

When the last one was dead, Gohn collapsed to his knees to thank God. He let the jawbone fall from his hands. His palm was sore from gripping the jawbone so tightly.

He had not one scratch on him.

"With a donkey's jawbone, I've made donkeys of them," Gohn said, laughing, unable to contain his joy. "With a donkey's jawbone, I've killed a thousand men."

Not with his own might, he realized. But by the power of God.

He took the jawbone and made a memorial on the beach.

"I'll call this place Shu-Ah Rath," Gohn said. Which meant *God has delivered me with a jaw.*

Gohn waded into the water and began to wash off the blood of the soldiers which soaked his body and clothes.

When he did, he bumped into one of the boats that was rocking back and forth in the waves.

Then realized.

He had a way off the island.

30

The Church Apartment
Fifth Quadrangle

"That's the last of it," Marta said to Aria. She poured porridge out of the jar and into their bowls. Then shook out the last remnants to make sure none was wasted. The jar was definitely empty. They had no more food in the apartment and no way to get any.

When Mercury Protocol 666 was first announced and before measures were in place, Marta and Aria went to the store and stocked up. That's the last time they were allowed in a store to buy food and supplies. The Protocol stated that only AXX-E-nated people could buy and sell. If you didn't have the mark on your arm, you basically had no way to purchase anything on Mercury.

Turned out, those who took the AXX-E died anyway. It took several weeks, but eventually the mercury in the AXX-E poisoned their systems, and they went into convulsions and died a painful death. Most of them anyway. For some reason, the rich and very elite were not affected by the shots. Nor were the soldiers who were out in force harassing everyone who didn't comply with the protocols. The assumption was that the Eliminati had decided who got the shots with the deadly toxin and who was allowed to live.

Some argued that dying from the AXX-E was better than starving to death which appeared to be Marta and Aria's fate. The two women refused to believe they were going to die. In fact, against the advice of most, including the elders of the church, they didn't ration their food. They insisted that God would provide whatever they needed when they ran out. So, they continued to eat and drink as they normally would, and their food supply lasted for more than three months.

Now it had run out.

They were not short on hope though.

Somehow, miraculously, they believed God would provide. Marta actually didn't care either way. Gohn was gone and presumed dead. All that was left of the believers in the fifth quadrangle were a little over a thousand people. Maybe twelve to fifteen hundred. Those were the estimated number of believers who were unAXX-E-nated. A small group of them met once a week at church. They didn't dare hold large gatherings. None of them, including Marta, had the faith of Gohn nor the strength he had in his hair to defy the authorities.

Cutting Gohn's hair was something Marta regretted every single day. She was convinced that's why he was taken. With his strength gone, Gohn had no power to fight the soldiers who had, no doubt, come in the middle of the night and took him away. Cloyd hadn't been able to find out any information on Gohn's fate, and although they hoped for the best, they assumed the worst.

Marta went back and forth between hoping he was alive and knowing he'd be better off if he were in heaven with Jesus. Selfishly, she preferred believing he was alive, and that someday, he'd return home to her.

Foolish, she knew. Cloyd had argued that Gohn was better off dead. As a soldier, he knew firsthand what the authorities could do to prolong Gohn's suffering.

Cloyd was dead.

Shortly after the protocol was announced, he was forced to take the AXX-E, and died from it. Most soldiers didn't die even though everyone took it. They assumed Cloyd was given a lethal dose because of his affiliation with Gohn. The other soldiers were essential to the Eliminati to maintain control, and they were given a shot without the lethal toxin.

As far as they knew, Cloyd's wife, Lyla, was alive and living in the fourth quadrangle with a rich elite executive of a silver company. She'd been given the AXX-E but had lived. Somehow managing to worm her way into the inner circle of aristocracy. Probably because she single-handedly brought down the notorious pastor of Revelation Church. The anger still ran deep as Marta struggled to forgive her.

Aria took a big bite of the food and let out a loud slurp, bringing Marta back to reality. Neither of them had said anything for a good five minutes, and in those quiet moments, Marta's thoughts were often unbridled, like a horse let out of its corral.

"Obviously, we did the right thing by not taking the AXX-E," Aria said after she'd finished the last of her porridge. "I have no regrets."

"When you're not afraid of dying, death loses its sting," Marta said, as she also took her last bite. The warmth soothed her stomach and calmed any nerves she might've been feeling. She looked at her sister admirably. She'd watched her grow up over the last couple of months. The girls had become close through the trials, and Marta thanked God everyday she had Aria to go through it with her.

Marta stood from the table and went to the sink where she washed out the jar that had held the porridge. When she was done, she sat the empty container on the kitchen counter to dry. Aria brought the rest of the dishes over to the sink and helped Marta clean them up.

"I'm tired," Aria said with a yawn.

Darkness had already descended on Mercury, and they were ready for bed. After a short, meaningless conversation, they turned out the lights and fell asleep, their stomachs full even if their hearts weren't.

The next morning, Marta was up well before Aria and began her normal routine. The same one she'd had since Gohn disappeared. This morning would be different in one respect; they were out of coffee. They'd used the last of it the day before.

Normally, Marta brewed a pot and sat two cups on the table. One for her and one for Gohn. Then she sat at the kitchen table thinking about him and praying while staring at his empty seat. Nursing her own cup while looking at his until it eventually cooled. A slight gesture of faith in the waning belief that someday Gohn would show up at the door. If he did, she wanted him to know that she had thought about him every day and hadn't given up all hope.

Since Marta didn't have any more coffee to prepare, she boiled a pot of water on the stove so she could feel normal, then sat down at the kitchen table. After the "coffee," she'd go to the office. While there wasn't much to do at the church, she gave herself busywork to do. It kept her mind off everything else. While it reminded her of Gohn, she felt like she had a purpose for staying alive. Like the ministry was still viable.

The growling in Marta's stomach reminded her that they were out of food. She looked over at the empty jar of porridge and made a mental note to put away the dishes that had dried overnight.

Before she could stand up and do just that, Marta noticed something.

A smell.

A pleasant aroma really. Coming from the stove.

It smelled like coffee. The pot had steam coming from it.

Marta dismissed the thought. She'd either imagined it or it was leftover residue in the pot.

That wasn't possible.

Marta cleaned the pot every night. Meticulously.

When the aroma got stronger, her curiosity got the best of her, and she opened the top and looked inside. To her shock, the pot was filled with strong, black coffee. Marta took the pot off the stove and stared at it for nearly a minute. Not quite sure what to make of it.

Without question, the pot was full of coffee. She carried it over to the table and poured the liquid into her cup. Then put the pot back on the stove. She went back to her seat, sat down, picked up the cup, and put it up to her nose to smell it. Then she let out a moan. It might've been the best coffee she'd ever smelled.

Marta took a sip.

"My goodness!" she said aloud.

The texture and taste of the coffee were beyond description. She'd never tasted anything that good before.

What's going on?

Marta saw a whiff of steam coming out of the jar sitting on the counter that had held the porridge from the night before.

What?

Marta stood and walked over to the counter and stared at the jar. Trying to figure out why it had steam coming out of the top of it. She touched the side. It burned her finger slightly. Marta picked the jar up by the handle. It seemed full. Her arm strained to lift it.

Not sure what to do, she sat it back down. The indecision caused her to fumble with the handle, and what appeared to be porridge splashed out of the top and onto the counter. How could this be? She dipped her finger in the puddle and tasted it.

It was porridge!

Better than anything she'd ever made before. She took a bowl out of the cabinet and poured herself some of the piping-hot liquid. Marta got a spoon out of the drawer and took a bite while still standing at the counter. She sipped it slowly at first, then devoured the entire bowl.

What's happening?

Did someone from the church sneak in overnight to fill the porridge and coffee? Will maybe? If so, why was the porridge still hot?

Marta went to the back door and looked out to see if maybe Will had snuck in when she wasn't looking. Something was on the doorstep!

Marta opened the door and bent down to pick it up. Pieces of bread lay at the entrance. She gathered them up and took them inside. It appeared to be about a day's supply of bread for four people.

Someone must've left the bread there for them. Probably Will. She had told them they were about out of food. Will said his family was already out of food and supplies. So where did he get the bread, porridge, and coffee? Why did he give them to her when his family needed it?

Marta brought the bread inside and sat it on the table. She tore off a piece then put it to her nose and smelled it. It seemed perfectly edible. She took a bite. A nibble at first. The bread was delightful, and she let out another moan. She walked over to the table and dipped a piece of bread in the coffee and ate it, savoring the contrast in flavors.

Her whole body felt warm after she scarfed down the rest of the portion of bread.

I have to tell Aria!

Marta rushed into the bedroom and shook her sister out of a deep slumber.

Aria was groggy, but her eyes widened in surprise as she clearly thought something bad must've happened.

"You won't believe it," Marta said. She was out of breath.

"What's wrong?" Aria asked. "You're scaring me."

"Nothing's wrong."

"Why are you waking me up? What time is it?"

Aria sat up.

"Did I oversleep?"

Not that they could. They had nowhere to be and nothing that required their attention. Most of the days were the same. Boring tedium.

"No, honey," Marta said. "I have news. God has provided food for us. And coffee."

"Slow down, Marta. You're not making sense."

"Come on, I'll show you."

Marta grabbed Aria's hand and practically dragged her into the kitchen. Then stood there without saying anything to let Aria figure out what was going on.

"What's that smell?" Aria asked.

"I know! Can you believe it? It's coffee! Go sit at the table. I'll pour you a cup."

"What's this?" Aria asked, as she sat down at the table. The bread was spread out in front of her.

"It's bread. I found it on our doorstep this morning. Try some. It's delicious."

Aria tore off a piece, sniffed it, and then put it in her mouth, following the same routine as her sister.

"Mm. That's good," Aria said.

"I told you."

Aria scarfed down the rest.

"Is that porridge?" she asked, looking at Marta's bowl still on the table with the remnants of the brew from the jar still in the bottom of the bowl.

"It is. This morning the jar was full."

"No way! How's that possible? I thought we were out of food."

"We are. I don't know how it's possible."

"Did Will do this?"

"That's what I was thinking. Somehow, he found food and brought us some."

As if on cue, Will appeared at the back door. Marta motioned for him to come in. He took one look at the bread on the table and said, "You got some too!"

"It was on our doorstep this morning," Marta said. "We thought maybe you put it there."

"I didn't do it. We had some on our doorstep as well. Enough for the entire family. We also had tea in the teapot this morning."

"We had coffee!" Marta said excitedly.

"This has to be from God," Will said.

"We're going to go and get dressed," Marta said, as she realized that Aria and she were still in their night clothes.

"Don't go anywhere," Marta said. "We'll only be fifteen minutes.

Marta and Aria left the room to change clothes.

Ten minutes later they were dressed.

When they came back into the living room, Will and Gohn were sitting at the kitchen table, eating bread, and drinking coffee.

31

When Marta saw Gohn sitting in his chair at the kitchen table, she let out a scream. Then bolted across the room and threw her arms around his neck. Her heart was suddenly pounding in her chest to the point she could hear it in her ears.

"I can't believe you're alive," she said, kissing him profusely on his head, cheeks, and neck. "I missed you so much. How did you get here? Are you hurt?"

Gohn couldn't get a word in edgewise as the questions were coming rapid-fire.

"I missed you too," Gohn said.

Then Marta looked into his eyes, and dread came over her. He was staring off at a distance, past her, not able to focus on any one object or even look into her eyes even though Marta was only inches away from his face.

"Oh honey," she said as tears welled up in her eyes, and she was suddenly overcome with an intense sadness. She could see the scars on his face around his eyes and noticed that the pupils and whites of his eyes were totally destroyed. Like someone had poked them with a stick.

"What happened... to your eyes?" Marta's voice cracked as she asked it.

"When the soldiers took me away, the leader of the Eliminati ordered the soldiers to gouge out my eyes. I'm blind now. I'm sorry."

Marta gasped.

Why was he apologizing to her? This was her fault. She was the one who cut his hair.

"That must've been so painful, having your eyes gouged out. I can't even imagine. At least you're alive. Where have you been? Where did they take you? Did they torture you? We thought you were dead!"

Marta didn't even stop to catch a breath between questions.

"Ask him one question at a time," Aria said to her sister. She walked over to the other side of Gohn and kissed him on the cheek.

"Aria, my dear," Gohn said, looking up at her but clearly unable to see her. "I missed you. I missed all of you."

"I see your hair grew back," Aria said. She flipped the back of his hair with her hand. "It's so long."

"It did."

Marta didn't feel the least bit jealous of Aria. She was past all of that. At that moment, all she could think about was that Gohn was alive.

"My strength was in my hair," Gohn said. "Just like Pret said. When we cut my hair, the Lord was no longer with me. Or at least, no longer in my hair. He's always with us. My strength was gone. When the soldiers came later that night, I couldn't fight them off."

"It's my fault," Marta said. "I should've never cut your hair."

"You didn't know the soldiers were going to come back that soon," Gohn retorted. "Lyla was the one who led them here."

"She betrayed you and Cloyd," Will said.

"What happened to Cloyd?" Gohn asked.

"He's dead," Will replied. "He took the AXX-E. The Eliminati required it of all the people. They put poison in it. I don't know how many people are dead, but there are a lot."

"Two thirds of the population," Gohn said. "God showed it to me in a vision. Mercury Protocol 666. I came back to warn the people not to take the AXX-E, but I'm too late. I was afraid of that. I just... couldn't get off the..."

This time Gohn's voice was the one that cracked as he spoke. He'd obviously been through a devastating trauma.

"We refused to take it," Marta said, defiantly. "That's why we're still alive. The AXX-E makes a mark on your arm. No one is allowed to buy or sell without that mark. We refused to get it and decided to trust God."

"You did the right thing," Gohn said. "Otherwise, you'd be dead too."

"How did you escape the soldiers?" Will asked. "Where did they take you?"

"I've spent the last three months on the Island of Desolation."

Marta had heard of it but had never seen it. She knew only the worst of the worst criminals went there. It infuriated her that they considered Gohn a criminal. Then she realized it was a good thing that they took him there. That's why they kept him alive. Probably never believing he could get off the island.

"How did you get off?" Will asked.

Marta was about to ask the same thing.

Gohn's brow furrowed as he got a serious look on his face. "When my hair grew back, my strength returned. If the guards had been smart, they would've cut my hair again. When they had the chance. They hadn't been told, I guess. Or if they had, they forgot. Anyway... once my strength returned, I killed all the soldiers guarding me."

"All of them? Even though you were blind?" Marta exclaimed. "How did you know where they were?"

"I could sense them," Gohn said. "I could feel their movements. If they got near me, then I had the strength to fight them off."

"That must've been frightening," Aria said.

"I wasn't afraid. Not even when I didn't have my strength. I was surprised when they let me live. Anyway, for the last few months I've been on the island alone."

"How did you get off? Did you swim back?" Will asked for the second time.

Gohn shook his head from side to side. "No. The soldiers came back to kill me. A thousand of them came to the island on boats, and I killed them all."

"You killed one thousand soldiers!" Marta blurted out.

"Yes. I couldn't see them, but I could feel them. God was with me."

"How did you kill so many of them?" Aria asked.

"I slew them all with the jawbone of a donkey."

"No way!" Aria said. "That's amazing."

"Those jawbones are sharp," Will said. "Have you ever felt a donkey's teeth? Like touching the blades of a saw."

"Then I took one of their boats and rowed back to shore."

"How did you know which direction to go?" Marta asked.

"The Lord sent a dove. She guided me."

"But you couldn't see her," Aria said.

"But I could hear her. She cooed all the way and led me to the shore."

Gohn led out a chuckle. "When I got on shore, a dog was there. Almost like God had sent him too. I told him where to go, and he guided me here. Like he knew what I was saying. Really, God was with me the entire way."

Marta put her arms around Gohn's neck and squeezed tightly. "I'm so glad you're home. At least you're safe now."

"None of us are safe," Gohn said soberly. "We're not staying. I won't be here long. We all have to get out of here."

"You can't leave again!" Marta cried out. "I don't think I could stand it if you left. Not knowing what was happening to you."

"We're all leaving. God gave me a vision," Gohn said. "We're supposed to round up all the elect. The remnants. From quadrangles two through seven. There are 8400 of them."

"Who are they?" Will asked.

"The believers who didn't take AXX-E," Gohn answered. "We're to find them and get them all together in one place."

"What do we do then?" Will asked. "They won't fit in the church."

"We take them to the island. We'll all be safe there."

"How do you suggest we round up that many people?" Marta asked.

Her mind whirled with questions. That'd be an undertaking of mammoth proportions. She didn't even know where to begin.

"We can set up the image broadcaster and speak to them in the squares," Will answered for Gohn.

"Exactly," Gohn said, as he pushed out his chair and stood to his feet. "I will deliver a message to them. I'll tell them to meet at the shoreline. Later today."

"They'll be shocked to hear your voice," Aria said. "They all think you're dead."

"They'll be thrilled to see that you're alive! We'll praise God together. It's a miracle," Marta said.

"Will, is the broadcaster still in the sanctuary?" Gohn asked. "Is it working? Can we connect to the squares? Can you set everything up?"

Gohn suddenly had a sense of urgency in his voice. Before he was laid back. Peaceful. Content to be home. Now he was back in ministry mode.

"We can do it," Will said. "The broadcaster still works, and we still have a connection to the squares."

"I'll help," Aria said.

Will stood up from the table. "Let's go," he said. "We need to get the message out in time for people to get to the shore before dark."

They stood and left, leaving Marta alone with Gohn.

"I need to take a shower and get out of these clothes," Gohn said to Marta, who was now clutching his arm. She didn't want to let go of it. Even to let him take a shower.

"Of course. Did you get enough to eat?" Marta asked. Then chuckled inside. Always the hostess. Making sure everyone has had enough to eat. The house was empty of food. Except for what God had provided. She couldn't make him anything, even if he wanted her to.

"I did get enough to eat," Gohn said. "I ate some bread. Thank you, though. Food was never my problem. I had plenty to eat on the island. So, I wasn't starving. My problem was not being able to see. Will told me how God provided you with bread and drink and I ate some of it."

Marta had a burning question in her mind but was afraid to ask. Gohn took a couple steps like he wanted to walk somewhere.

"Can you show me the direction to my bedroom?" he asked.

"Of course. Let me guide you there," Marta said, still holding his arm. "Everything is just like you left it."

She led him into his bedroom. Took him from the bed to his desk, to the dresser and then to the entrance of the bathroom, making sure he had his bearings.

"Gohn," Marta said. Still hesitant.

"Yes."

She had to ask.

"Do you still love me?"

"Why would you ask me that?"

Her heart was pounding again, and she clutched her hand which was suddenly shaking.

"I have to know. Do you still want to marry me?"

A big smile came on Gohn's face.

"More than anything else in the world!" he said. "You're all I thought about when I was on the island."

Marta's heart skipped a beat as joy filled her heart like water fills a glass.

"I want to marry you too," she said.

Gohn reached out his arms and Marta stepped into them. Rested her head on his chest.

"I'm going to take a shower," Gohn said. "I can only imagine how hideous I look. Will you be here when I get out?"

"You look like a prince to me."

"When I come out from the shower, will you be my wife?"

Marta's heart fluttered. She thought she knew what he meant but wasn't sure.

"Do you mean what I think you mean?" she asked.

"Is that a yes?" Gohn asked.

"Of course. I'll meet you in bed."

* * *

An hour later, they were all in the sanctuary. Will put a microphone on Gohn. He was preparing to record Gohn's message to the quadrangles. Marta was behind the image broadcaster, and Aria stood next to her.

"I'm married," Marta whispered to Aria, whose mouth gaped open after she said it.

"What?" Aria said. "When?"

Aria put her hand over her mouth and her eyes widened like she suddenly knew. Clearly when Marta pointed toward the back of the sanctuary and the door that led to the apartment.

Marta let out a slight squeal.

"Gohn asked me to marry him, and I said yes. We made love. Just now. In his bedroom. Neither of us wanted to wait."

Aria threw her arms around Marta's neck. "I'm so happy for you," she said.

"Me too. I can't believe it. An hour ago, I thought Gohn was dead. Now we're married."

"With everything that's going on, will you have time for a honeymoon?"

Marta grabbed Aria's shoulder and turned her so they were facing away from Gohn and Will. Then leaned in to whisper in her ear.

"When Gohn finishes his message, he's going to go to the first quadrangle."

"Why? That's too dangerous!" Aria blurted out. Loud enough for others to hear, but Will and Gohn were distracted with their preparations.

"Gohn wants to destroy the Eliminati and kill the leader. Herodius. The one who took his sight."

"How's he going to get there? He can't see."

"I'm going to take him."

32

Gohn finished his message to the squares, and he and Marta left for the first quadrangle. Presumably to confront Herodius and the Eliminati. Gohn had given specific instructions for all of the unAXX-E-nated believers to meet at the shore of the lake in four hours. Enough time for Marta and Gohn to travel to the first quadrangle, exact whatever revenge Gohn intended, then travel back to the shore in time to meet everyone.

Marta had a thousand questions, but she mostly kept them to herself. With Gohn's strength, she felt relatively safe. If he was able to kill a thousand men on the island, then it seemed as though there was nothing the soldiers could do to them as long as she stayed with him.

Her biggest worry was the sky which had suddenly grown ominous. On Mercury, the bubble provided constant stability to the atmosphere. During the day, the rays shone through the sky above with a perfect mix of warmth and light. Creating ideal weather year-round. At night, the bubble held in just enough of the warmth of the day to keep things cool but comfortable. With the ocean above the bubble, the air and ground had a constant supply of humidity, and it always felt like they were in a shower without the water running. To the point that their hair and clothes felt continually damp but not wet.

The air was almost always cool and refreshing, and Marta only occasionally felt hot when outside on rare days when the sun's rays were stronger than normal..

Consequently, clouds were a rarity, and it never rained. Today was different. Unlike anything she'd ever seen before. Large, dark, billowing clouds had rolled into and covered the first quadrangle. She even saw flashes of lightning high in the sky. Thunderclaps resounded and caused her to jump every time they rumbled. Almost like clockwork. She'd see the lightning, then hear the thunder four or five seconds later.

"Do not fear," Gohn said to her. "The Lord's judgement is at hand. But not on us. We'll be safe."

"How can you be so sure?" Marta asked, as another loud roll of thunder shook their vehicle.

She was driving them from the fifth quadrangle to the first. About a two-hour drive.

"God is with us," Gohn said confidently.

"What about the Eliminati?" Marta asked. "What are you going to do when we get to the first quadrangle? Don't you think they'll be waiting for you? They must've heard your message to the squares and know that you're alive."

"If God is for us, who can be against us? God didn't deliver me from the island only to have me killed at the hand of the Eliminati. He told me to lead the people out of the quadrangles and to the safety of the island. I don't suppose I'll die in the first quadrangle."

Another bright lightning strike filled the sky. Seconds later, she heard the thunder. Louder this time. The closer they got to the first quadrangle, the louder the thunder became.

Gohn asked Marta to describe what she was seeing in the clouds.

She described everything to him in detail

"There is a coming destruction," Gohn said. "The great city will be destroyed. But the disaster will not overtake us."

Marta could see the buildings of the first quadrangle off at a distance. The buildings reached toward the sky, and the lightning strikes almost touched them from above. Gohn had said in the message that the city was going to be destroyed by fire. She couldn't believe that they were driving toward it. If the city was going to be destroyed anyway, why did Gohn need to go there and kill Herodius. It seemed like the fire would do the trick. It's almost as if Gohn had a personal vendetta. A score he had to settle himself.

While Marta refused to leave Gohn's side, it didn't make it easier to drive right into the heart of the enemy. She thought they were taking an unnecessary risk. Gohn's words in the message had been clear. "Flee for your lives! Don't look back and don't stop anywhere in the quadrangles! Flee to the islands or you will be consumed with fire!"

That seemed like good advice at that moment. She was tempted to turn the car and drive back to the shore. How would Gohn even know? He was blind, so he had no idea in which direction they were headed.

She couldn't make herself deceive him in that way.

The clouds had obviously spooked the populous as well because she saw hundreds of people scurrying around. Closing up shops. Securing doors and windows. Lines formed outside the grocery stores.

Once they were in the city proper, somehow Gohn was able to tell Marta where to go, even though he couldn't see it himself. God had shown him in a dream which building the Eliminati operated out of, and he led her right to it. Despite the chaos in the first quadrangle, no one stopped her, and traffic was light. Surprisingly, the checkpoints usually manned by soldiers were abandoned.

She saw numerous government vehicles heading out of the city. Marta wondered if the soldiers were heading toward the lake to confront the remnant. Nothing she could do about it if they were, other than pray for the safety of Aria and the others and get Gohn back there as soon as possible. They were in God's hands anyway.

When Marta arrived at the building, she parked the vehicle, got out, and went around to the passenger side to help Gohn out.

"Tell me what you want me to do," she said.

"Do you see two pillars?" Gohn asked. "At the entrance."

The building was a large four-story, white building with columns. The largest building she'd ever seen on Mercury. She presumed he meant the two columns in the center near the entrance.

"Do you mean columns?" Marta said. "I see several large, white columns. They're about four feet round. They look like they're holding up the roof. The two biggest ones are in the center."

"Those are the pillars!" Gohn said excitedly. "Put me where I can feel them, so I may lean against them."

Marta led him to the main entrance of the building. Dozens of people were running around, including soldiers, but none noticed them. She positioned Gohn so he was up against the pillars and could reach both.

"Stand back," he said to her sharply. "Get away from the building."

"Are you going to be okay?" Marta asked, still not sure what he was planning.

"Go! Now!" he said.

Rather than argue, Marta did as he said and moved away from the building.

"Sovereign Lord," Gohn cried out in a loud voice. "Remember me. Strengthen me once more and let me, with one blow, get revenge on the Eliminati, and Herodius for my two eyes."

Gohn reached toward the two central pillars on which the building stood. He braced against them. His right hand on one and his left hand on the other. Marta realized what he was about to do. Gohn was going to bring down the entire building. Problem was that it would land on top of him. He'd kill the people inside, but he'd be killed as well.

She shouted for him to stop.

Too late.

She saw him straining against the pillars. Pushing with all his might.

She let out a scream.

Was Gohn going to die? Did he even care? What about their marriage?

The building swayed.

She had to stop him.

She took off running toward him.

The whole building began to shake.

She was too late.

The entire building collapsed to the ground.

* * *

The Eliminati was meeting in the conference room of their headquarters. Herodius called the council together to discuss the new video that had surfaced of the Disorderly Pastor Gohn.

The discussion was heated.

"We should've killed him when we had the chance!" Botis said angrily.

A number of the council had argued that Gohn should be killed. Herodius wanted him to suffer on the island. Live out his days toiling away in the fields without his sight. The guards had been given instructions to give him minimal food and water, and they could torture him as much as they wanted but couldn't take his life.

The word was that Gohn had regained his strength and killed all the soldiers on the island. Herodius ordered a thousand men to go to the island and kill him once and for all. Apparently, they hadn't been successful. Herodius was shocked to see Gohn's face on the video earlier that day. Very much alive.

Worse than seeing him were the words he spoke. Gohn said that destruction was coming to Mercury and to the Eliminati. Herodius didn't know what Gohn was planning, but he was desperate to come up with a strategy to kill Gohn before he killed them.

"Gohn told all the Disorderlies to gather at the shore," Herodius said.

"That's a good thing," Incubus said. "They are the unAXX-E-nated. We've been trying to hunt them down and kill them. Now we know where they'll be. Let's send soldiers there and kill them all."

A loud agreement resounded through the room.

"I've already done it," Herodius said. "I've ordered all available soldiers to go to the shore and kill them."

"Excellent. What do you make of the sky?" Botis said. "Should we not seek shelter?"

"Yes," Herodius said. "I don't know what's happening, but we should adjourn and go to the bunker."

Under the main building was a series of tunnels that led to an underground shelter. A safe spot in case of a disaster. Herodius wasn't sure what was happening with the sky but didn't want to take any chances. They'd be safe in the shelters.

Everyone stood to leave.

Suddenly the room began to shake.

Herodius almost fell over. He would have if he hadn't reached out with his hand and caught himself on the edge of the table.

"What's happening?" someone cried out.

Tiles from the ceiling began to fall. The entire building seemed to be collapsing. There wasn't time to make it to the shelter.

"Get under the table!" Herodius shouted.

The six men cowered under the large conference table as the entire room shook. Violently. The entire building swayed back and forth.

Herodius heard a loud cracking sound.

Then a huge boom.

The lights went out. They were in total darkness.

Herodius could feel himself falling.

Faster.

The last thing he remembered seeing was the roof come crashing through the conference table. On top of him.

He felt no pain. He had the sense that he was dead but couldn't be sure.

The next thing he saw was a great light in the distance.

He was moving toward it.

33

Epilogue

Herodius was moving at a fast rate of speed. Toward a bright light. The heavens opened, and he stopped right in front of a white horse and He who sat on it. The one called Faithful and True. In righteousness, He judges and wages war.

The Righteous One's eyes were like a flame of fire, and upon his head were many jewels on a crown. He was clothed in a white robe. His name was called The Word of God. All mysteries of the heavens had been revealed to him.

"The first quadrangle has fallen," Herodius heard an angel say. "She had become a dwelling place for demons and unclean spirits. All of the quadrangles had drunk of the passion of her immorality. The merchants of Asiminia had become rich by the wealth of their sensuality."

Asiminia was the name God had given to the planet. The evil one had named it Mercury.

A vision appeared on the clouds.

Herodius suddenly saw the first quadrangle. The great city that he had built and controlled for hundreds of years. Fire rained down from the clouds and consumed every building and every living thing who had glorified themselves.

Herodius fell to his knees and wept. "Such great wealth has been laid waste in less than an hour," he said.

He was still thinking about the things of the world. Not realizing the fate that awaited him.

The headquarters of the Eliminati lay in rubble.

Then he saw Gohn.

Walking out of the dust. With a woman. The cloud of smoke and rubble were behind them.

They were suddenly transported to the sea.

A great throng of people greeted them.

Gohn had regained his sight.

How was that possible? Herodius had ordered his eyes poked out by the soldiers. Now he could see.

Where were his soldiers?

He saw. They were all dead. Consumed by the fire that came out of the clouds and burned the entire city. The ruins were smoldering.

The vision went back and forth between the destruction in the city and the rejoicing of the crowd by the sea. Why weren't they killed by the fire?

Herodius watched as the waters of the lake opened up and created a path for them to walk through all the way to the island.

A sound came out from among them. He heard the harpists and musicians and flute players. Trumpeters blasted a song of praise.

A voice came from behind Herodius, and the throng of people could hear it because they looked his way. Toward the heavens.

"Give praise to Our God, all you Bond Servants," the voice said. "You who fear him. The small and the great."

The crowd began to sing louder. Their voices ascended all the way to heaven.

They danced as they walked toward the island. When they reached it, the waters closed behind them. They prepared a great feast and ate food and drank wine at a large table until they were full.

Herodius saw the great city again. His city. It lay in ruins. The skies had cleared of the clouds, and all that was left was the smoke rising from the ashes. The fire had now consumed everyone in the other quadrangles except for the ones on the island.

An angel seized Herodius by the back of his neck. Violently.

"You have deceived the people," the angel said with fury. "You made many to take the mark of the beast on their arms. You persecuted and killed the prophets. Be gone!"

Herodius wanted to cry out for mercy. Before he could, he was suddenly propelled through the air. Toward a huge lake of fire. He could see the waves of fire lapping into the air. He landed in it.

Still alive.

* * *

The Lord spoke to the Father, "What is to become of the remnant on Asiminia?"

The Word of God and the Spirit of God were with the Father in heaven. Asiminia was the first planet to be given man. The evil one renamed it Mercury, but now that he was removed from power over the planet, the name had been restored.

Asiminia was thriving. The elect were repopulating the planet; and without the evil one in control, sin no longer abounded. Prosperity and healing had come to them. They were no longer only on the island but were living in all the quadrangles which had been rebuilt.

God provided their every need. Like the garden of Eden had been restored.

"They are my remnant. I'm going to leave them there until the end of the ages," the Father said.

The Word and the Spirit knew that the Father intended to bring life to every planet in the solar system. He would put on each a garden of Eden, an Adam, and an Eve, and give them life and the ability to sustain life. They'd all be given a perfect world to start with.

But with free will. The ability to choose life or death. On each planet would be a tree of the knowledge of good and evil. If they chose evil, sin and death would enter the world.

They would all eat from the tree. Every one of them.

The end was predictable.

The Father could already see the fate of each planet. Each planet would eat of the fruit and eventually destroy itself. The end of the ages would come when the last planet was uninhabitable. Then God would destroy the sun, moon, and stars and those who believed in Christ would live for an eternity in heaven. God would decide then what to do with the remnant on Asiminia.

"Will the other planets know about the elect on Asiminia?" the Spirit asked the Father.

The people of Asiminia were in a bubble under the ocean. None of the other planets would ever know they existed unless God the Father revealed it to them.

"We'll see," the Father said. "The last planet in this solar system will be Earth. I might reveal it to them. They'll be the first planet with the ability to travel to other planets."

"What planet do you intend to bring life to next?" the Spirit asked.

Many eons would pass before Earth would be given life. The Spirit was the one who brought life into existence from the spoken Word of God through the power of the Son, and he was prepared to act on God's command. The other planets would be given life before Earth.

If God intended to bring life to another planet soon, then he'd be ready.

"I will bring life to Tapei." God said.

Tapei was the farthest planet from the sun. The largest in the solar system. Twice as big as Jupiter. The evil one had named it Pluto.

When he was banished from Asiminia, he took up residence on Pluto, as far away from Mercury as possible.

Pluto meant underworld. Another word for Hades. Pluto was the God of the underworld in the copycat worlds Satan had created for himself.

Tapei, in contrast, meant lowliness of mind. Humility. The things of Satan were always opposite of God. For whatever reason, man adopted Satan's names rather than God's.

"When do you want to start?" the Word asked.

"Now," God said. "Let there be life on Tapei."

With those words, man was created on Tapei.

The second planet.

What would be their fate?

THE EDEN STORIES

GET YOUR FREE GIFT

As a thank you for finishing my book, I want to give you a free gift. Go to terrytoler.com and sign up for my mailing list and I'll give you the first three chapters of *The Launch*. A Jamie Austen novella.

About the Author

TERRY TOLER is the author of the Jamie Austen and Alex Halee book series along with *The Eden Stories*. He is a minister, public speaker, counselor, and retired entrepreneur. Impacting the lives of people worldwide through storytelling has become one of his passions in life. He can be followed at terrytoler.com.

www.ingramcontent.com/pod-product-compliance
Lightning Source LLC
Chambersburg PA
CBHW050403260626
47156CB00003B/848